#STARSTRUCK

#STARSTRUCK

SARIAH WILSON

Montlake
Romance

This is a work of fiction. Names, characters, organizations, places, events, and incidents are either products of the author's imagination or are used fictitiously.

Published by Montlake Romance, Seattle

www.apub.com

Amazon, the Amazon logo, and Montlake Romance are trademarks of Amazon.com, Inc., or its affiliates.

ISBN-13: 9781503949362
ISBN-10: 1503949362

Cover design by Michael Rehder

Printed in the United States of America

For Shiloh—who wanted to know why there wasn't a book dedicated to her and for being my favorite daughter.

CHAPTER ONE

Do you know that feeling you get in the pit of your stomach when you've reacted and said something maybe you shouldn't have? As soon as I pushed the Tweet button, I regretted it.

In my defense my favorite movie star, Chase Covington, had asked:

The film was a depiction of Caesar Augustus (known to his family as Octavius) as a young man and his rise to power in Rome. And apparently I was the only one who thought he was kind of flat in it.

Every other response was typical of his fangirls, who called themselves Chasers. Of the *OMG I luv u have my babies!* variety. As I scrolled through the responses, I realized I was the only one who wasn't heaping praise on him.

And it would be only a matter of time before my fellow fans started attacking me. I went to push DELETE, and this happened.

Chase. Covington. Just. Tweeted. Me.

Me. Regular old Zoe Miller.

My heart froze in my chest, and I might have blacked out for a minute. He had like ten million followers on Twitter. He tweeted pretty regularly and tried to engage with his fan base, but how on earth had he seen what I had written? And responded so quickly?

I knew I should play it cool. That I should come up with something witty and amazing so he'd never forget me. But I was so excited that Chase Covington had actually responded that I couldn't help myself. With shaking hands, I tweeted him right back.

Thirty seconds later:

Chase Covington ✓
@realchasecov

Following

@zomorezoless Feisty. You don't give a guy a break, do you?

💬   ⟲ 271   ♡ 1.1K

Was he upset? Amused? Chase never used emojis, unlike his Chasers, who treated them like decorations and their tweets were Christmas trees. I was anti-emoji, so I appreciated that about him. But sometimes it made it impossible to read context.

Zoe
@zomorezoless

@realchasecov I do when he deserves it.

💬   ⟲ 0   ♡ 0

People with usernames like @chaseluvr and @chasesbabymama started noticing our conversation and, predictably, sent me hate tweets, asking how dare I be mean to Chase, I should die, my mother should have killed herself before I was born, blah, blah, blah. I'd seen these flame wars before, and I wasn't interested in being their target.

I was about to turn off my phone when I noticed Chase had tweeted again.

Chase Covington ✓
@realchasecov

Following

@zomorezoless I want the list.

💬   ⟲ 409   ♡ 1.3K

My first thought was creating that list wouldn't be hard. Like I said, Chase was an extremely talented actor, easily one of the best in Hollywood, and he'd been in the business since he was four years old. He started out on a family sitcom called *No More, No Less* (hence my Twitter username) and graduated to a string of other highly successful TV shows after that one was finally canceled. At seventeen he had switched to movies, and now, at twenty-five, he already had one Academy Award under his belt and was one of the highest paid actors in the world. And he never let anyone pigeonhole him; even now he would do anything from rom-coms to moody historicals to indie dramas.

The second thought was wondering what his game was. Why did he need a list from me? I understood that actors liked to have their egos stroked as much as the next dude, but why did he care what some random fan thought? Wasn't his other 9,999,999 followers' adoration enough? Did it have to be unanimous?

I really didn't have time for this. I had to turn in my celibacy paper to my women's studies class tomorrow, and I still had about five more pages to write. If Chase needed validation, he could head to his closest mall and let the tweenyboppers scream and fall at his feet.

Before I turned off my phone, one final tweet landed in my notifications. It was from @twihardchaser and said:

twihardchaser ✓
@twihardchaser

Follow

@zomorezoless U suck & UR #notspecial prob just his asst #Chaser #WantToMarryOctavius

💬 ♻ 5 ♡ 11

Which was followed by a string of poop emojis. Well, there was no arguing with someone who thought marrying a butcher like Caesar Augustus was a good idea.

I took one last look at the picture Chase used as the header on his account, his golden hair and bright-blue eyes making him look like a total California beach god, and turned my phone off. I was determined to focus on my paper, but that last tweet had sucked all the giddy, joyful hope out of me. She was probably right, and I had been chatting with an assistant or his publicist. That would be pretty par for the course for me. To get all excited over something that turned out to be absolutely nothing.

Story of my life.

A couple of years ago I might have immediately agreed with her. There was a period of time when his tweets sounded different. Off. But for the last year or so, he'd gone back to sounding like himself again, and while I didn't have a reason to doubt, I still did.

Why was it that people wouldn't let you have one good thing and wanted to destroy it before you even got to enjoy it?

Sighing, I turned my attention back to my paper. Being in my senior year, I had learned the fine art of BSing my work and writing essays in a way that made the professors happy. A few footnotes and quotes, some basic discussion you expounded on to make your paper longer, and you were golden.

So a couple of hours later, I was done. As I gathered up my laptop and phone, I looked at all the other students in the university library, studying and working. Part of me wanted to climb up onto one of the library tables and announce to these strangers that I (might have) just had a Twitter conversation with Chase Covington.

I settled for going back to my apartment instead. I was nearly to the complex when I remembered I had turned off my phone. I restarted it, and my phone dinged repeatedly with notifications. I couldn't help myself—I checked to see if Chase had said anything else. With a frown of disappointment, I realized he hadn't, what with the ball being in my court and all.

As I wondered whether I should send him a list of what I thought was his best work, I realized my best friend and roommate, Lexi, had texted me like thirty times, and the texts were all variations of

> OMG, CALL ME RIGHT
> NOW!!!!!

She was a theater major and, as such, was often prone to dramatics, but this was over the top, even for her. Nearly home, I decided to hold off until I saw her in person. In part because I wasn't sure what to tell her about Chase Covington.

Lexi was the reason I'd become a Chaser. I was homeschooled by my formerly Amish (not kidding) grandparents until my mother married, had a bunch of kids, and decided she wanted to be my parent again. The first thing she did was enroll me in public school, and at twelve years old I had absolutely no idea how to make friends.

It was Lexi who had come to my rescue. She had approached me at recess, where I stood alone, not knowing what to do, and said, "Do you love Chase Covington? Because I love Chase Covington more than anything in the world, and if you love him, too, we're going to be best friends."

I remember how lonely I felt, and if she'd said, "Do you think it's fun to eat your hair and tear out your fingernails?" I would have agreed and done it just to have one friend. She was true to her word. We became best friends in Ms. Ogata's sixth-grade class and still were, ten years later.

She was still pretty much my only friend. After she discovered my lack of pop culture knowledge, she'd made it her personal mission to rectify it, not even caring that I'd been just a bit untruthful about loving Chase, since I hadn't even known who he was. Lexi had been a cheerleader, the lead in every school play, and the homecoming/prom queen. Everybody loved her, and everybody wanted to hang out with her. People were nice to me because we were friends, but I never really felt a part of things. It wasn't until I took an Intro to Psych class that I realized something important about myself—I was the biggest introvert who had ever lived. It was why everything was so difficult for me—parties, hanging out, trying to make another friend besides Lexi. She, meanwhile, was the quintessential extrovert. We were the epitome of opposites attracting.

And she was almost as devoted to me as she was to Chase Covington. Because she hadn't been kidding about the loving-him thing. She bought teen magazines by the truckload and cut out every article and picture of him. It was a very serious process deciding whether a picture should be put up on her wall or into her scrapbook. We spent hours discussing the merits of each photo and where it should go. Somewhere along the line it had gone from being Lexi's obsession to a shared one.

Even now in our bedroom, she still had Chase Covington posters hanging on her side of the room, and she blew them kisses before she went to bed for the night. After we'd graduated from high school, Lexi had wanted to head immediately for Los Angeles and start auditioning. But her grandmother had made her a deal—if she went to college and graduated, her grandma would fund Lexi's acting ambitions for two years.

She agreed, but the delay had frustrated her. Lexi was determined to find Chase Covington and make him fall in love with her. I didn't doubt her ability to do it—with her half-Italian heritage, dark hair, dark eyes, and flawless skin, she was never without male company. None of her relationships lasted for very long because, as she would always tell me, "He's not Chase Covington."

I did have hopes for her latest conquest. His name was Gavin, and he was majoring in software engineering. He was actually the kind of guy I would normally have a crush on—tall, dark hair, slightly nerdy, wore glasses. An approachable, nice man. Nothing like Chase. But

Gavin and Lexi had been dating for two whole months, and it was already her longest relationship. He seemed to have mastered the fine art of giving Lexi the attention she needed but being frequently unavailable to her. Which made her want him more.

When I walked into our apartment and she pounced on me, my hope was that her news was something good about Gavin. My fear was that she had somehow seen my Twitter exchange with Chase. I didn't know how that would happen, given that Lexi detested Twitter and refused to use it, but with all the negativity pointed at me earlier in the evening, I was worried.

She would be jealous, and a jealous Lexi was not fun—as Valentina Sokolov had discovered our senior year when she'd made out with Lexi's boyfriend-of-the-week behind the bleachers.

"Zoe Miller! Where have you been? Why didn't you answer my texts?" she demanded, jumping up and down.

I let my book bag slide to the floor. "At the library. I turned my phone off. What's going on?"

"What's going on?" she repeated, still hopping around. "Only the greatest thing in the entire world. My flirtation subterfuge has finally paid off. We're going to meet Chase Covington!"

It took me a minute to figure out what she was saying. About three months ago, Lexi had been at a club in LA and met someone who knew someone who had Chase's publicist's cell phone number. Lexi got the digits and had been carefully cultivating Mr. Aaron Mathison since then for information. And her digital flirt-texts hadn't even bothered Gavin, who somehow seemed both unaffected by, and understanding of, his girlfriend's addiction.

"What do you mean?" It felt like a big cosmic joke that I had finally (possibly) had some real interaction with Chase, and now Lexi was saying we were going to meet him.

Which was nearly impossible to do, because Chase didn't seem to care about the fame thing. He didn't do meet and greets. He barely showed up in the tabloids and seemed particularly gifted at avoiding paparazzi. People didn't get to meet him in real life.

And now Lexi, her eyes glittering, was announcing that we would. "Aaron let slip that Chase is going to do some radio stuff early tomorrow morning at KHWV. I think we should leave now, go down there, and stalk him until he talks to us. What do you say?"

Los Angeles was a little more than an hour away if the freeways were clear. Which they never were. I didn't want to drive all the way out there and all the way back. I wanted to crawl into my bed. But I had never been able to tell Lexi no. "I have class at eleven, so we have to be back by then."

"Zoe!" she screeched, throwing her arms around me. "You're the best friend a girl could ever have! We have to pick out our outfits, and you have to let me do your hair and makeup. Then we'll just stay up all night so we don't mess anything up. Ack! I'm so excited!" She started for our bathroom; then she suddenly stopped. "Oh, I forgot to tell you. Laura Henderson called here looking for you because your phone was off. She said she needed you to call her right away."

Santa Isla University was a small college not far from the sleepy beach town where we had grown up. As was the case with most people who lived nearby, the Hendersons were fantastically wealthy, and they began hiring me in high school to watch their kids for a couple of hours every afternoon while Mrs. Henderson Botoxed or waxed or did whatever it was women in their forties who were trying to look twenty-eight again did. Lexi had once asked me why they didn't have a nanny, and I explained that Mrs. Henderson's father had left her mother for their nanny, so the Henderson household was a nanny-free zone. They paid me an obscene amount of money, in part because they could and because, thanks to my much younger siblings, I was a pro at babysitting. I had been working for them since I was sixteen.

Their housekeeper answered the phone and went to track down Mrs. Henderson. I could hear her three boys yelling in the background as she said, "Hello?"

"Hi, this is Zoe. My roommate said you called."

"Oh, Zoe! Yes. I'm glad I got ahold of you. I have some bad news, I'm afraid."

Concern bloomed in my chest. "Are the boys okay?"

"Yes, the boys are fine. I'm sorry to have worried you. No, it's nothing like that." I could just imagine her lounging on the couch while she talked to me, how she might be trying to frown or make a facial expression and would be unable to. "It's just that Mr. Henderson has been offered a promotion. In New York. And he's going to take it."

"When?"

There was a long pause. "He was actually offered the promotion weeks ago, and he finally found us a suitable place, so we're moving out to be with him. This Saturday."

That was only three days from now. I had noticed boxes and things around their house, but I had assumed she was just redecorating for the millionth time. It had never occurred to me that they would move. Or that I wouldn't be seeing Tevin, Carson, and Freddie any longer.

I was now out of a job.

A job I depended on for silly things, like paying rent and eating food.

I was so screwed.

She kept talking, apologizing for not telling me sooner, saying she didn't know how to explain. The petty part of me assumed she hadn't wanted me to look for another job so I could be available to her for as long as she needed me.

But I decided to be generous. "I will really miss you and the boys."

The relief in her voice at me not freaking out and calling her names was evident. She asked me to come by before they left, and we set up a time for me to say goodbye to the kids. She went on to assure me she would give me two weeks' severance pay, but I didn't have much in my savings account, and I was concerned that it was late in the school year to be trying to find a job. All the on-campus ones were already filled.

I tried to process everything while she continued to talk, saying this was best for her family and how much she appreciated everything I'd done for them. She finally ran out of steam, and we hung up.

I was officially jobless.

I still had my internship, but that didn't pay any money.

How was it that your life could change completely in such a short amount of time?

Lexi chose that moment to come bounding back into the room. "What do you say, best friend? You ready to meet Chase Covington?"

CHAPTER TWO

Lexi was appropriately sympathetic when I told her the news, but seeing as how she was well off and didn't understand the whole not-having-money thing and was relentlessly optimistic, she was sure I would have another job soon and that it wasn't worth worrying about.

She had texted Gavin, and he had offered to drive us, but she explained that this was a Zoe and Lexi–only event. She had set up "Operation Chase" when we were in seventh grade. It was one of the various ways Lexi thought we could meet Chase. Like getting on one of his TV shows. Or throwing ourselves in front of his limo so he'd have to rush us to the hospital. Or he would read one of her many fan letters and realize she was the girl for him, and he'd ride up to our school on a white horse and declare his love. (What can I say? We were thirteen.)

We stopped at an IHOP along the way and sat in a booth eating pancakes (my possible last meal if I didn't find new employment soon) and practicing exactly what Lexi would say to Chase. She had so many variations, I lost track. She considered improv to be one of her specialties, so I knew she'd figure it out. I didn't expect I would get to say anything.

Even if I did, what would I say? "Hi, I'm the girl who insulted your acting ability on Twitter last night. How are you?"

"This may not work," I warned her once we were back on the road. She danced along to the pop tunes played by KHWV—The Heatwave. We didn't normally listen to the radio, but Lexi was all about getting into character, and for some reason listening to the station we were about to lay siege to helped with that.

"It will work," she said confidently. "You're still up for being my maid of honor?"

"I don't know if I can pull off the lime green," I said, which made Lexi smile. When we were fifteen, Lexi had planned her wedding to Chase (the wedding scrapbook was still at her grandma's house). Chase had said in an interview that his favorite color was lime green, so my bridesmaid dress obviously had to be lime green. But paired with my fair skin and strawberry-blonde hair, I would look deathly ill.

"It doesn't have to be lime green. I still hope you're not taller than him."

Yet another way Lexi and I were opposites—she was a good six inches shorter than I was. We had many discussions about how tall Chase actually was; both of us were into very tall men. He said he was six three, but Lexi always insisted it wasn't true. "Actors do that all the time. They say they're five eight, but that means they're actually five three. They want to seem taller. I'm the one in the drama department. Trust me, they're almost all short." When I started sprouting up in high school and the girls' basketball coach wouldn't stop bugging me about joining the team, one of my biggest concerns was that I would be taller than Chase.

"I guess we're about to find out."

"You bet we are! Oh, we are going to have the prettiest babies," she said with a laugh.

As I pulled into the empty parking lot, I realized how our actions might look to someone who didn't care about Chase. It was weird to be part of a fandom. It was like the rational part of my brain recognized the things I did were crazy, but the rest of me didn't care that my actions would not be what other people would consider "normal."

It's something only other fans get.

"Now what?" I asked. "We just stand in front of the station and hope we see him?"

Lexi shrugged. "I guess."

We got out of the car, and I zipped up my jacket. Lexi refused to wear one because she wanted Chase to see her skimpy, club-worthy outfit. I had repeatedly warned her that she was going to freeze, but she didn't care.

I checked my phone. Still a bunch of hate tweets I hadn't looked at yet. It was four o'clock in the morning. When we got closer to the building, we realized it had a high fence with a locked door. Lexi tugged on the door twice, letting out a moan of frustration. "I didn't know it would be locked!"

"What? But your plan was so well thought out and perfectly calculated."

She smacked me on the shoulder, and I tried not to laugh. She began rubbing her hands up and down her arms.

"I think I have an extra sweater in the car. Do you want me to get it?"

"No," she said, her teeth slightly chattering. "He has to get the full effect. I want him to see me like this. He can't fall in love with me if I'm all covered up."

It was not the time to have the love-versus-lust conversation with her again. "Unless he has a Smurf fetish, he's not going to think your blue skin is attractive."

"Quiet for a second. I need to think." She started pacing back and forth while I leaned against the fence, eyes closed. This was a better plan than the one where she wanted to call in a bomb threat to the studio where his sitcom filmed and be waiting outside when they evacuated. It was her favorite plan until I convinced her the FBI would get involved and we would go to prison, and she looked terrible in orange.

There was a creaking, metallic sound from somewhere behind us, and we both turned to see a gate sliding open.

Behind the radio station.

"No!" Lexi wailed. She pulled out her phone and began to furiously text. It was still dark out, but the building had several outdoor lights. I saw a man emerge from a black SUV, and my heart started thumping when Chase got out of the back seat. He was wearing a ball cap. Although I couldn't see him clearly, I knew it was him.

The man stopped and took a phone out of his pants pocket. He said something to Chase, and Chase went into the building while the man began to walk toward us.

"Take off the jacket," Lexi hissed. "You look great. How do I look?"

"Perfect, like always," I told her. "What did you just do?"

As he came closer, I realized the man had dyed his hair so blond it was almost white, and he had frosted the tips light blue. But he was wearing a polo shirt and khakis. He was the kind of guy who so desperately wanted to be cool that he mimicked someone else, but it just came off looking clueless and stupid. I couldn't tell how old he was. He had one of those LA faces where he could have been anywhere between twenty and forty.

"Sexy Lexi," he said. His voice sounded oily, which grossed me out. "You're even hotter in the flesh."

This had to be the publicist. Aaron Mathison. Lexi must have texted him that we were here.

She batted her eyelashes at him, hunching her shoulders together to push her boobs up. I'd seen her do this maneuver on so many guys that I rolled my eyes.

But it worked. He couldn't take his gaze away from her cleavage.

"You said you'd be here, and I wanted to meet you," Lexi said. "And my friend, Zoe, really wants to go into radio, so I thought this would be such a great chance for her." She gave him a seductive smile, lowering her voice as she added, "And such a great chance for you."

Aaron cleared his throat and shifted from one foot to the other. "Let me see if I can find someone to let you in. Be right back. Don't go anywhere."

After he left, I said, "Gavin's going to kill you."

"I haven't done anything other than flirt, which is not cheating," she replied. "And ew. Give me a little credit. I'm not doing anything with that skeevy pervert."

If she were anyone else, I would probably be upset, but I was the one person in the world who not only understood but also shared in her obsession. "But you might want to do something with Mr. Covington when you finally meet him."

She ignored me. "Zoe, this is it. We're finally going to meet him." If ever a moment called for screaming, this was probably it. But we were both cold and a little in shock that it was actually happening. It didn't seem real.

And it wasn't.

At least for me.

A heavyset security guard came to the fence a few minutes later. "Lexi Antonelli?"

"That's me," she said, leaning against me for warmth.

"You can come with me." He pulled out a key ring and thumbed through the keys until he found the right one. He put it in the lock and pulled the door open. The bottom of it scratched against the concrete.

She stayed put. "What about my friend? She's supposed to come in, too."

"I was only told to bring in Lexi Antonelli. And this door's about to close."

Lexi looked at me frantically, and I understood her dilemma. This was a dream we shared together, and I knew she wanted to go but also didn't want to leave me.

"Go without me," I told her. "If anyone deserves to meet him, it's you."

Her eyes darted back and forth, and I could see how torn she was. "But . . ."

"Time's up, girlie. What's it gonna be? You coming or not?"

I nudged her. "Seriously. Go. And give me every single detail."

She took a few steps forward and turned back to look at me. "Are you sure?"

"I'm sure. Go!"

"I will tell him all about you. Maybe I can get him to come out here! Love you!" Without further hesitation Lexi went through the gate, and the guard locked it behind her. I watched until they'd entered the building, then decided to wait for her in my car. I turned it on, running the heater and wondering what was happening. Obviously I was disappointed, but if it couldn't happen for me, I was glad it was finally happening for Lexi.

My phone beeped. I looked at it, expecting a text from Lexi.

It was Chase.

Chase Covington ✓
@realchasecov

Following

@zomorezoless I'm still waiting for my list.

⟲ 526   ♡ 1.2K

Aaron's leering expression popped into my head. This was probably him. Lexi was most likely totally ignoring him and fawning all over Chase, leaving Aaron free to text Chase's fans, pretending to be him.

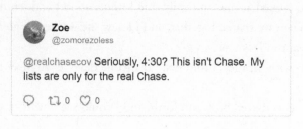

A few seconds later, I had a notification on my Twitter app. A new follower.

Chase Covington was following me. Which was significant, given I had, like, seven followers, and one of them was my mom.

He sent me a direct message, which was private, unlike our tweets.

If I'm Chase, I think you should make me some of your famous spice cookies.

Now I knew it wasn't him. How would Chase Covington know about my spice cookies? Aaron had just tipped his hand. Had Lexi told him? It was the only plausible explanation. How else could he possibly know? Was that what he spent his free time doing? Trolling for dates among Chase's fans? So gross.

> You're on. Prove it's you.

A few seconds later, there was a picture of Chase wearing the ball cap I'd seen him in. He was holding up a piece of paper that said, "Hi, Zoe Miller."

It was him. He was tweeting me. My heart pounded so hard I was afraid I might have a heart attack. This was happening. And it was four in the morning. How did he still look so beautiful this early?

> How do you know my name?

I was pretty sure my full name wasn't on my account. I didn't want anybody from school or the Ocean Life Foundation, the charity I interned at, to know about my movie-star obsession.

> Followed a link you posted and it mentioned you by name.

He followed a link? What? What was happening?

> Why?

It was the only thing I could think of to say. It seemed like an eternity before he responded, but it couldn't have been more than a minute.

> To be honest, something about you intrigued me. It might have been your use of complete sentences or lack of emojis. And I probably shouldn't admit this, but I stayed up most of the night reading your posts. They made me want to meet you.

OMG, OMG, OMG. Now I understood why the other Chasers constantly tweeted in all caps. I felt hysterical and giddy. Excited that I had caught his eye but freaking out as I realized all the crap I had posted on Twitter. Stuff that made me laugh, politics that pissed me off, pictures of me and Lexi in avocado masks with our hair in big rollers.

Bragging about my spice cookies.

I was going to have to go through my account and delete every single thing I had ever put up.

But it was too late. He'd already seen them. Every sarcastic, snarky, self-deprecating remark I'd ever posted.

And all the gushing ones about how much I loved him.

OMG.

> Now you owe me a list and some cookies. When can I expect them?

Another girl, probably every other girl on the planet, would have jumped at the chance. But I didn't believe it. He didn't really want me to make him cookies. He was just joking. Teasing.

And maybe if my mom hadn't spent most of her life chasing fame, I might be more starry-eyed and less of a keeping-both-feet-on-the-ground type of gal.

> You know that's kind of weird, right?

> I'll have you know the clinical term is "crazy." I know it's weird. But I have to go. I have to meet a fan and then work. Later.

The person he was about to meet was Lexi. What would she think about her future husband asking me to make him baked goods? I laid my forehead against the steering wheel. I didn't trust things I couldn't understand.

And I most definitely did not understand this. Chase Covington could literally date any woman he wanted. He had already dated some of the most beautiful women in Hollywood. Supermodels. A pop star.

This insanely handsome man did not flirt with formerly home-schooled nobodies.

Maybe I was being presumptuous. Maybe he wasn't flirting. He was probably just being polite. Or friendly.

Why?

And at four thirty in the morning?

It didn't seem to matter how many times I asked the question, I couldn't make sense of it.

Did celebrities try to punk fans? Maybe he was high. That made more sense. Then he would just forget that all of this ever happened.

Which was probably for the best. I decided to not think about his possible motives and just chalk it up to a fun experience I would some-day tell my children about.

I turned on the car's interior light and decided to study until Lexi returned. Might as well be productive instead of endlessly speculating on what Chase Covington was doing.

It didn't really work.

About an hour later, the sun had come up enough that I could turn off the light and wait for my best friend. I saw her come out of the studio with Chase and Aaron, and she hugged each of them goodbye. I felt a swell of envy, but I tamped it down by reminding myself that I'd told her to go. She walked toward me, swinging her hips and stomping her heels like she was on a catwalk. Aaron watched her go, but Chase had already climbed into his waiting SUV.

She looked over her shoulder, and once she realized they were gone, she ran to the gate, urging the now-on-duty security guard to open it. I could see her grin as she rushed to the car.

Lexi threw open the door and jumped inside. Her eyes danced as she bounced up and down on the seat. "Zoe . . . I can't even . . . there's so much . . ." She closed her eyes for a second and clapped her hands together. "Okay! First things first. I have the most amazing news in the entire world. Literally. I mean, I know I've said that before, but this is better."

A lump formed in my throat. If she was going on a date with Chase, I would be happy for her. I would. Because what could be better than that?

She sucked in a deep breath and then let it out, smiling at me expectantly. She wasn't going to just tell me. She wanted me to ask.

"The suspense has been adequately built," I said, starting to get annoyed. "What is it?"

"We, you and I, the founding members of Chase Covington's Marabella fan club, are going to be extras in Chase's new movie!"

CHAPTER THREE

Zoe
@zomorezoless

1,089 x 9 = 9,801. #Math #Trivia #CoolStuff

💬   🔁 0   ♡ 2

For a second I couldn't feel my face. "What?"

Lexi looked like the cat who had swallowed an entire flock of canaries. "It's all arranged. We report to the set on Monday." She put on her seat belt. "Can you imagine? An actual movie set. Where we will be in an actual movie. That's going to be so much more helpful on my résumé than a bunch of college plays."

We had to get back. I had class. I started up the car and drove it through the parking lot, putting on the blinker so we could get back on the road. The movements were all automatic because my brain was so scattered. "Extras?"

"Okay. So I went with Aaron, and he took me into the radio station, and we said hello to the morning deejays that were there, and we had to wait because Chase was taping a bunch of sound bites for different stations in a booth, and he was so gorgeous I thought I was going to die. Oh, he is definitely six three, and his eyes are actually that blue. They do not edit them. Have you seen my phone? I forgot to bring it in with me. I didn't get a picture of him."

We both looked around, but I didn't see it. Lexi reached under the front seat and emerged with it. "It must have slid out of my purse. Anyway, I finally got the chance to go in and say hi while fending off Aaron's advances, and Chase freaking Covington hugged me and said hello, and I said, 'I'm an actor, too.' Like, of all the things I could have said to him, all the conversations we'd practiced for years, that's what I say. It was so stúpid. But he was so polite and chatted with me, and instead of getting my crap together and not acting like a moron, I decided to tell him you and I had been his biggest fans for years. And this is where it got weird."

"Weird?"

"He stops and goes, 'Zoe Miller? The one who works at the Ocean Life Foundation?'"

It's a good thing we were at a stoplight, because I slammed my brakes. Hard. That must have been the link he'd clicked on to find my name. I had linked to an article about a bowling fund-raiser that I'd helped organize for the Foundation. I could see how it would have caught his eye, because he'd spoken out repeatedly about our need to protect marine life. It was his pet cause. I'd never quite been able to figure out if I came by my love of the sea naturally because of where I grew up, or if I loved it because Chase loved it.

Even though she was flung a little bit forward, Lexi didn't notice. She just kept talking. "And I was like, 'Yeah, she's my bestie.' I thought it was weird that he knew your name, but then I thought about how he's all dedicated to ocean conservation and figured he probably recognized your name from that or something. Isn't that strange?"

She had no idea how strange this all was, especially since everything she assumed was totally inaccurate. Lexi used only Instagram and thought all other social media was a total waste of her time. Which was why she still didn't know about our Twitter exchange.

"Super strange."

"He must have an amazing memory or something. Which makes sense, considering how many scripts he's always memorizing. I told him the Foundation doesn't pay you, and you just lost your job. I don't know why I did that. I was seriously just babbling at that point. But it is so good that I did because he offered to get us parts as extras in his movie. I don't even know how much we're going to get paid, but who cares because WE ARE GOING TO BE IN A MOVIE WITH CHASE COVINGTON!"

She reached into her pocket and pulled something out. "Not to mention, I stole his straw. Now I own something his lips have been on." It was one of those coffee straws—skinny, short, and brown. She'd always daydreamed about snagging a souvenir from him, something he had touched.

It was almost everything Lexi had ever wanted. "And then did he ask you out?"

She leaned her seat back as far as it would go. "Not yet. But I have time now, right? My heart was pumping so hard. You don't even understand. He was even better-looking in person. I am seriously in love."

"What about Gavin?"

"I really like Gavin. You know that. But if Chase is interested . . ." She didn't have to finish that sentence. I knew exactly what would happen. Lexi would drop Gavin like a radioactive potato. Which was a shame, because he really was a great guy and seemed perfect for my best friend.

Despite my wanting to beat the morning rush hour on the freeway, I was denied. We were stuck in bumper-to-bumper traffic, and I listened as Lexi relived her experience over and over again. How Chase had said her name several times, and how while talking to him she felt like the only person in the whole world who mattered.

I was happy for her. I was. I only wished I could have been part of it. And maybe asked him what he was doing by sending me tweets and DMs.

As if he knew I had just been thinking about him, my phone chirped at me. I had my account set up to notify me whenever he tweeted. And he said,

Chase Covington ✓
@realchasecov

Following

Is coincidence a thing? Or is it the universe trying to send you a message? Do you think fate is real?

○   ⟳ 9.6K   ♡ 65K

Was that about me?

Or did he think meeting my best friend was fated?

As I settled into my Introduction to Women's and Gender Studies class, I kept wondering if Chase was interested in Lexi. Because men usually were. I should have expected it. Instead, it was bothering me, and I didn't really understand why.

This was a required class I had kept putting off and probably should have taken while I was an underclassman. Er, underclasswoman. But I forgot, and when I met with my counselor to go over my graduation requirements, she pointed out that I hadn't taken it yet. Which made me the only senior in a room composed mostly of rabid, men-hating freshmen. Freshwomen. Who would probably make women's studies their major. Our section was small, and I often felt bad for the three guys in the class who never, ever spoke. They probably feared for their lives.

The desks were arranged in a circle, as our professor employed the Socratic method. She didn't believe in lecturing and felt we would learn more through discussion. I wasn't sure what they paid her for, since she was essentially an academic version of a reality TV competition host—trying to stir up trouble and restate the obvious.

Our current unit focused on "body politics," and I handed my paper to my professor when she went around collecting them. I felt her come to a stop behind me, flipping pages. Was that my essay she was reading?

After she had gathered all the papers, she sat down at her spot in the circle, something she did so we would all be on equal footing. "I hope she doesn't mind, but Ms. Miller turned in an essay entitled 'Feminist Celibacy.'" She put my essay on her desk. "I thought this would be a good starting point for today's discussion. What did you mean by calling celibacy feminist?"

I was well aware of the fact that some second- and third-wave feminists advocated against celibacy, which I found to be highly hypocritical. "I thought it was interesting that people of our generation have a lower number of sexual partners and are twice as likely to be abstinent as previous generations. Even though we're being told the only way to be feminist is to sleep around early and often."

I probably shouldn't have tacked on the last part. The room nearly exploded with competing voices.

"Celibacy is the patriarchy's way of exerting control over women!"

"Haven't you ever heard of owning your sexuality?"

"Why aren't you sex positive?"

It wasn't so much a discussion as a dog pile. Professor Gonzalez raised her right hand, signaling she wanted quiet. "One at a time, please."

"I can answer those questions, if you don't mind. No one controls me. I've made up my own mind." I turned to the next girl who had spoken. "I own my sexuality more than anybody else I've ever met. In that it's totally mine, and I don't share it with anyone." Then to the next woman. "How is celibacy not 'sex positive'? I'm not slut-shaming or judging anyone else. This is a personal decision that I've come to, and I don't understand why you don't want anyone telling you what to do with your junk, but for some reason you think it's okay to tell me what I should or should not do with mine. It is the worst kind of hypocrisy because it's coming from people who should know better."

So, that happened. I'd just confessed to my entire class that I was celibate. I probably should have kept it in the abstract, but it was something I felt strongly about, and I spoke before I thought about the consequences.

As I sometimes do when I'm passionate about something.

There was silence as everyone stared at me. Like I'd just said I had a third arm or twelve toes.

One of the Three Stooges spoke up. "This is just to get dudes to do what you want, right? A way to force us to fall in line?"

We finally had one of the guys contributing to the conversation, and that was what he decided to share? "How am I making men do anything? They're free to date me or not date me. It's not some reward I'm dangling above them to ensure good behavior. It's off the table. Which is actually kind of nice, because it weeds out the losers and makes it so you really get to know someone without sex getting in the way."

A sorority-ish girl in a sweater set leaned forward and said, "I don't get why you would deliberately place those kinds of restrictions on yourself. Don't you want to be free to do whatever you want?"

"I feel very free. I've never been worried about missing a period. I've never worried about contracting a sexually transmitted disease. I've never shared something so personal with a man and then had my heart broken when he didn't call me again."

She was undeterred. "But don't you think it's important as a woman to understand that part of yourself?"

I shrugged one shoulder. "I guess I reject the notion that whether or not I do it is the most important thing about me. That my sense of self and value should be tied up solely in that one act."

The professor finally took the pressure off me by intervening. "Cultural gendered social messages tell us that women should not only be young and sexually appealing, but also be available to men at any time, any place, for any reason. Can you see where feminists choosing to be celibate might help negate that premise?"

That led the discussion to the topics of advertising and pornography as they related to what Professor Gonzalez had just said, but I was finished speaking up for the day. It wasn't that I was embarrassed about the choice I'd made. It was that people treated me like I was some kind of alien life form to be studied. Why couldn't it just be a valid life choice?

My phone buzzed, and I put it in my lap and turned it on. The professor had a no-phones-in-class policy, but I couldn't help myself. Another tweet from Chase.

Chase Covington ✔
@realchasecov

Following

Why can't I get her off my mind? #crush

🗨 ⟲ 22K ♡ 81K

My heart did a funny flip when I read that. There were hundreds of replies from fans offering to help him out with his problem. He hadn't said who he was talking about.

It couldn't be me. Could it? Maybe it was Lexi. That made more sense. Or I was being completely presumptuous that it had anything to do with either of us. For all I knew, he was falling in love with a costar. Or his dry cleaner.

Realistically, I accepted that it couldn't be me, which was good. It was one thing to daydream about a movie star, but it was probably totally different to actually date one. I didn't have any desire to be famous or have my life available for public consumption. It was bad enough telling twenty people that I had chosen to be celibate. I couldn't imagine it on a larger scale. Having it dissected by entertainment bloggers or being mocked by the public for it.

Which was another reason to stop being so pathetically hopeful. There was no way Chase Covington would be interested in dating someone who would never sleep with him.

There comes a point in your day when you realize you're no longer going to be productive. Mine happened at 11:52 this morning when Chase liked my tweet.

Zoe
@zomorezoless

#ProTip Rented a car and don't know which side the gas is on? The gas icon on the dashboard has an arrow that points to the correct side.

I was a font of useless information. The only thing that had ever rivaled my Chase obsession was my love of all things trivia. Trivial Pursuit games ended with me drinking the tears of my fellow players and leaving a trail of their bloodied hearts all over the board.

After my grandparents left the Amish in Pennsylvania and moved out to California, one of the first things they bought was a TV. When I lived with them decades later, they still had that same television. The only program they ever watched was *Jeopardy!*, and I remember sitting on their uncomfortable couch in between them as they missed so many questions. My guess was that my love for weird cultural minutiae came from them. Alex Trebek was kind of my hero.

So I tweeted out random facts. Which was better than having to hear Lexi say, "If you say one more thing about stoplight colors, I will slip arsenic into your orange juice."

Twitter was a good outlet for my useless knowledge. And now Chase had liked my post. I again wanted to read meaning into it and again felt that pointless, bubbly excitement that someone so well known and so incredibly hot had noticed me.

It was probably what it felt like if you were a nerd in high school and the quarterback started paying attention to you.

A situation I had absolutely no experience with.

"Are you trying to see if telekinesis exists?"

I blinked a couple of times, caught up in my Chase-centered world. I put my phone down and saw Noah standing at the door to the conference room. "What?"

"I'm pretty sure you have to actually use your hands to fold the papers yourself and stuff them into the envelopes." He sounded amused, and I was glad I wasn't in trouble for not doing my unpaid internship.

I wanted to work at the Ocean Life Foundation after graduation, so I came in twice a week to do things like fetch coffee and send out letters asking for donations. Which I was supposed to be doing right now but had stopped to stare at the notification that "Chase Covington liked your tweet."

I smiled at Noah. He had started at the Foundation three months ago as an intern in the accounting department, which is where I hoped to work. The first thing I noticed was that he had the same name as one of Chase's characters on this dramedy called *Noah's Ark*, in which his parents had died and Noah had taken over the family farm and raised his two sets of twin brothers and sisters. It had lasted only one season.

Anyway, the real Noah was awkwardly cute. He had sandy-brown hair and dark eyes and was a little bit taller than I was. I'd had a crush on him since he started. We had flirted. (Well, he flirted. I said stupid things.) He was the kind of guy I usually dated.

The anti-Chase.

"Right. I don't have that X-Men mutation. I can't stuff envelopes with my mind." See? Stupid things.

But Noah just kept smiling at me, ignoring my strangeness. "Are you coming to the meeting?"

"The meeting. Yes. I had totally forgotten about it."

I walked with him, and he asked, "What do you think this month's theme will be? Dolphins are awesome? Fish are friends, not food? Meat is murder?"

"I'm going with shoot for the moon. Even if you miss, you'll still land among the stars. Or the starfish." Our supervisor, Stephanie Wheeler, ran these meetings expecting that she would inspire and rally the troops. We were all here because we already wanted to make a difference. Her telling us there was no *I* in *team* didn't really do much to up our game.

And none of us was as obsessed with saving ocean wildlife as Stephanie. I had googled her once, and I'd found all kinds of pictures of her from protests, her mouth wide open, midscream. She was the kind of person who thought animal lives were more important than human ones. Which struck me as a tad deranged, but I figured her heart was in the right place.

We were sitting in the back of the larger conference room trading clichéd inspirational quotes when Stephanie's assistant, Miriam, came by and handed me something metallic. I looked at it. It was a key chain with a shiny blue fish.

"Does this remind you of the rainbow fish?" Noah asked, and it took me a second to place it. My brother, Zander, had gone through a phase where that was his favorite story. It was about a beautiful fish that gave away his shiny, multicolored scales to other fish so they could all be the same. It had always seemed kind of communist to me.

Stephanie called the meeting to order. "As you know, we are only a few months away from our biggest annual fund-raiser. Our charity dinner and silent auction always does very well for us. But this year I thought we should aim higher. I thought we should collect some rainbow fish of our own who can share their scales with us. Add some luster to our event."

I nodded at Noah, acknowledging his excellent guess about the key chain. He winked back at me.

She turned around and wrote the words *Kevin Bacon* on the whiteboard. "I'm sure most of you are too young to remember, but has anyone heard of the Six Degrees of Kevin Bacon?"

I knew what that was. But I also knew better than to interrupt Stephanie when she was on a roll.

"It was a theory that everyone in the world is six degrees away from one another. That everybody in this room knows someone who knows someone who knows a celebrity. We've been trying for years to get some stars to our dinner, and I think if we can pull it off, it will be our biggest year yet. My challenge to you is to talk to everyone you know and find someone famous we can invite to our fund-raiser!"

Stephanie went on about some of the details and deadlines for the event. My first thought was my mom. She had some notoriety. People didn't usually recognize her, but when I told them what she had done, everybody immediately knew who I was talking about.

But my boss was probably looking for a different kind of celebrity.

Someone like Chase Covington. Who I was about to start working with and could probably talk to.

How lame would that be, though? "Hi, you don't know me, but want to do a charity event for the place I want to work at someday? Awesome."

"This year is particularly important," Stephanie said. Her smile no longer reached her eyes. "We've lost a major donor, and it's beyond vital that we bring in enough from our fund-raiser to keep the Foundation going."

That didn't sound good. It worried me, because getting a paying job at a nonprofit was nearly impossible. I had applied for internships at about fifty different charities before I finally landed this one. Even then it was an administrative internship and not the accounting one I had been hoping for. With all the effort and time I'd spent here, I needed there to be a payoff. A real future and career for me, all while making a difference in the world. If I was going to be stuck in the corporate rat race, it was important to me that I work for a company dedicated to making things better.

The meeting finished, and I added the sparkly fish to my key ring. I knew Stephanie took this kind of stuff seriously, and I could earn brownie points for showing her I took it seriously, too.

Even if I thought it was kind of dumb.

On my way out of the room, Stephanie asked Noah and me to stay for a minute. Noah raised both eyebrows at me, as if asking what we'd done. I shrugged. Other than spacing out earlier, I was usually a pretty perfect employee.

"What's up?" I asked.

"Zoe, Noah, I just wanted to let you both know that I'm aware of what a great job you've done for us. And that I would love to be able to promise both of you jobs here when you graduate, but given our current financial situation, I think the only way we can do that is if we raise enough money at the dinner. Anything you can do to help us land someone amazing would go a long way to securing your futures with us. We may be able to hire only one intern."

Jeez. No pressure or anything. I glanced at Noah, wondering how he would take the news that we were basically now competitors.

Stephanie left after that, leaving Noah and me alone. He took off his glasses and rubbed the lenses with a cloth he pulled out of his pocket. "So we have to land a big fish to get jobs here." I grimaced at his pun. "Maybe we should strategize over dinner about how to keep ourselves gainfully employed."

Only two days ago I would have been over the moon with excitement at Noah inviting me to dinner. But Chase and his tweets had turned my attention away from him. My crush didn't feel as strong as it once had.

Which was dumb. I should still be excited. Because Chase was fantasy, and Noah was reality. He was someone I enjoyed being with, and I had been waiting months for him to ask me out.

I smiled at him, reminding myself to keep both feet on the ground and appreciate what I had right in front of me. "I think that sounds like fun."

CHAPTER FOUR

That happened about five minutes into my dinner with Noah. He had gone to use the restroom, and I sneaked a quick peek at my phone. Another Chase tweet that again got my heart furiously pounding. That definitely had to be about me. Presumably he had a housekeeper or a personal chef or assistant who could whip up some baked goods for him if he really wanted them. But for some reason, Chase had said he wanted *me* to make cookies for him. He was using "zo" like in my Twitter username. A tiny voice reminded me that the *Z* and *S* keys were close together. It could have been a slip of a finger.

But it didn't feel that way.

It was all I could think about. I didn't focus on Noah like I should have.

It didn't help matters that whatever teasing banter Noah and I shared at the Foundation did not translate to real life. I knew he was a hipster, but the newsboy cap, suspenders, and bow tie were a step too far even for me. I felt a little silly sitting there with him, as if I were underdressed. We talked about Stephanie's unreasonable request, brainstormed some possible connections to celebrities, and then . . . the conversation died.

Admittedly, it was partly my fault for being distracted by Chase's tweet. Because half an hour after the first one, he posted this.

> **Chase Covington** ✓
> @realchasecov
>
> Following
>
> First time I can remember being excited for Monday.
> #anticipation #realorimagined
>
> 💬   🔁 11K   ♡ 61K

Monday. The day Lexi and I would be on the set of his new movie. It was one of those ensemble superhero movies, a franchise where Chase would play a new hero. Dr. Super Captain something.

"Something important happening on your phone?" Noah asked, giving me a pointed look. I immediately felt guilty. My grandma had been big into not being rude. I should have been giving Noah my full attention.

But all I could think about was Chase and his tweets.

I placed my phone in my purse, putting the temptation away. "Not really. Just . . . nothing."

"I thought maybe I was boring you." Noah folded his arms against his chest and seemed a little angry. "Or that you'd prefer to be somewhere else."

"No!" My throat felt tight, the guilt over his anger making me anxious. I picked up my fork and pushed the food still on my plate, my stomach too upset to eat anything else. I couldn't make eye contact with him. "Of course not."

A long, tense silence passed between us as my mind went completely blank. I couldn't think of a single thing to say. I sneaked a glance at him, and his lips were pressed tightly together. Like I'd failed some kind of test and disappointed him.

The quiet went on for so long that I felt sweat dripping down my lower back. "You go to UCLA, right?"

"Yes."

I was about to ask him what his major was, but I already knew. Accounting. Like me. My thoughts scattered as I tried to talk to him, and I asked him more questions I already knew the answers to. Like, "Do you still live at home?" and "How long have you been at the Foundation?"

We even veered into, "So, how about those Dodgers?" And I didn't watch baseball.

My introverted weirdness had reared its ugly head, and it was like Noah decided he wasn't into it or my pathetic attempt at making conversation. He didn't ask me anything, and his responses were as brief and of as few syllables as possible. Which made me more nervous and awkward and sweaty. I couldn't remember the last time I'd felt so completely self-conscious and uneasy. I'd never been so relieved to get the check. I offered to split it, and he didn't say anything as he took my debit card and slid it into the little leather folder.

Noah drove me back to my car at the Foundation in total silence and mumbled good night. His tires squealed as he sped off, not even waiting for me to get safely inside.

As I unlocked my front door, I decided to not dwell on yet another total social failure. Instead, I thought about Chase's tweets and put Noah out of my mind. I considered showing the tweets to Lexi. I wanted her opinion. But on the other hand, I didn't want to make a fool of myself. If I had built something up in my mind that was not even a little bit based in reality, I couldn't bear her pity.

My decision was made for me when I arrived home and found Gavin and Lexi cuddling on the couch, studying. Maybe I'd show her later.

"Where have you been?" Lexi asked, twirling a strand of hair around her finger.

I set my purse down on the counter and threw my keys into the ceramic bowl. "I think I was on a date." Or being tortured in my own personal hell. One or the other.

That got my best friend's full attention. "With who?"

"Noah."

She put her book down and turned to face me. "That guy from the Foundation you think is cute?"

"That's the one." I went over to the fridge and pulled out a bottled water.

"And you didn't come home to change and get gorgeous first?" She said this like it was some kind of personal affront to her.

I sat in the armchair across from her, the one we'd found at a flea market for ten dollars. "According to my women's studies class, I'm not supposed to get dressed up to please a man. Where's your feminism?"

"You mean that thing that murdered romance?" she retorted.

"Says the girl with a bouquet of red roses from her boyfriend on the counter."

That earned me a warm smile from Gavin. He was super romantic, and Lexi adored being treated so well. It was another point in the pro-Gavin column. Not only did he treat my best friend the way she deserved to be treated, but he had also made a real effort to become my friend. He didn't take my introversion personally (like some other guys, *coughNoahcough*, seemed to). He didn't think something was wrong with me or that I needed to step out of my "comfort zone." He just accepted me as I was and went out of his way to make me comfortable with him.

Lexi folded her arms. "It's not about pleasing him. It's about feeling good about yourself."

I felt good about myself in that moment, but it had absolutely nothing to do with Noah. I took a swig of water.

"Although if he chooses to enjoy your visual confidence, all the better for you. By the way, where are my details? Did he at least kiss you?"

Gulping down the water in my mouth, I shook my head. "Nope. Just dropped me off at my car." And drove off like his tires were on fire.

"What kind of date is that?"

"I don't know if it was a date."

Lexi narrowed her eyebrows at me. "Did you talk only about the office?"

"No." That was true, but the only time I felt okay was when we did talk about the office. "We talked about other things." Sort of.

I didn't want to tell her how weird it had gotten because Lexi lived in fear that I would become a spinster cat lady since I never got past a third date. Which was partly due to my social awkwardness and also to the we-wouldn't-be-sleeping-together thing.

Sometimes I thought about starting a blog called *Things Men Say When I Tell Them I'm Celibate*. Such as:

"I'm not fifteen. I'm not interested in dating like I still am."

"Oh. Great. Hey, I gotta go. I just remembered my grandmother's cat is having emergency surgery tomorrow, and I really want to be there for that."

"Thanks for letting me know this isn't going anywhere."

"Are you trying to become a nun?"

"I can take care of that for you." (Still makes my skin crawl.)

"Cool. Cool, cool, cool. This was fun, but I have a term paper due tomorrow that I spaced and have to go finish." (That guy had already graduated.)

"I'm not interested in being serious right now. I thought you were down for being casual."

"I can respect that." (He respected it so much he never contacted me again.)

And so on and so on. Reactions ranged from some combination of fear to being weirded out or being a little too into it. Lexi kept telling me that with the right guy, it would be a nonissue. That if he really liked me, Mr. Perfect would be willing to wait.

I hoped she was right.

"Who paid?" Lexi demanded.

Paid? Oh right. My "date" with Noah. "We split the check."

"Did he ask you, or did you ask him?"

"He asked. Kind of. It wasn't like a formal invitation, more like, 'Let's hang out and keep talking about our insane boss.'"

"I'm finding for the defendant. I say it was a date," she concluded, settling back onto the couch. "What do you think, Gavin?"

That made me blink a couple of times in surprise. I'd never known Lexi to ask one of her many suitors his opinion before. She was more of the informing-them-what-they-should-think type.

Gavin looked up from his laptop with a thoughtful expression. "I think he's a wimp. He should have let you know whether or not it was a date and if he was interested. People play too many games. It's a waste of time. It sounds like he was trying to hedge his bets. It would have been a date if things had ended the way he wanted. It was a work thing if nothing happened. Dude should have manned up."

He was a little bit right. Noah had not been straightforward about whether it was a date or just a work thing. I hadn't helped things with my inattentiveness and subsequent crashing and burning. Maybe even Chase Covington should bear some of the responsibility.

Tired of the subject and not wanting to share details that would only disappoint my friend, I asked how their days had been. We chatted for a while longer until I excused myself to my room, giving them some privacy.

I had a test to study for, a presentation to work on, and a new job to find.

I didn't have time to be thinking about another failed date.

Or about Chase Covington.

I said goodbye to the Henderson boys. I cried; they didn't. I stopped by and saw my siblings and played with them for a couple of hours. My mother asked me if I could help her out on Tuesday night because her sitter had canceled due to a family emergency. I told her I would. Then I started my job search. Mrs. Henderson was willing to give me a reference, but all of her ladies-who-lunch friends already had nannies.

The problem was I needed a lot of flexibility. Over the next few days, I went around to some of the downtown shops, but there weren't any employers who were interested in hiring me for two or three hours in the middle of the afternoon. They wanted time commitments I couldn't give them.

Next thing I knew, it was early Monday morning, and Lexi was dragging me out of bed. "Today's the day. Let's go, let's go!"

Even though she was caffeine-less, she was like a rabid squirrel on Adderall. Darting all over the place, checking her reflection, running to the closet to look through her clothes, brushing her hair for the ninetieth time.

Although I wouldn't have admitted it, I spent a little more time on my appearance than I normally did. Mascara, blush, and lipstick were even involved. A production assistant had called Lexi Sunday night and told us to dress like New York bowlers. We didn't know what that meant, so we both wore jeans, and I wore a light-gray T-shirt that matched my eyes while Lexi had poured herself into a tight black tank top.

We pulled up at Daylight Studios and were allowed in after we showed our identification and the guard found us on his list. He told us where we would be filming and directed us to park. Once we found the right area in the parking garage, we started the long trek to Building 20B. There were rows and rows of big beige buildings and people walking around in costumes, talking on their phones, driving in golf carts.

Lexi still hadn't managed to calm down. "We're actually here. Can you believe it? We're going to be in a movie!"

I was more interested in seeing Chase in real life. Especially because he'd gone uncharacteristically silent on Twitter all weekend.

We found the right building but were stopped by a PA (short for production assistant). He sent us to get our hair and makeup done and told us where to go afterward, along with the other extras. The makeup trailer was like an assembly line—people were in and out of their chairs in a matter of minutes. My guess was that a lot more time was spent on the stars. I got some foundation and powder and a darker shade of lipstick than I might normally wear and was told to move along. I waited outside the trailer until Lexi was done, and together we made the short walk to the soundstage.

It struck me as funny that when you watch a movie or TV show, the actors look like they're in actual apartments or bedrooms. But there was no ceiling, and one whole wall was missing. It was like a giant one-story dollhouse. There were massive lights, thick black cables, and cameras everywhere. We were directed to a set that looked like a real bowling alley. A director's assistant explained that in this scene, the superhero, Captain Sparta, would be thrown through a wall and into the back of a bowling alley. A stunt double would be performing that part, but Chase Covington would be filmed getting back on his feet and running out to confront the villain. There were a lot of excited whispers and tittering at that part. The DA told us to be serious and not screw up the shot or else we were done. Lexi was chosen to stand at the front of the lane, as though she was about to bowl, and I was a member of her team, sitting on the bench behind her. We were told to look surprised and scared when Captain Sparta went crashing through the wall.

Lexi was told that Captain Sparta would nod to her, and her job was to look shocked. She nodded seriously, but I could tell she wanted to squee.

Wardrobe came in and handed us bowling shirts to wear. Lexi put hers on but didn't button it and tied the bottom ends together at her waist.

There was a lot of waiting involved as the lights were set up and conversations were had, and I didn't know why Lexi wanted to be an actress so badly. It seemed like a lot of boring. My best friend, however, was in her element. She couldn't stop grinning and preening in her spot. It made me smile. I was happy she was getting the chance to live her dream.

A loud whisper rumbled through the room, starting at the door of the soundstage and making its way over to us.

Somebody next to me said over their shoulder, "Chase Covington is here."

I heard the DA hiss, "Be professional!"

He was here.

It was him.

Chase freaking Covington.

CHAPTER FIVE

Zoe
@zomorezoless

Did you know that movies were produced without sound until 1927? #Trivia

Captain Sparta's uniform was a white-and-gold molded bodysuit with a red cape and a Spartan helmet. Chase carried his helmet under his arm and came over to the director to shake hands and presumably say hello.

My heart was beating so hard in my chest that for a second I couldn't hear. It was actually him. Lexi was right. He was even better-looking in real life, and I'd already thought him the most incredibly handsome man alive. I looked down and saw that my legs were shaking. I was grateful I was already sitting.

It was strange seeing him. Up to that point, Chase hadn't been a real person to me. He was a character in a movie or a faceless entity sending out tweets. It was like it suddenly dawned on me that he was an actual human being. Like me. Or Lexi.

Obviously way hotter and taller and more amazing than Lexi or me, but still.

In all those years when we planned on meeting him, my imagined reactions usually involved screaming and jumping up and down, with tears streaming from my face.

I didn't feel the urge to do any of those things. Turned out I had some dignity where he was concerned.

It was a nice thing to discover.

The director showed Chase where he wanted him to lie down—at the end of the lane where Lexi was bowling.

"Let's do a quick run-through," the director said. Chase got down on the floor, and an assistant came over to hand him his weapons—a long, pointed spear and a battered Grecian round shield.

"Quiet on the set! Places!" the assistant called out, raising both of his hands. I sat as still as I possibly could, watching Lexi as she held up her bowling ball, poised as if she were about to send it down the lane.

"Boom! Explosion! Everyone is scared!" the director yelled, and I did my best to react.

Chase had put his Spartan helmet on, and it covered most of his face. He leaped to his feet. He brushed off some imaginary dust and marched down the lane, stopping when he got to Lexi.

"Sorry I ruined your score, miss," he said to Lexi. And there it was, that bone-melting, deep voice that sounded like smoke wrapped in velvet. It made me shudder.

Where I was falling apart even though he hadn't been speaking to me, my friend had no problem stepping up to the plate. She put one hand on her hip and with a flirtatious smile said, "If you want to help me score later, call me."

There was some loud laughter from the crew, and the director called, "Cut." We had been told there wouldn't be any dialogue in this scene.

Was Lexi going to be fired? Chase had spoken to her first. She had only responded. It would kill her if they made us leave.

I might also die a little on the inside if I was forced out after I'd finally gotten the chance to ogle Chase in person.

Okay, I would die a lot.

The same assistant as before came to collect his spear and shield. Chase took off his helmet, and some strands of sweaty blond hair stuck to his forehead. He was so sexy I couldn't breathe.

"Marty doesn't like it when I ad lib. That's why I do it only on test shots," he said to Lexi in a conspiratorial voice. "Kudos to you for that comeback. Hey, you're that girl from the radio station, right? Is your friend . . ."

His voice trailed off, and he turned, looking dead at me. Ignoring Lexi, he walked over and offered me his hand. "You must be Zoe Miller. I'm Chase. Covington."

He added on his last name like I wouldn't know who he was. It was kind of endearing. I stared at his hand until the girl on my right nudged me, and I gave him mine. A zap of raw electricity sparked at his touch, his hand warm and strong and big. It shot up my arm and spread throughout my body, making every part of me tingle.

"Hi, Chase Covington." I don't know how I was able to form words. Or how I hadn't dissolved into an incoherent, blubbering pile of Zoe goo.

"Hi, Zoe Miller."

We were still shaking hands, which was basically holding hands at this point, as it had gone on so long. He was just grinning at me like I was some long-lost friend he was excited to catch up with.

I didn't want to imagine what my slack-jawed, overwhelmed face looked like. He probably thought I was an idiot.

A guy with dark-brown hair and wearing a Bluetooth device in one ear came over. "Chase, Marty wants a word."

Chase finally let go of my hand. "Thanks, One-F. Stick around, Zoe Miller. There's more to say." He walked backward a few steps, like he didn't want to stop looking at me. With a wink, he finally turned and headed toward the director.

The girl who had nudged me said, "You are the luckiest wench in the entire universe. How did *you* catch Chase's eye?"

I understood she was basically insulting me, but seriously, I had no idea.

I tried to watch him out of the corner of my eye, but I didn't think I was doing a good job of being subtle. Especially since he kept catching my gaze and smiling at me, like he knew something I didn't.

Every cell in my body felt alert and aware, like I was a walking exposed bundle of nerves.

"Zoe!" Lexi ran up to me, out of breath. "Can you believe it?"

Certain she was here to talk about the parallel universe that had just opened up, where Chase not only knew my name but was also looking for me and told me he wanted to talk to me and had basically held my hand, I sighed deeply. "I don't really know how to explain it—"

She cut me off. "Neither do I! The DA just told me the director liked what Chase and I did. I'm going to get to say that line in the movie. I'm going to be an under-five! I mean, the line will probably end up on the editing room floor, but this is going to be such a great credit for me. I'm going to say a line in a Chase Covington movie!"

So not where I thought that conversation was about to go. "That's amazing, Lexi. I'm really excited for you." I stood up to hug her.

"Can you hold this for me?" She handed me her bowling ball, and I was surprised it was an actual, heavy bowling ball. I guess I thought it was like those fake rocks from old sci-fi TV shows that were hollow inside but looked heavy. It spoke to her dedication that she'd been holding it this entire time. "I seriously have to pee."

Lexi had the bladder of an ant, so I wasn't surprised she needed to use the bathroom. I was impressed she had lasted this long.

I felt a hand on my shoulder and whirled around, dropping the bowling ball.

A man swore and yelled, "Ow!"

Some tiny part of me was relieved when I realized it wasn't Chase. It was the guy he'd called One-F. He was hunched over, grabbing his left foot.

"I'm so sorry. Are you okay?"

"I think it's broken," he said through clenched teeth.

Chase was there and calling for a medic. The medic rushed over and had One-F sit down. She carefully took off his shoe and sock and did a couple of tests. One-F grimaced and winced the entire time.

"It seems broken. I'm going to call for an ambulance to take him to the hospital."

I put a hand over my queasy stomach. They were definitely going to fire us now.

"Do you want me to come with you?" Chase asked. Which meant One-F was somebody important to Chase. I felt light-headed and seriously considered sticking my head between my knees.

"No, stay here. If you come, it will just delay production."

I apologized two more times, and One-F told me it was fine, accidents happen. The ambulance arrived quickly, and two EMTs got him onto a stretcher and out of the building.

"Excitement's over! Let's set up for another shot!" the director's assistant called out.

"I'm sorry I broke your friend," I told Chase. All I kept thinking about was that scene from *Dirty Dancing* where Baby was trying to act cool and impress Johnny and went to that party and blurted out, "I carried a watermelon!" and then beat herself up afterward for saying something so stupid. That was how I felt. It was my "I carried a watermelon" moment.

"One-F is not just my friend. He's also my personal assistant. Which means I am down one assistant, and I rely on him a lot."

And he was telling me this why?

Noting my confusion, he went on. "I think it's customary that when you maim someone, you have to take over their job. Like a life debt or something."

What? "That's when someone saves your life, and then you have to follow them around and protect them. Which only happens in movies. But people out in the real world don't take over someone's job when they hurt them in an accident."

Chase smiled at me then, a smile so intense and bright I wanted to shield my eyes. "I was teasing. But seriously, your friend mentioned you needed a job. And now I need an assistant. It seems like a mutually beneficial arrangement. What do you say?"

My girl parts said, *Yes, yes, a thousand times yes! What is wrong with you?* But the rational part of my brain resisted. "I don't have any experience as an assistant."

"You used to babysit, right?"

Where had he found that out? From Lexi or Twitter? "I did. They just moved."

He crossed his arms, causing his forearms to flex. Wow. I had never noticed what sexy forearms he had. They were all rugged and strong and corded. "It's basically the same thing."

"So you're a child who has to be watched? I have to make sure you behave?"

Now his smile was sly, sneaky. "You can come over and watch me. I won't object. And I may or may not behave."

I was so seriously out of my depth here. I swallowed hard, twice. I was feeling physical things I'd never felt before. I reminded myself that he was a flirt. I had read the tabloids. I had helped Lexi cut out said tabloid articles. He changed girlfriends more often than I changed my underwear. I needed to remember that.

I also needed to remember that I needed the money. And if I were his assistant for a little while, maybe after One-F got back on his feet (no pun intended), I could ask Chase to help with the Foundation benefit.

Win-win.

"You're considering it." He sounded like he'd won something important.

"Coming over to your house to watch you, or taking the job offer?"

He leaned in, and I almost blacked out when I smelled him. It was light and rich and expensive. Intoxicating.

"Both." He whispered the word, and it felt like a physical touch, making me go weak-kneed.

Gah, he was right. I was considering both. "I am not."

"That's funny. Usually girls as pretty as you are much better liars."

I was overcome with a tongue-tied flush that I felt from the tips of my roots down to the white part of my toenails.

"Which is unfortunate, given that it's such an important life skill."

"Only for actors," I retorted.

Another brilliant smile from him. The same one that had been plastered across millions of movie posters to entice women into spending a lot of money to watch him. He was seriously charming. Why couldn't he have a troll personality? It seemed highly unfair that God had made him both gorgeous and likable.

"You don't even know me," I pointed out.

"Actually, I feel like I do know you."

Before I could ask him what exactly he meant, we were interrupted. "Chase, they need you back in position," someone said behind us. It was his publicist. Aaron with the blue-tipped hair.

"Yep. Coming." Chase put one hand on my arm, and my lungs suddenly felt too small for my body. "You may be here awhile. I have another scene to shoot after this one. Come by my trailer. I have your money for today there. If I'm not back, just wait for me."

For a full thirty seconds, I couldn't move. Then I forced myself to go back to my spot and sit, his words ringing in my ears. The girl next to me was trying to get me to spill, but I couldn't talk. My tongue had grown three sizes and was too thick to use.

Lexi came back. "What did I miss?"

Um, everything.

"Zoe, where's my ball?"

The bowling ball. I had left it. "Sorry, it's over there on the floor." I pointed at it.

She ran over to retrieve it and went back to her mark. She gave me a confused look. I knew I was acting weird. I couldn't help it.

Maybe Chase was chatting me up to get to Lexi. It wouldn't be the first time a guy had used me to get close to her. He totally didn't have to, though. Lexi was more than willing. All he had to do was say the word. Any word. I knew she wouldn't be picky.

We did the scene over and over again as they got different angles for Chase and Lexi. After what felt like a hundred times, the director was finally satisfied. Chase shook Lexi's hand and thanked her. He smiled at me as he left the set.

I thought that was it. Instead, we had to stay and film the scene with the stunt double being thrown through the wall into the bowling alley. It took a while for the stunt guy and special effects people to get set up. When they were finally ready, there were a lot of wires attached to the double, and fake debris was strewn about everywhere (which was good, as I didn't want to see anyone else get bones broken today). The first couple of times my reaction was real because it did surprise me. But it just went on and on, and I felt totally worn out even though all I'd done was sit there and pretend to look shocked. They gave us breaks and pointed us toward the craft services table (which was awesome), but it was still so boring.

It went on for so long that I missed both of my Monday classes, which I hadn't been planning on. I knew I could go in on Wednesday, come out of my introvert shell, and ask some classmates if I could borrow their notes. I'd been asked on more than one occasion; I hoped they wouldn't mind returning the favor.

The DA finally announced that it was a wrap, and a woman with a headset approached Lexi. "We need you to come to the production offices so we can have you sign some paperwork and releases," she said.

I told Lexi I'd meet her at the car, which is where I intended to go next no matter what Chase Covington had said. If he wanted to go out with Lexi, he could pursue her without my help. She hugged me and said she would pick up our paychecks and see me in a few.

I hadn't gone far when I was stopped by a man with a beard. "Hey, I'm Brett. I'm Chase's on-set PA. He asked me to walk you to his trailer when you were done."

"Oh, I was actually just going to leave . . ."

"Come on, he said it was important. You don't want to get me in trouble, do you?"

Having just lost my own job, I certainly didn't want to be the cause of someone else losing theirs. It surprised me when we went outside and I realized it was dark. Brett whistled as he led me past the buildings and into a pack of trailers. "Chase's is right here," he said, opening the door for me.

I stepped inside, not sure what I was supposed to do. I was about to ask Brett, but he had already shut the door behind me and left. The lights were on, and I realized this trailer was nicer than my apartment. Probably bigger, too. It had a full living room and a kitchen. There were some shut doors that I had to assume led to a bedroom and bathroom. I wasn't brave enough to investigate. Especially because I didn't want to catch Chase in a possibly compromising situation. "Hello?" I called out.

No response.

The trailer felt like a generic man cave. Black leather sofa, big-screen TV with video game systems. A couple of vintage movie posters on the wall. Stainless-steel appliances in a kitchen that looked like it had never been used. I sank down onto the couch, surprised at how comfy it was.

And then I nearly jumped out of my skin when a half-naked Chase walked through the front door and said, "I'm glad you're here."

CHAPTER SIX

Chase Covington ✓
@realchasecov

Following

Special thank you to Friends of the Ocean for awarding me their "Sea Star." #noplasticplease #marinedebris #doyourpart

💬   ↻ 8.7K   ♡ 24K

He had peeled off the top part of his costume, and I got to witness firsthand that the molded muscles on his rubber suit had nothing on what was happening underneath. My mouth went completely dry, and all the hairs on my arms stood straight up. Totally unfair. The governor should pass some kind of law saying that movie stars were not allowed to be shirtless in front of mere mortals.

It was like somebody had drawn the perfect man. I had the urge to run my fingers over his abs because I wondered what they felt like. Purely out of scientific curiosity, of course. He must work out constantly to look so—

"Want something to drink?" He interrupted my train of thought as he moved into his kitchen and opened the minifridge.

"No." I hadn't intended it, but my reply came out in a raspy whisper. I cleared my throat. "No, I'm good." So good. So very, very good.

Chase took out a glass bottle of water, twisted off the cap, and took a big drink. I could not stop watching his lips. His blond hair was still wet, and when he pushed it back off his forehead, it took everything inside me not to sigh. He was so effortlessly sexy. Like he had majored in it in college and then graduated with honors.

"About that assistant job . . ."

"You were serious about that?" Why did my voice sound so high?

"I do need the help," he said almost apologetically. He came over and sat next to me on the sofa, and I almost jumped out of my skin.

His eyes really were super blue. Ice blue. Like the sky over a Scandinavian fjord on a summer day—

"I'm operating under the assumption that you're not crazy," he said with a smile to take some of the sting out of his words.

"I'm not crazy." I paused. "Although I acknowledge that is what a crazy person would say. And you don't need to do all this to get to Lexi. Just so you know."

Confusion made his eyes go a shade darker. "Who's Lexi?"

"My friend? The girl you did the scene with today on the bowling alley set?"

"Right." He shook his head. "I'm not interested in Lexi." Then he flicked me a glance that made me think he might be interested in *me*.

I really hoped that set medic was still hanging around. I needed her to perform CPR on me. Because my heart had stopped.

"Anyway, One-F said he'd be willing to e-mail you anything you need to know. The ER doctor said it was a minimal fracture, and he should be in a cast for only a few weeks."

A few weeks? I wasn't sure I could be around Chase for a few weeks. My body might spontaneously combust. But instead of telling him that, I just latched on to something innocuous. "Why do you call him One-F?" A single drop of sweat escaped Chase's hair and made its way down his broad shoulder, over his pec, and then dropped into his lap. I forced my gaze up to meet his.

"His real name is Jef, and he spells it *J-E-F*. And whenever he meets someone new, he always introduces himself as 'Jef. One F.' When I was first starting out in film, one of my directors misheard him and called him 'One-F' for the entire shoot, which we thought was hilarious. It just sort of stuck."

I probably should not have been wondering what his skin tasted like. If the sweat had turned it salty. Which, I acknowledge, is slightly gross, but don't judge.

"Before I forget." Chase leaned in toward me and instantly fried all of my nerves. My pulse exploded, hammering hard inside me. What was he doing? Was he going to kiss me?

But he was only reaching across me to get two envelopes off the side table. "This is for you and Lexi."

I prayed he didn't notice how badly my hands were shaking when he handed them to me. I opened mine and saw a few hundred dollars. "Lexi said something about getting a check from production for today. What is this?"

He looked a little sheepish. "I told one of the producers I was going to add a couple of extras to today's scene. She said that hadn't been budgeted for, so I took care of it."

"You just told your boss you were adding extras, and nobody told you no?"

"People generally don't tell me no."

Boy, did I believe that.

And boy, did I blush at his underlying implication.

"So"—my voice sounded wobbly—"you're paying us out of your own pocket." Why was I repeating things he'd already clarified?

His eyes twinkled at me. "Don't worry. I can afford it."

"But . . . why?"

Had he moved closer to me? I could feel the warmth he gave off, and I wanted to lean into it. Wrap it around me. Like his bones were made of magnets and mine out of metal. I found it almost impossible to resist the pull.

"Because I wanted to meet you. You are the first fan who ever told me I wasn't amazing at something. And it was so refreshing. Like I told you in that message, I started reading everything you've posted. It made me realize you can learn a lot about a person from their Twitter time line." He put his hand over mine, and the entire world ground to a halt. "Something about you intrigued me. I wanted to get to know you better. Then Lexi showed up, and it was like this huge sign from the universe."

There were so many questions I wanted to ask him about what he had just said, but all that was going through my brain on repeat was *CHASE COVINGTON IS TOUCHING ME!*

I was incapable of speech. Even when he slowly pulled his hand away, I sat there frozen, like I'd accidentally side-eyed Medusa. He started talking about the assistant job and what it entailed, and it essentially sounded like running errands and being available in case he suddenly needed me to run said errands. Then he told me the hourly rate, and it was more than double what Mrs. Henderson had paid me, and they had been overly generous.

"I can't . . ." I closed my eyes for a second. I could form words. I had been doing it for decades. I knew I probably should turn him down. But I wanted it in a way that I'd never wanted anything before. "I have responsibilities. I'm in my last semester of college, and I have a twice-a-week internship. Plus, my family and other obligations. I can't be available to you twenty-four/seven."

"That's a shame." His voice was low and teasing, and I felt his words humming inside me.

"I'm serious. I can't be your beck-and-call girl." OMG, I had just called myself a call girl.

Which he totally caught, given the size of his grin. "I didn't expect you to be. We'll work something out. If that's a yes."

"Yes." I hadn't intended to say yes. I had intended to thank him for his very nice offer and go back to my regularly scheduled life.

But the word just slipped out.

"Awesome." He stood up, and I did the same. "Send me your e-mail address and cell number through DM when you get a chance. I'll be in touch."

"K." It was like I couldn't even manage two syllables. "Okay" wasn't that hard to say.

We just stood there. Me because I was an idiot, him because I was standing there like an idiot.

He pointed his thumb over his shoulder. "I'm going to go take a shower now."

Unbidden images filled my head. "Right. Right. And I'm going to go . . . not be here." That finally got my feet moving, and I headed to the front door.

"You know, a good assistant would offer to scrub my back," he said in that teasing tone that made my bones turn into Jell-O.

"A great assistant would remind you that the sexual harassment laws in California are pretty severe."

He laughed. And it was a sincere laugh, full of warmth and magic. It made me realize that all the times he'd laughed on TV shows or in movies had been fake. Because it had never sounded like this. Something tugged on my heart.

"I was right. You don't ever give a guy a break."

"I sure do. Just ask One-F." Figuring that was the perfect exit line, I let myself out and closed the door, his laughter following me as I made my way to the parking structure.

I folded my arms together, unable to keep the smile off my face. Chase Covington had wanted to meet me. He seemed interested in me, which gave me this fizzy, airy feeling. I could have floated back to the car.

Busy reliving our conversation in my head, I jumped when I almost tripped over Lexi. I had totally forgotten about her.

"There you are!" she said, getting to her feet. "I was afraid I was going to have to call on Captain Sparta to find you."

I opened my mouth, intending to tell her everything that had just happened. But something stopped me.

"Here," I said, giving her one of the envelopes. "This was for our work as extras today." I unlocked the car, and we got in.

As I was putting on my seat belt, she tried to give the envelope back. "I know today was hard and long and boring. Take it. So I don't feel so guilty."

I was the one who had something to feel guilty about. I should tell her.

I didn't.

"No, it's okay. You keep it."

She sighed. "Stop being proud. Let me do this. I know you need it."

"Actually, I found a job today." I looked over my shoulder as I backed out, then put the car into drive to take us home.

"You did? That's amazing! Doing what? Babysitting?"

I remembered how Chase had joked earlier and couldn't stop a smile from forming. "Sort of." More like movie star–sitting.

There was an accident up ahead, and Lexi told me to take a side street to Sepulveda Boulevard and then hop on the 405.

"It was so amazing going into the production offices," she said, starting a play-by-play of what had occurred while we were apart.

That nagging, guilty feeling returned. I should tell her about Chase. And the job. It seemed too incredible to be real. I was going to be hanging out with and working for Chase Covington. Who would believe that? I hardly did myself.

"You know who I saw in there? That skank Amelia Swan." Amelia Swan, Hollywood's newest ingenue, did interview after interview about her crush on Chase. She was willowy tall with perfect, shiny red hair and full lips. Lexi hated Amelia Swan. Not for any rational reason, of course, but because she was pursuing Chase and had an actual shot at him. "Who does she think she's fooling with that plastic surgery? She looks like a broom with boobs."

An uneasy feeling settled in the pit of my stomach. Lexi's hatred was based solely on Amelia's quest to land Chase. What would Lexi think if I told her he had flirted with me? Because I was pretty sure he had.

Which really didn't matter, because obviously this wouldn't go anywhere. How could it? He was Chase Covington, and I was just me.

And how do you say to your best friend, "Hey, know that famous star you've been in love with and dreaming about since you were nine? Yeah, he likes me and not you." I didn't want to hurt her. And I didn't want her to feel like I had somehow betrayed her or the Girl Code.

It was nothing. Chase was just a relentless flirt. Nothing would come of it. There was no reason to get Lexi all upset over nothing.

Part of me wanted to keep my interactions with him private. They had been just for me, and I didn't want to share them with anyone else. Not even her.

Which made me think back to the conversations I'd had with Chase that day. I realized I had felt like myself the whole time. But in a good way. I didn't feel like I had to compensate or behave differently. I could just be me, dumb comments and all, and I never felt "less than" or like he was judging me or I'd put him off. He reminded me a little of Gavin. There was this underlying current of comfort between Chase and me. One that was instant and didn't have to be cultivated.

Of course, it had been way buried under all the physical tension I'd felt. Like he was some live wire and I didn't know where the next surge of power was going to come from. Or whether I'd get electrocuted by him. He seemed exciting. Maybe even a bit dangerous. It was certainly something I'd never experienced with a guy before. Just thinking about being close to him on his couch gave me goose bumps.

People always said, "Don't meet your idols." But they were wrong. Because real-life Chase was a million times better than on-screen Chase.

I sent Chase my information after I set up a new e-mail account. There was no way I was going to tell him my e-mail was truechaser@siuc.edu. About five seconds later, I got a message from One-F. He sent me some documents he wanted me to sign, including one called a nondisclosure agreement. Which basically meant that I wasn't allowed to talk to any-one about anything related to Chase. I was happy to sign that one. It gave me a legal reason not to tell Lexi everything.

Then One-F asked me to pick up Chase's dry cleaning and sent me a picture of the receipt. He also wanted me to stop by Chase's agent's office to get his fan mail. Apparently the agency was overwhelmed by it and wanted it gone. He said I could drop everything off at Chase's house, and he gave me the codes to the gate and the front door. He promised to forward the production e-mails with Chase's daily call sheets. Which were basically the schedules for each day of shooting, listing what days Chase was to be there and his call time—when he was supposed to show up.

There were a lot of clothes to pick up at the dry cleaner's, but the tsunami of fan mail I had to retrieve was ridiculous. It literally filled up my entire trunk. Just boxes and boxes of it. I decided to drop everything by his house on Wednesday morning, as my mom needed my help that night.

I drove out to Marabella, making sure to cruise down the main strip. I loved this quiet little town. The main street was comprised of Wild West–type storefronts in fanciful colors like pink, turquoise, and purple. It was the kind of place where the locals tore down freeway signs so tourists couldn't find it. Marabella had the most beautiful, pristine beaches, and the natives didn't want to share them.

Nobody had been happy when Google Maps became a thing.

As I pulled into the driveway, I got a text from Chase. He had stopped direct-messaging me on Twitter and now just texted me instead.

> Did you get my dry cleaning? They have a tux I need for an event tomorrow night.

It was kind of hot that he owned a tux.

> Yes, I got it. I'll bring it by tomorrow morning. I'm helping out my mom tonight.

My mother had enough time to say hi and bye before she was gone, leaving me with my four half siblings: Zander (ten), Zane (eight), Zelda (four), and Zia (almost two). I asked them what they wanted for dinner, and Zia clapped her hands together and screamed, "'Acaroni and cheese, Zo-Zo! 'Acaroni and cheese!" I knew it wasn't exactly healthy, but it was her favorite food in the whole world, and she was so adorable I couldn't say no. I put my hair up into a messy bun and got started.

I somehow managed to get all their hands washed and everyone sitting at the table and eating in a reasonable amount of time. Zane was obsessed with superheroes and had on his Spider-Man costume. I convinced him it was okay to take off his gloves and remove his mask in order to eat. Zia happily got more of the mac and cheese on her face than in her mouth, Zander was more interested in his iPad than eating, and Zelda kept trying to give noodles to Mr. Wriggles, her purple panda.

"Spider-Man doesn't eat," Zane grumbled.

"He does eat. All the time. His aunt May makes sure of it," I said, catching Zia's sippy cup before it ended up on the floor. "All the superheroes eat. Even Captain Sparta."

This was indicative of how much real estate Chase Covington currently occupied in my brain.

"Which one is he?" Zander asked.

"The awesome one!" Zane shouted, giving Zander a dirty look.

Time to intervene. "He's the former tomb raider who found a gem that had all the spirits of 'The 300.' They were Spartan soldiers who single-handedly held off a Persian invasion. Some of the greatest warriors the world has ever known. And the gem gives him all the strength and abilities of 'The 300' combined. He goes off to New York to fight with all the other superheroes."

Which made me think of Chase in his Captain Sparta costume.

And when he was partially out of his costume.

As if sensing my distraction, Zia announced, "I pooped."

Sighing, I got her out of her booster seat and took her to the bedroom she shared with Zelda. Too late, I realized she had managed not only to fill her diaper but also somehow to shoot it all the way up her back to her neck. I gagged a little. "Gross, Zia."

"Luboo, Zo-Zo."

"I love you, too." I sighed, carrying her at arm's length into the bathroom. I got her cleaned and rinsed and in her pajamas fairly quickly, but it wasn't quickly enough.

Zander and Zane were in the living room. Zane was trying to see if he could stick to walls, and Zander was ignoring him. "Don't you have that science thing you're supposed to be working on?" I asked. Zander rolled his eyes as he put down his tablet and got his backpack.

I couldn't find Zelda, and it was never a good thing when she was this quiet. Not to mention I still smelled poop, which meant it was probably on me somewhere. I needed to change out of my yoga pants and old T-shirt and take a shower.

I found my sister on the floor of the pantry, her mouth stuffed with chocolate chips. "No!" I exclaimed, grabbing the bag from her. "Hurry, we have to get you to a toilet."

She stood up when I pulled on her arm and mumbled something that sounded suspiciously like, "I feel sick."

Then she proceeded to projectile-vomit chocolate all over me. Although she wasn't allergic to chocolate, Zelda had an intolerance to one of the ingredients. Our mom had been working with an allergist to figure out which one, and despite the fact that it made her throw up every time she ate it, the girl just could not stay away from it. Which I understood, because it was chocolate, after all.

Somehow she managed to get none of it on her and all of it on me. With a smile she announced, "I feel better!"

"You need to go brush your teeth," I said, slowly backing away toward the kitchen sink, trying not to drip all over the floor. "Zane! Come help Zelda brush her teeth."

"Why do I have to?" he whined.

"Because superheroes help their sisters!" I yelled back. He stomped into the room, clearly unhappy with me, and pulled Zelda away.

Then the doorbell rang. I went over to the kitchen sink and used a paper towel to scrape off as much vomit as I could. "Zo! Door!" Zander called. I was tempted to tell him to get it, but Mom had a rule. He was too young to open the door at night.

The bell rang again. It was probably Mrs. Wittemore. She had been a very good friend to my mom over the last two years, and she did not like to be kept waiting when she stopped by. "Hold on, hold on," I muttered.

I opened the door, and there, on my front porch, stood Chase Covington. "Hey. I was nowhere near your neighborhood—"

I did the only thing I could do. I slammed the door shut on him.

CHAPTER SEVEN

Zoe
@zomorezoless

A kindle of kittens, a sounder of swine, a sloth of bears, a crash of rhinoceroses, a tower of giraffes. #Trivia #animalgroupnames

♡ ↻ 0 ♡ 1

I'd just slammed the door in Chase Covington's face.

Taking in a deep breath, I reopened it. He looked adorably confused. He wore a pale-blue T-shirt that made his eyes impossibly bluer and jeans that had been created solely to be worn by him. And I was covered in poop and puke.

"Nobody's ever shut a door on me before." And I'd never shut a door on anyone before. "Bad time?"

No, I was so glad he'd decided to visit when I had one sister's regurgitated chocolate and the other's fecal matter all over me. "You could say that."

"I just needed to get my tux. I thought I would save you the trip."

My eyes flicked past him to the dark, quiet street. I thought celebrities were chased by paparazzi everywhere they went. I stepped back to let him inside. As he came in, I pushed myself against the wall so I wouldn't get puke on him, acutely aware the entire time that he looked like, well, a movie star, and I looked like something the cat found in the dump, dragged across town, and then shoved under the dryer.

Zia toddled in, sucking on her thumb, as I closed the front door. She walked over to Chase and looked up at him from under her lashes. "I Zia."

Chase crouched down so they were eye level. "Hi, Zia. I'm Chase." She reached out and patted his cheek. "Hi, Cheese."

"Chase," I corrected her, and she glared at me. "He Cheese."

He straightened to standing with an amused smile. Zia held up both her pudgy hands and reached for him. He complied, picking her up. She quickly nestled her head against his shoulder and sighed. "I loves him. My Cheese."

My baby sister was seriously flirting with him. Not that I could blame her.

"You should take it as a compliment," I explained. "Cheese is her favorite food."

Chase smiled. He had Zia propped on one side like he'd been holding kids his entire life. He didn't look even a little bit uncomfortable. His gaze traveled up and down my body, only this time it felt like a question instead of a compliment.

"My four-year-old sister barfed on me. She got into some chocolate chips. Which she's kind of allergic to. Leaving me with this lovely candy-coated shell." Great. Another watermelon-carrying moment. He hadn't asked, but I had to overshare.

"Hmm. Does that mean you'll melt in my mouth and not in my hands?"

A wave of want slammed into me. I was pretty sure I would melt either way. The offer was completely gross on its surface, given where said candy-coated shell had come from, but somehow still hot.

As if he hadn't just shifted my entire world on its axis, he cocked his head to the side, and I realized he was looking into the living room at my other siblings. "There's four kids total?"

"Yes. Why?"

"Go take a shower and get changed. I'll watch them."

"Seriously?"

"I'm not completely helpless. When I did *Noah's Ark*, I spent a lot of time with the sets of twins who played my siblings. They wanted us to bond and seem like a real family during filming. I learned how to take care of little kids. Go on." I still hesitated. "Trust me."

Without waiting to see if I would take him up on his offer, he went into the living room and started introducing himself to my brothers and other sister. I watched as he put Zia down on the couch, took off his jacket, and settled on the floor. Zelda showed him Mr. Wriggles, and Zane lifted up his Spider-Man mask.

As much as I wanted to stand there and be totally impressed at how well he was interacting with them, I really did need a shower. Part of me felt bad—I was supposed to be *his* assistant, helping him and making his life easier. Not the other way around. I stopped by the laundry room and threw all my clothes into the slop sink. I'd rinse them out later. I grabbed a towel from the dryer and wrapped it around myself as I stepped over mountainous piles of clean and unclean laundry and headed to the bathroom.

The water took forever to heat up, even though I kept willing it to hurry. When it finally hit lukewarm, I hopped in and scrubbed every square inch. I washed my hair, too, just in case.

The water finally became hot as I finished. I went to my mom's room to borrow some stuff. I hadn't planned on spending the night, so I didn't have any extra clothes. Borrowing clothes from her was always a little iffy. I was at least four inches taller than she was, and her clothes were either heavily Moms R Us, nurse's scrubs, or clubbing outfits from the early nineties that she couldn't bear to get rid of.

I settled for an old worn but soft SIU shirt that sort of fit and a pair of plaid pajama pants that had belonged to my stepdad, Duncan, before he died. They almost went to my ankles. I yanked the drawstrings tight. Like I was girding my loins, ready to do battle. I grabbed an elastic band from the bathroom and pulled my hair into a ponytail. I looked at the messy pile of toothbrushes and toothpaste. Should I brush my teeth? I decided against it, knowing it would keep me from throwing myself at him.

As I walked down the hallway, I thought for a second there were strangers in the living room. Then I realized all the voices were coming from Chase. He was sitting on the floor, Zia in his lap, Zelda snuggling up on his left side, reading one of Zane's Batman comics aloud, doing completely different voices for each character. All the kids were entranced. Even Zander, who was supposed to be doing his homework, had stopped to listen intently.

Chase finished the comic, and the kids groaned when he said, "The end."

"Can we read another?" Zane asked. "Maybe we can download a Captain Sparta one."

The knowing look in Chase's eyes made my cheeks turn pink. "Yes, I heard about your great love for Captain Sparta. How you were telling them all about him earlier."

Little traitors. "That's not quite what happened," I informed him, but I could see he didn't believe me.

"Did you know that sometimes at my job I get to dress up like Captain Sparta and pretend to be him?" Chase asked Zane, whose eyes grew impossibly big. Another victim of his charm.

"Hey, Zo, what's a school of squid called?" Zander asked. Most likely for his project. I probably should have made him look it up, but I was still a tad scatterbrained over the fact that Chase Covington was in my home.

"Regular or giant?"

"Uh, regular."

"A shoal."

That appreciative look was back in Chase's eyes. "I think it's cool you know random stuff like that."

More blushing that I felt all the way down to my feet. "Okay, bedtime." I would get the kids in bed and the movie star out of my house and everything would be fine.

"I want to say prayer!" Zelda shouted, raising her hand. I had hoped we might skip our family prayer, but no such luck. We knelt down and held hands. Chase offered me his, and I took it. That electric current was still there, the one that made me feel excited and freaked out at the same time.

Zelda prayed for Mommy to be safe, and for Daddy to like his wings, and for Chase to be her new friend, and for me not to be mad at her for throwing up, and for Mr. Wriggles to not have a headache.

We said amen after she did, and I told the boys to brush their teeth and get into their pajamas. Zander complained about not finishing his homework, and I was tempted to tell him it was his fault for waiting so long, but instead I said he could finish it in his room and then go to bed. Which led to Zane whining about the light being on and my telling them to knock it off and just go.

I marched them down the hallway, stopping by the girls' room to grab some pajamas and a Good-Nite diaper for Zelda. After I got the boys brushing their teeth, I came back and helped Zelda change, feeling Chase's gaze on me the whole time. Figuring she'd already brushed her teeth after the puking episode, I sent her off to her room.

"Come on, Zia," I said, offering my hand.

She shook her head adamantly. "No! Cheese put me bed!"

"I'd be happy to," he offered. I told him her bedroom was the third door on the left, down the hallway.

He picked up Zia, and on his way out of the living room, he came to a halt way too close to me. I could feel his warm breath on the side of my neck. "Is there anyone else you want me to put to bed?"

It sounded innocent, but I caught his unspoken meaning. That made me suck in a huge gulp of air as I ordered my legs to keep me vertical. He chuckled like he knew exactly what he had done to me. I reminded myself that it wasn't a big deal for him to say stuff like that. He probably said a lot more explicit things to a lot more experienced women. But it made me all flustered and nervous. Like a junior high school girl at her first dance.

So I did what any self-respecting, awkward junior high girl would do. I hid in the bathroom.

And I brushed my teeth.

Just in case.

When I had collected myself enough that I felt like I could face him again, I heard his voice in the girls' room. He was singing to them. Which was so sweet it made me put my hand over my heart. If I could have bottled up that feeling and sold it, I would have been a billionaire.

Not wanting him to catch me eavesdropping, I returned to the living room. Which I suddenly realized was an absolute pigsty. It was one of those things where you get accustomed to a mess because you live with it all the time and it seems like no big deal, but when you realize how it must look to an outsider, you're embarrassed.

"I hope you're not doing that on my account." Chase leaned against the living room wall, hands in his pockets, looking so utterly delicious that I froze. "I've already seen it."

Yep, totally humiliating. I sank onto the couch and put down the basket of clean laundry I had planned on stowing in another room. I started folding it to give my hands something to do. "My mom's got a lot on her plate. I try to help out when I can. She has this ongoing to-do list. Or as I call it, the Ta-Da List. Because it would be magic if we actually accomplished anything on it. But when you have this many small kids, it's like continually cleaning up by yourself after a raging party you didn't attend that happens every night. Which means my mother's housekeeping style can best be described as 'There appears to have been a struggle.'"

He let out another laugh as he took in his surroundings. He looked at all the pictures on the walls, the knickknacks, and the books on the shelves. He didn't seem to notice I was nervously babbling. Or else he was polite enough not to comment on it.

"What about the giant ones?"

What the what? "Giant ones?"

He picked up one of the wooden toys my grandfather had carved for me when I was little. "Groups of giant squids. What are they called?"

"Oh, schools. Like fish. And a group of little kids is called a migraine."

Chase laughed, that same real laugh, and I felt it in the lower part of my stomach. "I love that you know random stuff like that."

"It's Alex Trebek's fault."

He put the wooden horse on the shelf. "Why? Did he hold you down and force you to learn things?"

"I always wanted to meet him and be on *Jeopardy!*. I used to read trivia books all the time." It occurred to me that I hadn't picked up a book like that in years.

His fingers drifted across my grandma's old Bible. "The prayer was nice. My grandmother was religious."

Not like mine. "I'll see your religious grandmother and raise you an Amish one."

"Really?"

"Really. It's a long story, though. I'll have to tell you about it another time." Because didn't he need to leave? I needed him to leave. I was running out of clothes to fold. "I didn't ask you before, but how did you know where my mother lives?"

"It was on those forms you filled out for One-F." Right. I'd had to provide previous addresses and emergency contacts. He could have put two and two together. That seemed like a lot of effort, though. He must have really loved that tuxedo.

He found a photo album and held it aloft. "May I?"

"Sure, stalker."

He grinned and settled onto the couch next to me. "Trust me, this is a new experience for me, too. Usually it's the other way around." He opened the album to the back page and saw a baby picture of Zia with her name on it. "Your parents seem pretty committed to this 'Z' thing."

Parents? Another can of worms not worth opening just then. "My grandpa's name was Zev, and my mom's name is Zerah. She carried on the theme."

He flipped a page. "I bet that gets confusing."

"It does. You should hear her when she's trying to yell at someone. She will run through every name except for the kid she's mad at."

I finished folding the laundry in the basket. Which made me all fidgety and not sure what to do with my hands. I figured I should probably run and get more, but I wondered if that would seem pathetic. I mean, I was sure he was super impressed with my glamorous lifestyle of staying in and doing laundry and watching small children. Would getting another load make it worse?

Chase perused the pictures, sometimes turning the album slightly to better see the photo. He had really nice hands. Long, tapered fingers. I thought of earlier when he'd held my hand during Zelda's prayer. I'd really liked it.

But sitting in that silence, not sure what to do or say next, it suddenly dawned on me.

I was alone in my childhood home with Chase Covington.

CHAPTER EIGHT

Zoe
@zomorezoless

Dr. Henri J. Breault invented the childproof cap in 1967, dropping child poisoning by 91%. #Trivia

I took the only escape I could think of. "Can I get you something to drink? We have water, milk, and possibly apple juice in boxes."

"I'd love some water."

As I hopped up and hurried into the kitchen, I wondered if he knew the water would be from our tap. No bubbles, nothing sparkling, and nothing infused with any kind of fruit. When I walked in, I realized I hadn't cleaned up the remainder of Zelda's version of sharing.

"Did you need help?"

Chase so startled me I nearly dropped the Swiffer mop. "I'm fine. I just realized there's some mess. From earlier. That I need to clean." I must have been seriously impressing him with my mastery of the English language.

"I can get the drinks. Where are the glasses?"

"In that cabinet there. Left of the sink. You'll find them behind the sippy cups and bottles."

He wasn't anywhere near me, and I was still shaking. Shivers skated up and down my spine. Like someone was dripping ice water on my bare back, a single drop at a time. Would I ever feel totally calm around him?

Part of me whispered that I wouldn't want that. I liked the physical sensations he caused.

"What kind of sorcery is this?" he muttered, and I turned to see him struggling with the cabinet lock.

"The whole house is childproofed. But somehow they keep managing to get in." It was one of my mother's favorite jokes, so it just sort of slipped out. It did make him smile, though.

It was too late when I realized what I was doing. He stayed put, and I leaned in close to undo the latch. I should have moved back.

I didn't.

"Thanks," he murmured, feeling his breath against my still-wet hair.

"You're welcome," I whispered. We weren't touching, but it felt like we were. All I had to do was take one step back and I'd be flush against him. Or just turn my head and we'd practically be kissing.

Instead, I reached inside the cabinet. I almost exploded in flames when he put his hand on my wrist. "I said I could get it." His voice was low, gruff. Exciting.

"I'm supposed to be the hostess." He didn't respond, and he didn't let go of my arm. My skin pulsated underneath his touch. Gulping, I extricated myself, pulling my arm free. Even though I didn't want to.

Which was surprising.

"You could mop. If you want to help," I said when I could speak again.

"Selfishly, I'm happy to let you clean up the kid puke." I heard him put the glasses on the counter, open the freezer to look for ice, and break out cubes from a tray. Then he opened the refrigerator. "Where's the water?"

"In the faucet." I sneaked a glance at him, sure he would be grossed out or surprised. He was neither. He just lifted the tap and filled the glasses.

"So is this a new service you're offering all your fans? Free babysitting?"

He let out a short bark of laughter. "Um, no. I don't even take pictures when I'm asked."

"Really? Why not?" That seemed harmless as far as fan interactions went.

"A couple of reasons." He leaned against the counter, his drink in hand. "When I'm filming, on a typical day almost every minute is scheduled. And if I'm stopping thirty times to take selfies, that adds up and puts me behind. Which isn't fair to the people who are waiting for me, and it isn't very professional. Plus, when you take a picture with a fan, they immediately upload it to social media, and then there's electronic evidence of where you are right that minute. I don't want people to know that. Especially not tabloids."

"I have to tell you that I was surprised when you showed up without a trail of paparazzi behind you."

"They're easy to avoid. There's some places it can't be helped—big events, award ceremonies, movie premieres. There's certain restaurants they stake out. Which is why celebrities go there. They want to be photographed. Those actors and singers you see complaining about their lack of privacy? Those are the ones who have a paparazzo on their payroll, and they pay them to show up and take pictures everywhere they go. You can absolutely avoid them and have real privacy."

"What about the airport? They always have pictures of celebrities going there."

"Again, that's on purpose. The airlines offer private entrances and will make elaborate arrangements to get you out of the airport so no one even knows you were there."

That wasn't what I had thought. I thought stars like him couldn't even walk outside the door without being accosted.

"I'm usually fine in big cities like Los Angeles or New York. The people there generally leave you alone. The problem is when I go to small towns. But wear a hat, put on some sunglasses, and people overlook you."

"I doubt that," I said. Because there was something special about Chase. I had seen it earlier when he'd had my siblings eating out of his hand. Most people were just average. You didn't notice them when you were in a store or walking down a street. But Chase was different. It was like he gave off a special glow. I couldn't stop looking at him or being drawn to him, and I'd witnessed him having that effect on every person on set yesterday. He was larger than life. I couldn't imagine any scenario where he'd be out in public and wouldn't draw the eye of every woman in the vicinity.

Finally finished, I threw away the pad and returned the rest of the mop to the pantry. I washed my hands and grabbed a paper towel to dry them off. Then Chase handed me my glass.

"To new beginnings," he said, holding his glass aloft. Would I ever get used to looking at him? To not having my breath catch every time our eyes met?

I nodded and clinked my glass against his. My mouth had gone so dry that I was parched. Like I'd just spent a week crossing the Sahara.

If there was a seductive way to drink a glass of water, my mouth decided to do the opposite.

I tipped my drink back too quickly and almost choked. I put the glass on the counter, and Chase patted me on the back a couple of times. I waved him off. "I'm okay." Mortified and wanting to run into the bathroom to hide, but okay.

"Yeah, I hate when I'm drinking and the ice just attacks my face," he teased.

He was funny. Why did he have to be funny?

"Yesterday when I assured you I was normal, I may have exaggerated slightly." I was obviously an insecure freak who should be kept away from regular people.

"I think you're kind of amazing," Chase said, reaching out with his hand like he was going to touch my face. I backed up until I hit the sink. I braced my arms behind me, trying not to collapse in a heap. Because even though he hadn't made contact, my skin felt like he had.

He put his hand down, his expression puzzled. A few beats passed before he said, "I make you nervous, don't I?"

Uh, understatement of the year. But his movie-star ego didn't need to hear it. "I'm . . . I'm not nervous."

He inched fractionally closer to me, one small movement with each loud, slow thud of my heart. "I don't normally make girls nervous. Excited, yes. Overwhelmed. Shocked. Up for anything, usually. But not nervous." This time he did touch me. His fingers tucked some stray hairs behind my ears. I closed my eyes and dragged in a sharp breath. All those sensations . . . I totally got the overwhelmed reaction. And the excited and shocked thing.

And possibly even the up-for-anything impulse.

I opened my eyes and tried to deny it, but now Chase stood directly in front of me, his heat warming me, pulling me in. He put his hands against the counter on either side of me.

He'd trapped me.

"I think I know why I make you nervous."

"I told you, I'm not nervous."

A playful smile lit up his entire face. "Like I said, you're a terrible liar." He focused his gaze on my lips. He ducked his head toward mine. We were almost touching. So close, but not enough. I put my right hand on his chest, but whether it was to stop him or pull him closer, I didn't know.

It was like a scene out of my favorite movie, complete with my favorite movie star.

His lips hovered above mine, his slow, steady breaths a huge contrast to my short, shallow ones. "Zoe." Chase whispered my name, and it sounded like both a question and a promise. It made my knees buckle, my stomach tighten, and my pulse explode.

"Wait," I told him, pushing at his chest. "Do you hear that?"

"Hear what?" he asked.

"The garage door," I hissed, breaking the spell he'd cast over me. "My mom is home. You have to go. Right now."

Although my mother had matured over the last eleven years since she'd married Duncan, I didn't want her to meet Chase and get all fangirlie and weird or talk about her own brush with fame. It was humiliating enough in school; the last thing I wanted was for him to find out.

But he wasn't budging. I pushed against him again, and it was like trying to move a brick wall. A hot, muscular, well-defined brick wall, but still. "I'm serious. You have to go."

"Are you embarrassed by me?" he asked in a voice that was both bewildered and amused. But at least he finally took a step back. I grabbed him by the wrist and dragged him into the living room. I grabbed his jacket off the couch and shoved him toward my mom's bedroom at the back of the house.

"That's not it. It's . . . difficult to explain."

"Aren't you a little old to be in trouble for having a boy over while you're babysitting?"

"You just need to leave." I opened a window, pulled out the screen, and dropped it on the ground. I'd put it back later. I indicated that Chase should use the exit I'd just provided.

"Do you seriously want me to climb out a window?"

I heard the door from the garage to the kitchen open and shut. My mom called out, "Zoe?"

Frantic, I started pushing him, trying to force him out. He laughed quietly but gave in. "I'm going, I'm going. But you have a lot of explaining to do."

"Whatever," I said.

He sat on the windowsill, hanging one leg over the ledge. His attention was drawn to the massive poster that hung over my mother's bed. It hadn't occurred to me to try and block his view or take it down. "Is that your mom?"

That stupid picture had made my life miserable for years. I would have kept it from him if I could have.

My mother called my name again. It sounded like she was coming down the hall.

I was about ready to throw all my weight against him. "Yes, it's my mom. Now go!"

Laughing, he swung both legs through the open window and jumped the three feet to the ground, landing easily. Then he made a dramatic Shakespearean-type bow. "Till next we meet, my lady."

Okay, it was sweet. But I still rolled my eyes and closed the window. I had just finished lowering the blinds when my mom opened the door. "Oh, there you are."

The shock of her entering the room made my stomach clench and my heart freeze. "Sorry, I didn't answer because I didn't want to wake anybody up."

She didn't seem to buy it. She came over and yanked the blinds up. Part of me was afraid Chase would still be standing there, waiting for his chance to go all Romeo on me. Fortunately, he was gone.

And it was dark, so she didn't notice the missing screen.

"Mama? Mama!" Zia's voice crackled over the baby monitor. Like she'd been awake this entire time, waiting.

"Looks like your plan didn't work," my mom said, taking off her purse and jacket and laying them on her bed. I followed her to the girls' room, where Zia was standing with her arms held out. My mother picked her up and rested her cheek on Zia's corn-silk-blonde curls.

Oh, I didn't know about that. Even if the baby had woken up, Mission Get Chase Out of the House had gone very well.

Until my favorite little saboteur took her thumb out of her mouth long enough to say, "Zo-Zo's boyfrien' is Cheese."

Icy panic gripped my throat, making it impossible to respond. How did she even know that word? It wasn't like I'd ever had boyfriends.

"Good choice," my mom whispered as she gently rocked Zia to sleep. "My boyfriend is brick-oven-style pizza."

"No," Zia said, sounding fully awake. "Mommy's boyfrien' is Daddy."

I couldn't see her, but I felt my mother go still and heard her choke back a sob. Her voice was thick with emotion when she replied, "That's right. Daddy will always be Mommy's boyfriend."

Zia's words affected me, too, like a punch in the gut. Duncan had been my stepfather for ten years and had been such a good man and a good father. The only one I'd ever known. I tried not to think about how much I missed him.

"Hey, I gotta head back to school," I told my mom, my chest feeling tight, my voice rough. I briefly wondered whether Chase had left or if I'd run into him in the front yard.

"Thank you so much," she said as she sat in the rocking chair, trying to soothe Zia. "And I hate to do to this you, but Shelly's aunt is still sick, and she canceled Saturday, too. Would you mind? I'm working from eleven to seven."

I planned on meeting with a study group then, but I could reschedule. Family first. "Yeah. Of course. See you on Saturday."

I hurried outside before Zia could rat me out further.

As I put on my seat belt and started up my car, I glanced in my rearview mirror. It was then that I realized what had happened, and I let out a groan.

After all that, Chase had forgotten his tux.

CHAPTER NINE

Chase Covington ✓
@realchasecov

`Following`

I'll be putting that on my Ta-Da list. #shemakezmesmile

💬   🔁 9.9K   ♡ 31K

The next morning before class, I texted Chase to remind him about the forgotten tuxedo he said he had to have that night.

> Can't really text right now.
> Can I maybe just call you?

> Sure. And did you just Carly
> Rae Jepsen me?

> LOL

I actually prefer SALTS to LOL. Smiled A Little, Then Stopped.

A second later my phone rang. I considered making him wait, picking up on the fourth ring so I wouldn't seem too eager.

Instead, I answered immediately. "Hey."

"Hey. Sorry about leaving that tux last night. But somebody was shoving me out a window."

"I did not shove. I forcefully encouraged." His phone sounded crackly. "Where are you?"

"I'm running in Runyon Canyon. Want to join me?"

Running? That probably meant he was shirtless, right? And that his muscles flexed as he ran, and the sweat probably made his chest glisten in the sun . . . I told my mind to knock it off.

Shoving my laptop into my book bag, I switched my phone from my left ear to my right. "No, thanks. I'm allergic to running."

"What?"

"Last time I ran, my skin was all flushed, my heart raced, I got sweaty and short of breath. I looked my symptoms up online, and the Internet diagnosed them as an allergic reaction."

"If that's true, then I'm allergic to a lot of very fun, enjoyable things."

Did he ever not flirt? I was glad he couldn't see how much he made me blush.

"So anyway, about your tuxedo . . ."

"Right! I'm having some people over for a business lunch today, but we should be done about one thirty. Would you mind bringing it by then?"

My last class would be done at noon, giving me plenty of time to eat and then drive his tux over. "I can do that."

"Do you have my address?"

I remembered he lived in the Hollywood Hills and that One-F had e-mailed me Chase's address and security codes. "Yep. One-F is very thorough."

"Just let yourself in when you get there. See you soon."

I made myself some toast and headed off to campus. As I walked along the busy main street toward the crosswalk, I wondered whether the tuxedo thing had been deliberate. Like a girl who left her scarf in a guy's apartment so he'd have to call her again.

But in Chase's defense, and as he'd pointed out, I was the one who had all but shoved him out a window.

This one was probably on me.

Gorgeous wouldn't do the Hollywood Hills justice. There were tall, leafy trees (not the palm trees I was used to) and well-manicured greenery everywhere I looked—and beautiful mansions built on ledges of hills. I wondered which one was Chase's.

When I got to his neighborhood, a line of cars was waiting. I saw a gate and a guard. One-F hadn't mentioned that. The Porsches, Ferraris, and Bentleys in front of me were waved through, but the guard stopped me in my ancient Honda Civic.

"May I have your name, miss?" If someone asked you to imagine a security guard, you'd probably think of some old grizzled man or a middle-aged guy with a huge gut. But this very in-shape good-looking man bore a striking resemblance to Chris Pratt.

Then again, Chase was so rich that for all I knew the guard actually was Chris Pratt. "Name, please?"

"Zoe Miller."

He did something on his tablet and then asked, "May I see your ID?"

My stomach twisted. I had a bad feeling for some reason. Memories of my poli-sci professor, a former ACLU lawyer, turning red in the face as he screamed that we weren't required to turn over our identification to anyone flitted through my head, and I wondered what the guard would do if I said no. He'd probably call Chase down to his phone-booth office, which would be embarrassing. I was supposed to be assisting Chase, not making his life harder. I reluctantly gave my driver's license to Parallel Universe Chris Pratt.

He input some information and then handed it back to me. "Thank you, Miss Miller. Do you know how to get to Mr. Covington's house?"

One-F must have put me on a list. "I have directions on my phone. Thanks." I considered telling him how much I loved him in *Guardians of the Galaxy* but decided against it.

The guard pushed a button, and the wrought-iron gate slowly retracted. As I drove past, the neighborhood around me got even more beautiful. Lush, emerald-green, perfectly manicured lawns were visible between hedges and trees, as were flowers in every color. I saw fountains and mini waterfalls and caught glimpses of massive white mansions.

I definitely wasn't in Kansas anymore. I mean, I loved my quaint beach town, but this was like another universe.

My GPS indicated that I had arrived at Chase's house. I couldn't see anything but bushes and trees surrounding the driveway. I entered the code on a keypad near the gate, and as the heavy doors swung in, I started up the steep incline.

The driveway curved, and suddenly his house was visible. It appeared as if by magic. "House" wasn't right. I should say the glass-and-white-stone mansion that ate other houses for breakfast appeared.

I got out of my car, unable to imagine anybody could own something this beautiful. The front of the house was white stone with huge windows and several balconies, and from this angle I could see that the back of his house was almost entirely made of glass. An infinity pool on the left side of the backyard sparkled in the sunlight, and it looked as if

Sariah Wilson

you would just fall off the hillside if you swam to the edge. I understood why Chase had all the large windows. The view from here was one of the most breathtaking I'd ever seen.

Speaking of breathtaking, I drew in a long breath, trying to calm the knot in my stomach. I walked up his steps and realized the soft breeze carried the scent of lilacs. I faltered at the door, trying to decide if I should knock or just let myself in like he'd said I could.

The decision was taken out of my hands when he opened the door and beamed at me. "Hi, Zoe. Come on in."

I wondered how he had known I was there until I saw a small camera pointed at the door. The front foyer was all white tile and high ceilings, with a massive modern chandelier overhead.

"In case you were wondering, that's how you greet people when they come to your home," he said with a smile, shutting the front door behind me. "See how I didn't slam the door on you?"

"Ha ha."

Chase hesitated as if he wanted to do something he couldn't bring himself to do. He shoved his hands in his pockets instead. "Come and meet some of my friends."

I followed behind Chase, afraid to touch anything or breathe wrong. I didn't know much about art, but it looked like I would have to sell an organ if I somehow wrecked any of the vases or paintings.

We walked into an open family room that was next to a massive kitchen with an eat-in dining area. "Zoe, I want to introduce you to Benjy, Kevin, and Chan. We're talking about a project we're hoping to do next year. But we just wrapped everything up, and I was about to walk everyone out."

My jaw hit the floor so hard my face should have ached. Standing around his dining room table were Batman, Silent Bob, and Magic Mike.

They said hello to me, nodded, and waved, and when I couldn't answer, they returned their attention to Chase. I just stood there with

86

his dry cleaning in my arms as they walked out, talking to one another and promising to be in touch soon.

I heard Chase bid them goodbye and close the door. When he came back into the family room, I said, "That . . . that . . ."

"So you're starstruck for them but not for me?" he teased as he went into his kitchen. "Can I get you anything? Water without vicious ice cubes? Milk that's not meant for toddlers? I even had my housekeeper, Sofia, pick up some apple juice boxes so you'd feel more at home."

"I'm good. Thanks." Now that the shock of meeting his "friends" had worn off, I could finally take in my surroundings. As expected, the view was unencumbered and amazing. There was a massive deck with a hammock, outdoor couches and chairs, and an actual fireplace. The decor inside his home was all white, gray, and steel. There was no question a man lived here. His kitchen looked like the kind you'd see on TV. Glittery stone countertops, white cabinets that went almost to the ceiling, and stainless-steel appliances that seemed brand new. I could just imagine the kind of desserts I could whip up in a place this beautiful, and it took all my restraint not to invade the pantry and start pulling out ingredients.

"I'll take those." Chase put out his hands for his clothing and then threw it over the back of one of his white couches.

"I thought lime green was your favorite color," I said, dazzled by his pale-gray glass fireplace that went all the way up to the top of the cathedral ceiling.

"Lime green?" he repeated with his mouth twisted to one side. "Why would you think that?"

How did you say to someone, *Because that's what you said in a March 2009 article in* Seventeen *magazine that I still have memorized?*

"I thought I read it in an interview once." It was supposed to be the color of my bridesmaid dress. I knew I hadn't imagined it.

"Not true. Just about everything I've ever said in an interview that was personal was a lie. I want to show you something."

"Do we have to have the sexual harassment talk again?" I joked.

Chase flashed me a wicked grin before heading for the floor-to-ceiling windows. He pushed open the sliding glass doors that slid in both directions until there was no wall between his family room and the outside. He sat down on an expensive-looking wicker lounge chair with dark-blue cushions. He patted the chair next to him, and I took a seat.

"This is such a gorgeous view."

He had brought out an energy drink, and he popped it open. "It never gets old. You should see it at night, with the city all lit up."

We sat in silence for a few minutes, but it wasn't awkward. Instead, it felt relaxing and comfortable. Or it was until Chase turned to look at me with an intensity and longing in his eyes that reminded me of our encounter in my mother's kitchen, which made my skin break out in goose bumps.

"Why do you lie in interviews?" I asked, desperate to think about something else besides wanting him to kiss me.

"When you're in the public eye, people think they have a right to know everything about you. I realized I was already giving them so much of myself that I wanted to keep some things just for me and the people I care about. Which means that whenever they ask something personal, I make up an answer."

"Thanks for letting me know you're a liar and I shouldn't trust you," I teased. "Better to find out now, I suppose."

"I try to be an honest person. But realistically? Lying's kind of my profession. I pretend for a living. Right now, with you? Is this an interview? Are you going to publish or post anything I tell you?"

"No. Of course not." I hadn't so far. That had to count for something.

"Right. You've already proved that. Which is why I've been overly honest with you." He sat up, turned his legs toward me, and leaned forward. "I promise you I'll never lie to you. Ask me any question you want, and I'll always tell you the truth. As long as you promise to do the same."

"Okay." Where that came from, I could not tell you. Trust wasn't really my strong suit.

"Then my favorite color is indigo blue. Although I'm starting to feel a little partial to gray with flecks of green and gold."

He was talking about my eyes. There was no way I could keep my blush in check, and I had to avert my gaze so it wouldn't get worse. I could go full cherry tomato with enough teasing.

Chase seemed to sense my unease and casually asked (as if he hadn't just done some mad flirting), "My turn to ask a question. What is up with that picture I saw in your parents' bedroom?"

No way to get out of this one. And I'd just promised to be truthful. "You mean the one with my mother on the hood of a Camaro? She's the girl from the Black Serpent video." Black Serpent was one of those big-hair rock bands that faded away in the early 1990s, and that particular group was famous for its one-hit wonder.

Recognition dawned on his face. "That was your mom?"

"Yep. We're all super proud."

Not picking up on my sarcasm, Chase said, "I saw her at the MTV Video Awards when I was, like, ten. Black Serpent had reunited for one night to perform, and they lowered an actual Camaro from the ceiling with your mother on it. The crowd went nuts."

My entire life people had been trying to show me that clip on YouTube. "I've heard all about it, but I haven't seen it. Or the videos. There's just some things you don't want to see your parents doing."

"I get that. My mom wants me to watch her show, but I'm not up for scouring my retinas after I see her in a love scene." Chase's mother was the star of a long-running daytime soap opera, one of the last few still left on the air. She'd joined the show as a teenager and had been the star ever since. Her character was never without romance and a leading man.

"I've never had to worry about love scenes, but not for lack of trying. My mom wanted to be famous more than anything. She left home and lied about her age. She was fifteen when she filmed that. She fell in love with the director of the video. My biological father." It had been a long time since I'd said that out loud. "He wasn't interested in having a kid, and once he bailed, my mom took me to my grandparents'. And they raised me. Until I was twelve."

"What happened when you were twelve?"

It was easier to look at the view than the pity in his eyes. "My mom chased after fame for a long time. Made some really poor life choices." Life choices that had seriously affected me and my decisions. Like getting pregnant with me at fifteen. That was one of the biggest reasons I had chosen to be celibate. "Then one day it was like she grew up and realized she'd been wasting her life. She went back to school to become a nurse, and she met my stepfather, Duncan. They married about a year later and then had Zander. That's when she took me to live with her. While she was pregnant with Zia, Duncan had a heart attack and died." My voice caught on the last word.

Chase reached out to put his hand on my arm. "I'm so sorry."

Usually I could tell that story without tearing up. I wiped my eyes with my free hand. "It was totally unexpected. He ate well, exercised, was in perfect health. The doctors said sometimes it just happens."

He left his hand there, as if he could infuse me with his strength. The gesture did make me feel better. "I lost my dad, too. But that was because he wrapped his car around a telephone pole when I was seven."

"Seriously?" How did I not know that?

"My mom's PR team spun it as an accident, but he was an alcoholic who was fond of driving drunk." It was the first time I'd heard Chase sound angry. "And then my mother's new boyfriend didn't want to raise another man's kid. I was raised by my grandmother, too."

I hadn't realized we had those things in common. I put my hand on top of his, wanting to comfort him the way he had just comforted me.

He stared at our joined hands, and my heart started to race as my palm threatened to go clammy, so I pulled away. After a moment, so did he.

"That just got heavy, didn't it?" I asked, wanting to lighten the mood. "So I'm going to go out on a limb and guess that skydiving is not your favorite hobby."

"No." He smiled. "It's surfing. Or it was. That's one of those things where if the waves are good, the paparazzi are waiting."

"You should come surf in Marabella. A lot of the beaches there are private and only for the town's use. You could surf in peace."

Chase pulled out his phone and flicked over a few screens. "How about Saturday?"

I hadn't meant it to sound like I was asking him out or anything. Fortunately, I already had an excuse. Which left me feeling both disappointed and relieved. "My mom's babysitter canceled on her, so I'm watching the rug rats on Saturday."

"I don't know if you know this, but I think this thing between me and Zia might be getting serious. You should bring everyone with you. I don't think she'd mind."

I laughed a little, and I could see that had been his intent. I knew I should say no. I shouldn't allow myself to hope and dream when there were no possibilities. When his assistant would recover, and I would be sent on my merry way and never see him in person again.

But the other part of me desperately wanted to say yes. To use any excuse to see him and spend time with him. To stay on the ride for as long as I could. To live in a fantasy world where Chase Covington could be interested in Zoe Miller. Even though it scared me, I liked him. The real him, the one I was getting to know.

And the gorgeous outer shell didn't hurt things, either.

His phone buzzed. "Sorry, I have this meeting down in Studio City I have to get to. Can I walk you out?"

We went inside, and he shut and locked the glass doors. When we got to his front door, I stepped outside and expected to turn and say goodbye, but the expression on his face made the words die in my mouth.

"There's something I want to say to you. And I'm not sure how you're going to react." He paused, as if waiting for me to give him the go-ahead or do something besides stand there like a fan caught in a movie star's headlights. "California's sexual harassment laws aside, I really . . . I like you the exact amount that won't freak you out. I'd like to spend time with you. Not as employer/employee, but as Chase and Zoe. What do you think?"

At first my only thought was *Chase Covington likes me?*, but what I said was, "I think I don't trust in things I don't understand."

Now he looked confused. "What's to understand? You're beautiful, funny, smart, and kind, and I want to hang out and get to know you better."

It was like he was talking about someone else. He couldn't possibly think those things about me, right? "Because you could date Amelia Swan."

"Amelia Swan?" he repeated, sounding disgusted. "She's the world's biggest diva and the most self-centered person I've ever met. And I work in Hollywood, so that's saying a lot."

"There's something you don't know about me."

His phone chirped at him again. "I really do want to talk to you more about this, but if I don't leave now, I'm going to be late. And contrary to the actor stereotype, I like to be on time. We can talk more. Later. If that works for you."

I nodded. Chase walked me to my car and opened the door for me. I could just picture the faces of my women's studies classmates, but I liked when guys were gentlemen. I didn't feel like he was implying I was incapable of opening my own door. He was just being polite and thoughtful.

"This is your car? If you're going to be running errands for me, I should just buy you a new one. I don't want this to give out on you and strand you someplace."

"You're not buying me a car. You can't just buy people cars."

"Why not?" he asked, his expression earnest.

"Because nobody buys cars for people they hardly know."

"Oprah used to."

He had me there. "True, but don't buy me a car."

After I sat down, Chase leaned his head in the car, and I hoped he might kiss me. Instead, he just said, "See you soon, Zoe."

He headed around the corner to what I assumed was his garage, and I drove off quickly, not wanting him to pass me on the road and see me driving with a confused, goofy look on my face.

Chase Covington liked me. He had, in Gavin's words, manned up. He'd said he wanted to spend time with me and get to know me.

It was every daydream, birthday wish, and fervent prayer I'd ever said about him all coming true.

With a sinking feeling that made my stomach ache, I remembered we had no chance at a relationship. This would all end.

Especially once I told him I wouldn't sleep with him.

CHAPTER TEN

Chase Covington ✓
@realchasecov

Following

Life is so full of possibilities right now.
#Chasersarethebest

💬   🔁 104K   ♡ 323K

"What's so funny?" I asked my giggling roommate as I set down my purse.

"Oreo has started putting jokes on the side of packages. Listen to this—'Serving size: three cookies.' That's hilarious," Lexi said before shoving said serving size into her mouth.

I wanted to discuss the Chase situation, especially because I had no one to talk to about it. I had this fear that if I said anything to my mother, it would trigger something in her and make her regress into that person she used to be where fame mattered more than anything else. And I couldn't deal if she did that again.

And I knew I should tell Lexi. She was my best friend. My only real friend. We had stayed up late so many nights discussing every minute detail of the boys she liked. How they'd looked at her, the things they said, and what they actually meant. Now it could be my turn. I could confess all my fears to her. Lexi knew why I was so gun-shy when it came to boys.

I wanted her input and wisdom. I wanted her excitement and enthusiasm.

Which was the problem.

In a way Chase had been Lexi's first. She was the super fan and had pulled me into it. I worried that if I told her, she'd be mad. Or hurt.

I also worried that if Lexi knew I could put her in Chase's path, she'd do everything she could to nab him. And that he'd choose her over me. Which logically didn't make sense, given that he'd already met us both, and he didn't ask Lexi to be his assistant or tell her he wanted to hang out with her. But every crush I'd ever had in high school had preferred her to me.

A voice inside me whispered, *If he chose her over you, then you deserve better. You don't have to keep this to yourself. Stop being selfish.*

Maybe it was selfish, but for now it was fragile and new, and I didn't want it destroyed. I mean, that might happen anyway once I told him about the celibacy thing, but I didn't want Lexi to be the reason it ended.

Sometimes it felt like my entire life was devoted to taking care of other people. I could have one thing that was just mine.

Not to mention, legally I couldn't say anything.

"What?" she asked. "You're looking at me funny."

"I'm just . . . glad we're friends."

Lexi twisted off the top of her Oreo. "There's something different about you."

Could she tell? Did she have some kind of movie-star radar, and had she figured out I'd been with Chase? "What do you mean?"

She shrugged one shoulder. "I don't know. There's this, like . . . happiness about you. Wait! You've been seeing that guy, haven't you? Because you have that 'A boy likes me and we're dating' glow about you."

"You mean like the one Gavin gave you?" Not a great distraction, but it was the best I could come up with.

And it didn't work. "We're not talking about Gavin. We're talking about the cute boy who likes you."

The cutest boy on the entire planet. I really should tell her. "Look, Lexi, the thing is—"

"Have you told him about your Fortress of Solitude situation?"

She meant my celibacy. "Not yet. I'm going to. I wanted—"

"Are you going out again?" she interrupted me. "With that guy from work?"

Chase was now from work. "Yes. On Saturday. But—"

She squealed and ran over to hug me tightly. "I'm so excited for you! You'll have to tell me all about him later. I'm supposed to meet Gavin for a late lunch. I'm even being regressive and letting him pay."

I pointed at her cookies. "But you're already eating."

Lexi rolled her eyes. "Duh. So I don't eat a ton in front of him."

"You've been dating for a while. I'm pretty sure he knows you eat food."

"It's ingrained! I can't help it!" she protested. Her grandmother had been a serious Southern belle with plans to take Hollywood by storm. It hadn't quite worked out, and now she'd pinned all her hopes on her granddaughter (while still demanding Lexi get a degree first, "just in case"). Given her background, her grandma had raised Lexi to do stuff like feign helplessness and not eat in front of men.

I mean, I mocked her, but maybe there was something to it. She did always have boyfriends.

Another quick hug and she was gone.

I felt icky for having lied to her. Technically it hadn't been a lie, because Chase was a boy from work. Just work Lexi didn't know about. And I did try to tell her, like, three times, but in typical Lexi fashion, she hadn't let me get a word in edgewise because she was excited about me dating someone.

Someone she thought was Noah. Although Chase had played a character named Noah. So that made it not really a lie, right? (Yes, I knew I was reaching.)

My phone buzzed. And my heart did a happy dance when I saw it was Chase.

Is that a yes? For Saturday?

Say yes.

I didn't overthink it. I didn't list all the reasons why I should say no.

Yes.

What time should I pick you up?

I told him to come by around noon, and he offered to bring a picnic, which I thought was incredibly sweet.

If I don't have to cook, I'm definitely in.

> I thought you loved cooking?

> I love baking. So not the same thing.

> It seems the same. And speaking of baking...I'm still waiting.

> Maybe I'll bring something to add to your picnic basket.

> I can't wait.

Honestly, neither could I. Which he would know if he could have seen my face and the Joker-size grin I was sporting.

I had a (maybe) date with Chase Covington. A date that was going to involve all of my little brothers and sisters, but still, something like a date.

And there was no one I could tell.

Chase Covington ✔
@realchasecov

Following

Planning a day at the beach. Activity suggestions?
#wanttoimpress

💬   ⟲ 22K   ♡ 81K

There was nothing for me to do at work. I usually brought my laptop to do homework, but I was distracted by Chase's tweets. They seemed generic, but I knew they were about me. About our (possible) date.

It made me feel special in a way I'd never felt before.

And he wanted to impress me. Did he not know how unnecessary that was?

"Time for the meeting!" I looked up to see Amy in the doorway. She was a new volunteer who insisted on doing everything herself without any direction. I didn't see her lasting very long. Earlier I had tried to help her with reshelving some files, but she'd waved me off. I couldn't stay and watch. The only thing worse than seeing something done wrong was seeing it done slowly.

In the conference room I made awkward eye contact with Noah, and we both quickly looked away. I hated that my social ineptitude had made him go from work friend to work stranger. We didn't speak, tease, or laugh. He completely ignored me. It was like I didn't even exist.

I didn't know how to make it better.

Stephanie started the meeting, and again the emphasis was on recruiting celebrities for our fund-raiser. She had Francisco from HR come up to the front for an announcement. He gave a long, windbaggy speech that essentially boiled down to the fact that he had a college roommate who was a cousin of a guy who worked with a former contestant from the reality show *Survivor*, and the contestant had agreed to come to our dinner. The room erupted in applause, and Francisco looked smugly pleased with himself.

I had a momentary fantasy of standing up to announce that Chase Covington would also be attending, since I totally knew him and we might even be dating. In part because I'd never liked Francisco and would have loved to steal his thunder, but also because it would have been nice to let Noah know I had done so much better and I didn't care if he ghosted me.

Stephanie seemed thrilled by Francisco's announcement. I could only imagine how much more excited she would be about Chase. If we had him on board, we could probably double the ticket price and easily get it. "See?" Stephanie was saying. "Work your connections and we can make this happen! I just know this will be our best fund-raiser yet!"

Although I felt like I didn't know Chase well enough to ask him for this kind of favor, maybe I should just do it. Even if he was busy that night, he obviously knew and was friends with extremely famous people.

It would really help my future career. Not to mention that Stephanie would probably throw me a parade.

I resolved to ask him the next time I saw him.

I didn't see him again for the rest of the week. It was not quite what I was expecting when I'd agreed to be his assistant. I thought I would be constantly running errands for him, or making his travel arrangements, or whatever it was that One-F did. One-F sent me copies of Chase's call sheets, but he also sent them to Chase.

Chase did text me every day, though. Usually to say good morning and good night. We chatted a bit, but it was typically when he had a break on set, which wasn't often, given that he was the star of the movie.

I never texted him first. Not because I was trying to be Lexi-esque and force him to make the first move but because I couldn't believe he wanted to hear from me. And I didn't want to interrupt him at his job, where so many people's livelihoods depended on him doing well.

On Saturday morning I made my way to my mother's house, so giddy with excitement that I wondered whether people could have happiness attacks—like anxiety attacks only you felt overwhelmingly good instead of anxious. Although I was plenty anxious, too.

My mother gave me some last-minute directions. Zander hadn't been feeling well, so there was some kids' cold medicine next to the toaster for him, and Zia had shortened her nap, so she now went down at two. Mr. Wriggles had been washed, and Zelda was in the laundry room waiting for him to finish drying.

"Thank you again for filling in for me. I really appreciate it."

"No worries," I told her.

"Just to let you know, I'm a little concerned about Zane. He's been talking about how Captain Sparta is his new best friend. And Zia won't stop talking about how much she loves cheese."

"You know kids!" I tried to deflect. I honestly thought one of them would have ratted me out by now, but my mother was on this "no TV/movies" kick because she'd read some parenting article about screen time. Although she hadn't extended the rule to Zander's iPad. But it meant none of them had recognized Chase, which was the only thing keeping me safe.

My mom nodded thoughtfully but still looked concerned and distracted. "Call me if you need anything."

Realizing I hadn't run my plans by her, I figured I probably should. "I was going to take them to the beach today, if that's okay."

"Of course. Just make sure to put on sunscreen. And reapply it every couple of hours. I'll leave their car seats on the front porch."

I promised to keep them screened from all UV light, and once she'd pulled out of the driveway, I went into the kitchen and whipped up some soft-baked chocolate-chip cookies. By the time I was finished, a crowd of little people had gathered around me, begging for a cookie. I told them they could have one as soon as they were ready for the beach. Everybody whooped and cheered in delight, then ran off to do as I'd asked.

The swimsuit I'd worn since high school was more than a little ragged. In anticipation of today, I had gone out and bought a new one. I'd never really felt comfortable in a bikini but tried one on, thinking it might make me feel more confident. Instead, I felt overexposed. But it led me to a blue-and-gray tankini that covered almost as much of me as a one-piece would, and it was extremely flattering. It was expensive, and

I wouldn't have bought it even two weeks ago. But since I had some extra money, thanks to my new job, I decided to splurge. After I changed into it, I packed up a diaper bag for Zelda and Zia, making sure to include their swimming diapers, extra clothes and swimsuits, sippy cups, juice boxes, Zander's medicine, and a vat of SPF 100 waterproof sunscreen. I decided to throw in a hoodie for each kid, too. I didn't know how long Chase planned to be there, but I thought it was better to be prepared.

I got the cookies packed up, including some that didn't have chocolate chips in them for Zelda.

Zander followed me as I rooted through the hall closet looking for beach towels. "How are we going to get there? Mom took her car. We won't all fit in yours."

"Chase is going to pick us up."

At that, Zia poked her head out of her room. She had a ballerina bathing suit, complete with an attached tutu, but she had put her head through one of the armholes, and it was all twisted. "Cheese? My Cheese is coming?"

"Yes, your Chase is coming," I told her as I straightened out her suit and went to her room to find cover-ups for her and Zelda.

"I waits for him."

Zia stood on the couch beneath the window in the family room. She pressed her face against the glass, watching the front yard.

I had Zander and Zane gathering up boogie boards and floaties while I retrieved Mr. Wriggles from the dryer. I added the stuffed animal to the growing pile in the family room.

"He here! He here!" Zia screamed, hopping up and down on the couch.

My heart ricocheted off my ribs, bouncing like Zia, until it landed in my throat. I couldn't reprimand her for the furniture-jumping because I got it.

The doorbell rang, and I didn't know who was more excited to see Chase: me or Zia.

CHAPTER ELEVEN

"Hey, you," he said, nearly blinding me with his smile.

Would I ever stop catching my breath when I saw him? I realized I had missed him and, surprisingly, felt a little emotional at being around him again. "Hi."

"Cheese!" Zia threw herself around his legs. "My Cheese!"

"There's my favorite girl!" he said, sweeping her into his arms. She giggled, delighted. It seriously made my heart flutter to see him being so adorable with my baby sister.

Even though I never would have admitted it to another person, I was also the teeniest bit jealous.

"What do you need me to do?" he asked, forcing me to tamp down my ridiculous reaction.

"All this stuff needs to go in your car. I'll take care of the car seats." I stepped out onto the porch, intending to grab the seats, but instead was distracted by how pretty he was and how good he smelled.

And how close together we stood. Close enough that every molecule in my body flooded with heat. "Hi."

"You already said that," he responded with a sexy smirk that made those same molecules explode. His blue eyes darkened.

"Cheese!" Zia demanded, smacking him on the shoulder. "You my Cheese. Not Zo-Zo's."

That made him laugh. "Someone's staking her territory. Guess you should have shown some interest earlier."

Shown some interest? I had so much interest in him I was practically a bank.

"You're bringing all of this?" he asked as we went inside, and before I could formulate an awesome retort, he added, "You've got enough junk here for a small army. Were you planning on invading the beach?"

"Have you ever gone somewhere with four kids before? Trust me, it's all necessary."

I grabbed Zia's and Zelda's car seats and turned toward the driveway, surprised by what I saw. "You own a minivan?"

"I don't own a minivan," he responded, sounding offended. "I have many beautiful pieces of machinery, and I would not insult them by bringing something like that into my garage. I rented it. By myself. It was easier than I thought it would be. And I even remembered your tip about the gas icon and the arrow so I know the gas tank is on the driver's side." Now he sounded proud of himself, and I guessed he'd never rented a car on his own before.

It reminded me that despite my decade-long belief that I knew him, all those articles I'd read and interviews I'd devoured, none of the things he'd said were true. I didn't know him.

But I would get to know him as he was getting to know me.

"Is it locked?" I asked.

Chase pushed a button on his key ring, and the doors on both sides of the minivan opened, allowing me to buckle in the car seats. I felt a bit bad about installing those seats, encrusted with hardened liquids, gum, and what looked like melted crayons, into this pristine car. At least it had captains' chairs instead of a long row, like my mom's minivan. It would keep the girls from smacking each other when they were tired at the end of the day.

"Zo, can I bring my iPad?"

"No!" I called back. "You're getting some fresh air today. Leave it here."

Zander bore a mutinous look until I reminded him that if he accidentally dropped it in the ocean, it would be ruined.

Chase then corralled the boys into helping him bring everything out to the minivan while I got Zelda and Zia buckled into their seats. As Chase arranged things in the back of the car, I told Zane and Zander to get in. I went in the house to make sure we had everything and then locked the front door behind me. Chase and I got into the van at the same time, and we smiled at each other.

It almost felt like we were playing house.

"Everybody ready?" he asked, and the kids let out a chorus of yeses.

My siblings had the ability to make any car ride, no matter how short, totally miserable if they decided to. Fortunately, today they were all in a good mood and looking forward to spending time in the water. It probably also helped that the beach was only a ten-minute drive from our house.

When we arrived, I helped the kids get out of their seats and turned them loose. They had grown up going to the beach almost every weekend during good weather, so they knew to stay clear of the waves unless they had an adult with them.

I went to help Chase with all the gear, including the lunch he'd brought, and when I realized there was too much, I said, "We can make a couple of trips."

"No way. I got this." And in true male fashion, he loaded himself with so much stuff I worried he might fall over. "Lead the way."

With my own arms full, I decided to pick a spot not too far from the car. It was a good thing I'd brought a couple of blankets, as I discovered Chase hadn't brought one. He dumped everything in a pile, unloading bags, towels, and toys.

Wondering what a movie star thought constituted a picnic lunch, I peeked inside the basket as Chase set up our family's massive beach umbrella. I was pleasantly surprised to see fried chicken, mashed potatoes, and biscuits from a chain restaurant. "Huh."

"What?" he asked, turning the umbrella to keep the sun's rays off the blanket.

"I'm just surprised. I thought I'd find, like, caviar and capers in here."

"Caviar is disgusting," he said, plopping down next to me with a grin. "Capers aren't much better."

He smelled so nice. Like sunshine and oranges and sea breezes.

"Your hair looks red in the sun."

"That's why they call it strawberry blonde," I said, ignoring the way his observation made my heart skip a beat. It was like he was making this list about me, noticing all these little things that nobody else had ever bothered to see.

I cleared my throat and called for the kids to leave their sand castles to have lunch. Zane tore into the food like he hadn't eaten in a month. Zander was uncharacteristically not hungry, and I wondered if his cold was worse than Mom had let on. Zelda wanted only mashed potatoes, and Zia had three bites before she was ready to dash out and play. I made them all line up for sunscreen when they decided they were finished. Chase offered to help, which made it go twice as fast.

The kids scampered off to play, and Chase stood up to remove his T-shirt. I was so glad I was wearing sunglasses and could watch the interplay of his muscles as he stretched and tossed his shirt to one side. Then it got even better as he began to apply sunscreen in smooth, hypnotic motions over parts of his body I wished I could run my own hands over.

"Can you get my back?" He handed me the bottle.

OMG, OMG, OMG. Chase Covington wanted me to put sunscreen on his back. His very beautiful, well-defined back. He sat down and leaned forward, giving me full access to his sun-kissed skin.

I sat there for too long, overwhelmed and freaking out about what he wanted me to do. It wasn't until he looked over his shoulder that I squeezed some sunscreen into my hand and tentatively applied it to his back. His skin felt warm under my fingertips.

It didn't help matters when he sighed with pleasure and said, "That feels good." His shoulders lowered slightly, and his head drooped, as if he was relaxing.

It gave me a sense of feminine power that I could touch him and make him feel that way. It emboldened my moves, and I spread my palms flat against his back as I rubbed lotion all over. I probably applied more than was necessary.

"My turn." His voice was low and seductive, and I had never been so aware of the blood pulsing through my veins. He stood up and held his hand out for the sunscreen bottle. Aware that I still had a shirt and shorts on, I did my best to take them off without making eye contact. He sat behind me on the blanket, and I had to fight the instinct to lean back against him.

It was like every sense was heightened. The sound of the squawking seagulls overhead, the rhythmic ocean waves lapping against the shore, the sun overhead warming me, the coconut scent from the sunscreen, the taste of salt on the breeze. They were all magnified in a way I'd never experienced before.

I heard him squeeze the bottle, and my whole body tensed, waiting for the touch of his hand. The shock of the cold lotion against my hot skin made me gasp. I pulled my knees up to my chest and wrapped my arms around them. I needed something to hold on to.

He rubbed sunscreen on my shoulders first. And he didn't quickly brush it on. He carefully massaged the lotion into every inch of exposed skin.

My unsteady breathing sounded harsh to my own ears; I hoped he hadn't noticed. I tried to calm down, but his fingertips made that impossible. It was as if he possessed magic and was using his hands to cast a spell on me.

Hot, tingling pinpricks arose in every place he touched as my heart pounded in triple time. I was glad I didn't have any pulse points in my back so he couldn't see how hard it was beating. A pulsating pressure started deep in the pit of my stomach and spread throughout my body.

His movements felt hypnotic, tender, and sensual. I alternated between wanting to collapse into a gooey Zoe puddle and turning around and attacking him.

I'd known the tankini had a low back when I bought it, but I hadn't realized how low until his hands dipped down farther than I was comfortable with, breaking the spell. I started to say something, but my sisters came to my rescue. Zia clocked Zelda over the head with a bucket, and Zelda started crying loudly.

"Should probably go take care of that," I mumbled, pitching myself forward, grateful for the escape.

"I think you missed some spots!" he called after me, referencing the fact that the only parts of my body currently shielded from the sun were my shoulders and back.

"I'll get it later!" I called over my shoulder. Translation? *I don't trust myself to behave right now, and I'd rather not permanently traumatize my younger siblings. In fact, at this moment I would love to dig a deep hole in the sand, bury myself in it, and not come out until I can learn to control my reaction to you.*

Something I feared might never come to pass.

I separated the girls, reminding Zia that it was never okay to hit. They both protested and argued about their actions, but my mind was back on that blanket with Chase. I could still feel his lotion-covered hands against my skin. It was a long time before I started to feel normal again.

By then Chase had taken the boys out into the waves on their boogie boards. Zia had started to tire, and I convinced both girls to lie down with me on the blanket under the umbrella. She immediately fell asleep in my arms, and even Zelda nodded off.

Chase returned with my brothers, and they toweled off. Chase's wet hair reminded me of the day we'd met on set, and it put me back on edge.

He reached inside a bag he'd brought with him and pulled out what looked like a very expensive drone. "Do you guys want to try this out?"

"Yes!"

I had to remind them to be quiet, but neither of my sisters moved. Zander grabbed the remote and handed the drone to Zane.

"I hope you aren't super attached to that. My guess is it's not long for this world," I said as my brothers ran off. That wasn't exactly the kind of thing you should give to kids.

"I bought it just for today. I thought they might like playing with it. If they break it, they break it. Stuff happens."

That caused a light, fluttery sensation that started in my heart and filled my whole soul. He was so thoughtful. And considerate. Which honestly surprised me. Living in Marabella, I had met a lot of rich people whose defining characteristic seemed to be selfishness.

Chase was not only rich but famous. A double whammy of personality wreckers. Add in the handsomeness, and he should have been vain, self-centered, and careless.

I noticed him staring at me with an amused expression. "What?" I asked.

"I'm wondering if you'll still be as beautiful when you're completely sunburned."

"I'm not beautiful—"

"You are." He stopped my denial. "Why would you say you're not?"

His question stunned me into silence for a second. "Well, there's the daddy issues. When your own father doesn't want anything to do with you, you automatically win the lottery of insecurity, self-doubt, and trust issues." I had meant it to sound light and breezy, but my voice caught at the end.

There was a long pause. "That's not the only reason. Something happened to you."

I wanted to protest that he didn't know me, but he was right. I didn't know how, but he was.

"Would you tell me? I'm a good listener. And I hope you know you can trust me."

Trust had never been easy for me, but I realized, deep in my gut, I could trust him.

And maybe that was due in part to the exhaustion of running around for half the day or the heat of the late afternoon, but I felt that drugged tiredness that makes you let your guard down.

So I told him.

CHAPTER TWELVE

 Zoe
@zomorezoless

George Washington spent almost $200 on ice cream in
the summer of 1790. #Trivia #smartman

♡   ⊕ 0   ♡ 1

"In sixth grade, phones weren't allowed in class." Not that I had even
owned one. "So everybody went old school and passed paper notes. To
stop that from being a distraction, our teacher, Ms. Ogata, put up a mail
board on one wall. During breaks or lunch, anyone could thumbtack a
note for someone else on the wall."

Lexi left me daily notes about her love for Chase Covington, but
that wasn't pertinent to the story.

"One day I walked up and there was a note for me with handwriting I
didn't recognize. From someone who said they had a crush on me but were
too shy to say so. It went on for weeks. I tried to catch whoever was doing
it, but the board was always crowded so I never got to see who it was."

Zia blinked drowsily in my arms and rolled over. I shifted as she
repositioned herself and went back to sleep.

"In the notes, he said all the things he loved about me. How beautiful I was, how smart and nice, and at first I couldn't believe it. I thought it was a joke, but after a while it felt real, and I looked forward every day to a new note. I remember watching the boys in my class, trying to guess who it was. To see if anyone would sneak glances at me or give me a secretive smile. Something that would indicate who was responsible. It didn't happen."

As I got to the hard part of the story, I had to swallow down the lump in my throat. "The notes indicated that he would tell me his name on the last day of school, that he still felt too shy. I actually started a countdown, excited that somebody thought I was pretty enough and special enough to pay this kind of attention to. But on the last day of school, as I took my letter off the wall, that all changed. It told me how stupid I was. That all my classmates had spent the entire year laughing at me. Who would ever want somebody as ugly and stupid as me? He said he wasn't even human but a dog who had learned how to write because only a dog could ever be attracted to me."

I didn't start sobbing, which I counted as a victory. I did squeeze my sister a little too tightly, and she quietly protested until I eased up. "I cried for three days. Not just because everyone made fun of me but because I had let myself hope and believe. And my trust had been shattered. It made me question everyone's motives ever since. I never did find out who did it. And I've never told anyone this story. Not even my best friend."

Because if I had, Lexi would have pitied me, and then she would have punched people until someone confessed and she forced them to apologize. I had just wanted everything to go away. I didn't want to keep dealing with it and dragging it out.

But there was power in confessing. I experienced relief when I put down the burden of this secret and Chase picked up part of it so it no longer sat solely on my shoulders.

"I don't know if there's a right thing to say here, but I understand how the things that happen to us as kids can affect us our whole lives. I'm really sorry that happened to you. But whoever did that was an idiot. And completely wrong. And if you knew who it was, I would probably jump in that uncool minivan, find him, and kick his a—" He glanced at the sleeping girls. "Kick his butt."

I knew I was supposed to be opposed to violence, but the thought that he wanted to avenge my honor thrilled me in a way I didn't quite understand.

"That is a pretty uncool car," I agreed. "Even my Honda is better."

"So what you're saying is that you're cooler than me?"

I shrugged, which was not easy with Zia's weight pulling my arms down. "I didn't say it."

That wolfish, predatory grin was back. The one that sent fizzy bubbles of desire rocketing through my bloodstream. "If you're cooler than me, does that mean I'm hotter than you?"

Um, most definitely.

We were interrupted by Zane and Zander, who had returned because they couldn't agree on whose turn it was next. Their arguing woke up the girls, and everybody was grouchy and annoyed.

Everybody but me. This was the lightest I had felt in a long time.

As I tried to sort out my brothers' disagreement fairly, Zelda asked, "Where are the cookies?"

"Cookies?" Chase's blue eyes sparkled with excitement. "Did you finally make me cookies?"

What was his deal? "I made some this morning, yes."

I started looking through bags, and after a minute, Chase helped me. But we couldn't find them anywhere.

"I remember wrapping them up and putting them on the kitchen table. I must have forgotten them."

He shook his head. "I can't believe you made cookies and I don't even get to have any. I feel so cheated."

"If you want them that badly, I can come over and make you some." He was really hung up on this.

"Tomorrow? My place?"

"Sure."

"But I wanted dessert, Zo," Zelda complained, clutching her sandy Mr. Wriggles closer. He probably had another visit to the washing machine in his near future.

"We could go to the ice cream shop on the boardwalk," Zander suggested, and that made even Zia throw off her tiredness.

She crawled off my lap and stood in front of me, her big gray eyes pleading and her hands clasped together. "I want isacheme, Zo-Zo. Please."

"I don't know, you guys. It's getting late, and it's almost dinnertime. Mom will kill me for getting you all hopped up on sugar this late."

"C'mon, Zo," Chase said, mimicking Zia's expression. "It won't hurt just this once. Let's get ice cream."

"Your puppy-dog charm is not going to work," I told him. Even though it totally was.

"Oh, a compliment. You just called me charming."

"Did not. And if you weren't listening, I compared you to a manipulative puppy." One using his cuteness to get what he wants.

"All I heard was charming." He stood up, offering me his hand. "And if you keep saying no, we might have a mutiny on our hands."

"Okay, fine. We can have ice cream."

Amid their cheers, and Zelda making up a song about how much she loved ice cream, I made everyone put on their flip-flops. I took Chase's hand, and it was just like I remembered. Warm, strong, and completely electric. I quickly let go. I grabbed my sunglasses, grateful to hide behind them. I slipped into my clothes and shoes. Chase put on his shirt, a ball cap, and sunglasses, and I wondered if he was covertly watching me the same way I was watching him.

As we headed for the boardwalk, Zelda asked, "Can I get chocolate ice cream?"

Both Chase and I exclaimed, "No!" at the same time, which cracked us up. The kids joined in, even though I don't think they understood why we were laughing.

Zia grabbed my hand and demanded, "Hold hands, Cheese." She wanted us to swing her as we walked. We counted to three and swung her high in the air, and she laughed hysterically each time.

"It must be nice to be part of a big family."

"It is," I agreed. "Although sometimes I feel like a second mother because of the age gap. I mean, if I got married and had kids in the next few years, Zia would be an aunt at a really young age. That part of it is weird. But I adore them."

Chase stayed quiet for longer than was normal. "Is that something you think about? Getting married?" Given his tone, it was like he was asking, "Is that something you think about? Committing multiple murders and becoming a serial killer?" Such a stereotypical male reaction to discussing marriage.

"Not really." I mean, I had been thinking about it a lot lately, given my current situation with *People Magazine*'s three-time winner of "Sexiest Man Alive," but it wasn't something I had seriously considered. I hadn't even graduated yet.

When we got to the ice cream parlor, Chase opened the door for everyone, ushering the kids inside, where their voices echoed loudly. I put my sunglasses on top of my head; Chase left his on. The children gathered around the display case, deciding on flavors. Zelda had to be reminded more than once that chocolate was not an option.

They finally made their decisions. Zane opted for the Incredible Hulk flavor—mint ice cream with chocolate chips. I decided to get the same.

"No Captain Sparta flavor?" Chase murmured. "I think I should be offended."

I would totally eat that up. But instead of saying so, I just smiled. I noticed he was hanging back, standing behind me. As if he didn't want anyone in the parlor to know who he was. It seemed to be working, as the girl at the cash register was busy texting on her phone and ignoring us. I asked Chase what he wanted, and he said butter pecan.

"Ha. I knew your icky movie-star tastes would come out eventually. Your picnic didn't fool me."

"What's wrong with butter pecan?"

"Um, everything? Such a waste of good ice cream." I grabbed my purse and moved to the register to place our order. Chase put his hand on my wrist, preventing me from getting my wallet. He handed me some cash.

"It's on me. I'm the one who asked to spend the day with you guys, remember?"

I kept forgetting this was kind of a date. I knew the girls—er, women—in my women's studies class would want me to protest. Maybe even get angry and tell him I didn't need him or the patriarchy paying for me. But I gratefully accepted his kind gesture. "I'll get it next time."

It wasn't until later that I thought about how presumptuous that must have sounded. Like we were definitely going on another date when he hadn't indicated he wanted to. I gave him his change after the cashier rang us up. Once she had scooped our cones, Chase suggested we sit on the outdoor patio that overlooked the boardwalk and beach.

We got everybody situated at the table, and I wrapped the cones for the two youngest kids in enough napkins to soak up an oil spill. Chase seemed completely entertained by how much the kids loved their ice cream.

"Everybody tell Chase thank you!"

They all said thanks, including Zia, who said, "Fank you, Cheese" between delicate bites of pink bubblegum ice cream.

"I think this is a day they'll always remember," I told him. I knew it was one I would never forget.

"What's your favorite childhood memory?" he asked.

"Not paying bills," I immediately responded, which got the laugh I'd been looking for. "What about you?"

"I always paid the bills. Even when I was a kid. Sometimes I wish I'd had more of a childhood."

There was something so inherently sad about his statement that it made my heart ache. And I could relate. "I know it's not the same, but I didn't have much of a childhood, either. I was expected to work hard all the time."

Zander had already finished his ice cream and let out a loud sigh of boredom as he leaned his head back.

"He seems a little lost without his tablet," Chase said softly to me.

"Right? Like someday I expect to wake up and find that it's become permanently attached to his hand. I try to get him to go out and do real-life stuff like this. It tends to backfire. Like one night I was feeling inspired, so I told them no devices, no TV. That we were going to play board games."

"How did that go?"

"Let me put it this way—now I understand why all those parents in the 1960s were alcoholics."

"Hey!" Zane poked Chase in the side. "What kind of shorts do clouds wear?"

Chase pondered the question seriously. "I don't know. What kind of shorts do clouds wear?"

"Thunderwear!" Zane cracked himself up.

"I think Thor wears that, too," Chase added, making Zane laugh harder.

"Hey, do you guys want to play in the sand while we wait for the girls?" Before I had finished my sentence, my brothers fled the table.

Zelda had stopped eating her Neapolitan ice cream a while ago, and now it was running in pink, brown, and white rivers down her hand.

"Why aren't you eating your ice cream?" Chase asked as he reached for more napkins before everything dripped on her leg. "Did you lose your sweet tooth?"

"My sweet tooth?" Zelda asked in alarm. "Which tooth is that? Did the Tooth Fairy take it? I want it back!"

I tried to explain idioms as she grew increasingly frantic, so I settled for reminding her that she hadn't lost any teeth yet. I got her cleaned up and sent her off to play with the boys.

As we watched them play, some joggers ran past us on the boardwalk. "I used to love running on the beach. I miss it."

Again, I felt a pang of sadness for him that so many things in his life were abnormal.

"What about you? Do you ever come down here and run?"

I tried not to laugh. "Not unless I have to chase somebody down."

"You don't like running?"

"My stepdad used to say running was for criminals and masochists. Lexi used to be really into it, but it was never my thing."

He leaned back in his chair, putting his hands behind his head. It made his shirt lift up slightly, and I forced myself to look at his face. "So basically, if you ever have to run for your life, things aren't going to end well for you."

"Basically."

"What kind of exercise do you like?"

How did you tell somebody whose life revolved around being in the best shape possible that your exercise routine consisted of tossing and turning at night? "Climbing?" I was talking about the three flights of stairs at my apartment but left that part off.

"What gym do you go to?"

"I think about going to the gym, but the guy who works the counter at Wendy's is named Jim, so I figure that's close enough."

It felt like he was looking at me, but I couldn't tell with the sunglasses. "You're lucky you have such a fantastic metabolism."

My cheeks burned at his implication, and I ducked my head so he wouldn't see. It was true. I had grown up eating traditional comfort foods laden with butter and cream. I probably should be the size of a baby hippo, given my diet.

"I guess we can't have everything in common. That would be boring." I couldn't tell from his tone whether he was disappointed by my revelations. Was it a bad thing? A divisive wedge that would come between us, since I would rather have my fingernails ripped out one a time than go running with him in some canyon?

"We should probably go," I said. "It's getting late." The sun was setting, and the winds had picked up. I was glad I had packed hoodies for everyone.

I hadn't, however, packed anything for me. I started shivering as we walked back to our blanket. We had left everything on the beach despite Chase's conviction that we shouldn't. I told him that at a different beach I would have packed it all up, but in Marabella I always felt safe and didn't worry about stuff getting stolen. Sure enough, we found everything just as we had left it.

Chase rummaged around inside his bag and pulled out something dark blue and fuzzy. "Here. You can use my sweater."

I was too cold to protest, and we still needed to get the children and all their equipment in the car. I put it on, and it was the softest material I had ever felt. Like it had been collected from the bellies of baby Angora bunnies raised on organic carrots who had slept on cotton balls.

And it smelled like him. I wondered how weird it would be if I took it home and draped it over my pillow so I could be surrounded by his delicious scent all night.

Next thing I knew, we were home, taking everything out of the minivan. I told the weary kids to go inside, instructing the boys to take showers and the girls to wait for me so I could give them a bath.

Chase waited for me out front, but I needed him to leave. Not only so I could take care of my siblings, but also because even though my mother wouldn't be home for at least two hours, sometimes they sent her home early on Saturday shifts, and I couldn't run the risk of her seeing Chase Covington on our porch.

He had removed his glasses and hat, and he had that intense, hungry look in his eyes. I folded my arms, loving the feel of his sweater against my skin.

I would probably like the feel of him even more.

"So thank you for today," I said, finally finding my voice. "This was amazing."

"You're welcome. I really enjoyed it." For real? Was he just being polite? Was it acting? "And thank you."

"For what?"

I suddenly flashed to the part in his most recent rom-com where he thanked his love interest after a date. When she'd asked why, he said, "For the kiss." Only he'd never kissed her.

And when she'd started to say as much, he'd laid a kiss on her so hot that I had fanned my face the first time I saw it.

I'd heard people talking about feeling butterflies, but I hadn't understood that statement until right this second. Because I felt this flapping, fluttering sensation, not only in my stomach but also everywhere else. Like every internal cell had turned into a butterfly, fluttery with excitement and anticipation. The atmosphere between us felt thick, charged.

Only this wasn't a movie, and he didn't try to kiss me. He tucked a strand of hair behind my ear, and his fingers lingered on the side of my head for a moment, leaving a burning imprint. "Thank you for having no ulterior motive for hanging out with me. For being the first person I've ever met who didn't want something from me. See you tomorrow."

I echoed, "See you tomorrow," as he walked off the porch to his rental. I stood there, frozen, as he drove away. I didn't even wave.

Because the butterflies had been replaced by gross, slimy guilt worms that wriggled around inside me. I thought of Stephanie and how I had intended to ask Chase to help with the benefit.

How that would make me just another person who wanted something from him.

I hadn't told anyone. There was no way he could find out, right?

As long as I kept my mouth shut, everything should be fine.

CHAPTER THIRTEEN

Chase Covington ✓
@realchasecov

Following

The cookies are coming! #hopetheyliveuptothehype

💬   ↻ 14K   ♡ 63K

Last night when I got back to my apartment, it had occurred to me that I'd been so focused on Chase finding out about the fund-raiser that I had sort of blocked out the whole "Hey, Chase, guess what's completely off the table between us?" conversation.

And if he was the kind of guy who would bail over it, I needed to know. No more playing house or living in a fantasy. I had to face it.

Because it would be better to find out now before he so completely enchanted my heart that it would devastate me to lose him.

Again, I spent more time than I normally would getting ready to go to Chase's house. I finished putting on mascara and gave my reflection a last once-over. He had asked me why I didn't think I was beautiful. There was the traumatic stuff, but I just didn't think of myself that way. Men had found me attractive enough to ask out, but to be honest, there was always insecurity involved when you had a friend like Lexi. She was the hot one whom all the guys drooled over, and I was the smart one. Like we each had roles to play, and I'd spent so much time in her shadow that it hadn't occurred to me that I could be pretty and she could have brains, too.

In our tiny living room, Lexi and Gavin were cuddled together watching one of Chase's movies. It was based on a postapocalyptic YA novel about how the earth had turned into a giant desert and Chase's character had the magical ability to detect water. Dumb as it sounded, he was much better in that one than in *Octavius*.

"Somebody's all dressed up!" Lexi noticed, giving me a satisfied grin. "Off to see your man?"

I'd left Chase's sweater on the coffee table so I wouldn't forget to return it to him. I picked it up. "He's not my man. We're not dating."

"Yet. You're headed down the road to Relationship City."

"It's more of a flirtationship."

"Do you at least know if his intentions are honorable?" Gavin asked, pausing the movie.

Lexi giggled. I rolled my eyes. "We're hanging out. Not discovering Plymouth Rock."

I had started stroking the soft fabric of Chase's sweater, not realizing I was doing so. Lexi pointedly looked at my hands, and I stopped. "It's just really soft. Although I don't know what it's made out of." As if that would explain my anxiety.

"I do. Boyfriend material." She waggled her eyebrows at me, but I didn't laugh. "You're nervous."

"He makes me nervous," I confessed.

"You should feel that way in the beginning. It's exciting and scary to fall for someone. I always say when you first start dating someone, he should be like a cappuccino. Hot and sweet, and he makes you all jittery."

"Did I make you jittery?" Gavin asked.

"Obviously. Still do sometimes," she said, and they both smiled. Their smiles faded, and their expressions changed, like they were about to ravage each other.

I cleared my throat. "Okay. So I'm going to go."

"Before you do"—Lexi broke eye contact with Gavin long enough to look at me—"don't give up on him once you get past the honeymoon phase."

"Honeymoon phase?" I repeated, not sure what she meant.

"Everyone is amazing and wonderful when you first start dating, but nobody can keep up the pretense forever. Eventually he'll show his true colors. Everybody has skeletons in the closet."

I told her I would keep an open mind and said goodbye. As I headed to my car, I wondered how true Lexi's statement was. Because so far, Chase had been kind of perfect. He was thoughtful, considerate, and kind. Charming and funny. And the handsomest man I'd ever met in real life.

But I had skeletons in my closet. And personality defects. I was human, after all.

Chase was a movie star and had grown up in a completely different environment from me. He didn't just have skeletons in his closet. There were probably T. rex–size fossils in there. We would have to decide if we could deal with each other's shortcomings.

I'd offer to show him mine if he showed me his.

Um, I probably needed to think of a different way to phrase that before I saw him.

"Come in!" For some reason it surprised me that Chase answered his own door. Like, what was the point of being that wealthy if you couldn't have somebody else answering your door and fighting off solicitors?

"Here's your sweater. Thanks for lending it to me." I decided not to tell him that I'd seriously considered putting it on my body pillow, because that was too weird, even for me.

"Anytime." He closed the door behind me, and I followed him into the kitchen. He had a stack of head shots on the island. "I sign these for fans who write in asking for one."

I put my purse down as he sat on a bar stool and began quickly autographing one picture after another. "Shouldn't I be helping you with this?"

"Do you think you could forge my signature?" he asked. "If you can't, it has to be me. I promised my agent I'd get these signed by tomorrow morning." He tapped the Sharpie he was using against his lips, and I'd never been so jealous of a writing instrument in my life. "Was it tomorrow? My agent says I never listen to him. At least, I think that's what he says."

He tossed me a mischievous grin, pleased he'd made me smile. It was so adorable and hot that all I wanted right then was to kiss him. To shove the stack of photos off the counter, leap across it, and knock him over. My lips actually tingled in anticipation.

"I'd like to know what you're thinking right now."

I felt all the color drain my face. Did he know? "I'm not telling you. That's why I didn't say it out loud. Because that's how thinking works."

Chase laughed. "Sometimes in interviews they ask you what super-power you'd like to have. I used to choose being able to read people's minds. Then Facebook happened, and I got over that."

Now it was my turn to laugh. He seriously got cuter with each passing minute. I needed to keep my hands busy and think of the best way to tell him what I'd come to say. "Do you mind?" I pointed at the pantry, and it made his hand still.

"Are you making me cookies?"

"Yes, you obsessed weirdo."

"*Mi* kitchen is *su* kitchen. Help yourself."

I opened the door to his pantry. It was easily the size of a small apartment. I could have happily lived in there. And it was organized with bins and containers, the kind you see in magazines. I scanned his shelves, because a cake mix would be easier. I found white, chocolate, and yellow mixes, but no spice cake. I grabbed the containers marked flour and sugar, and boxes of baking powder and soda.

"Where are your spices?"

He pointed to a cabinet next to his stove. I set the oven to 350 degrees. I admit it took me a few minutes to figure it out because it had more buttons and dials than NASA's Mission Control Center. I quickly found cinnamon, and it surprised me when I found cloves as well.

"I can't believe you have cloves."

"Of course I have . . . whatever you just said. Do you think I'm a savage?"

Shaking my head, I got butter and eggs out of his Sub-Zero fridge, the inside of which resembled a small farmers' market. He had a ton of fresh vegetables and fruits. Like they were in there reproducing.

I located a medium-size saucepan and measuring cups and put the butter, water, sugar, and spices inside. I turned on the heat (more time spent figuring that out), intending to bring it to a boil.

"What are you making?"

"Spice-cake batter. You said you wanted my spice cookies, so that's what I'm making. Because you seem pretty determined to have everything your way."

"Another compliment."

I stopped my hunt for a spatula. "Then I must have said it wrong, because stubbornness isn't really a good thing."

"Says the girl who's looking a little pinkish. Is that a faint sunburn I detect?"

"That wasn't because I'm stubborn." I found the spatula and brought it over to the island.

"No, that was because you ran away from me."

I couldn't meet his eyes. "I didn't run away."

Yes, I had. I'd totally run away.

"I noticed you can be a little . . . skittish. I hope I don't make you feel that way."

I almost laughed. My heart was pumping so hard right then that if I'd been standing in Texas, it probably could have pulled oil out of the ground. "Have you seen you?"

"Every day in the mirror."

He said it like it was a joke, as if his appearance should have no bearing on this conversation. Like he couldn't make a nun give up her vows just by winking at her.

I'd basically just told him he was ridiculously hot. And here we were being domestic again, me baking for him in his ginormous kitchen. Clearly a subject change was in order.

"You know, I'm supposed to be your assistant. Shouldn't I be assisting you with those? Putting them in envelopes or whatever? I'm here. I could be killing two birds with one stone."

"Nobody needs to murder any birds. I've got this covered." There was an evasive tone in his voice.

"There's something you're not telling me." The ingredients on the stove started to boil, and I removed the pan from the heat.

He put the Sharpie down. "Okay, I'm going to be honest with you. One-F has been doing most of the assistant work. Not running errands but just about everything else."

"Wait. You're paying both of us for the same job? That doesn't seem right."

"I wanted to help you. It's weird, especially because we don't know each other that well yet, and I know this sounds bizarre, but it's like . . . I want to protect you. I've never felt that way about a girl before."

Little butterflies flapped around inside me at the thought that Chase wanted to protect me. Not that I needed his protection, but it felt amazing that he wanted to.

"Not to mention it got you here making these cookies you couldn't stop bragging about on your Twitter feed."

It was true. I was not humble about my baking skills. "I didn't come here as your assistant tonight. I came over as your . . ." I momentarily panicked. What was the right word here? Just because Chase felt protective didn't mean he wanted a relationship. He might see me as a little sister or something, and I was not about to make a huge fool of myself. "As your friend. And I don't want you to pay me to spend time with you. Do you know what that would make you?"

"Extremely lucky?" he answered with a wink that made my knees melt faster than the butter in the saucepan.

"I'm being serious."

"So am I." He leaned forward, and I realized his intent. To steal some of my batter. I smacked his hand and moved the bowl away, which made him chuckle.

"If you want to spend time with me, then let's just spend time together."

"Are you quitting?"

"You could always fire me, and I could collect unemployment." He didn't smile at my joke. "If we're . . . doing whatever this is, then I don't want your money between us."

The silence lasted so long that I almost started babbling just to make it less quiet. "Does that mean you want to see if there's something here?" he asked.

What was that supposed to mean? "If we're being honest, you're not really my type."

"Remember what I said about you being a bad liar?"

"It's not a lie!" I stirred the wet ingredients into the dry ones, thankful for the distraction. "I tend to go for more nerdy, shy guys." That feeling was back, the thick one that made it hard to breathe or concentrate, that made my pulse go haywire and my stomach do flips. So of course I had to make it stupid. "I mean, obviously, you're everyone with a pulse's type. I'm sure you're on the hall pass of every woman in America."

"Hall pass?"

"Yeah, you know—the celebrities you're allowed to cheat with and not get in trouble with your significant other. You did an episode about it on *Frenemies*."

"I know." His devilish smile made me want to smack him out of exasperation.

"Then why did you make me explain it?"

"Because of how cute you are when you get embarrassed." He stretched, and my eyes couldn't help but follow the lines of his arms. I enjoyed the way his muscles tightened. "I think we just established that we would like to hang out more. Without me paying you for it."

Did "hang out more" mean dating in guy speak? If we were dating, it was time to 'fess up.

"There's something I have to tell you first. And it may change your mind."

CHAPTER FOURTEEN

 Zoe
@zomorezoless

31% of Millennials prefer cookies to alcohol. #Trivia

💬   ↻ 0   ♡ 2

Why was this never easy? It didn't seem to matter how many times I'd said it, how many times I'd practiced it so I could sound cool and sophisticated and above it all. Instead, I came across like a cavewoman, lacking basic language. "You. Me. No do it."

It didn't help matters when he reached across the counter and took my hand in his. "I can't imagine anything you could say that would change my mind."

"I'm celibate." I blurted the words out without my usual buildup to explain my decision.

Three beats later he said, "What?"

"Celibate. I have chosen not to have sex until I get married."

Chase looked pensive, and I tried to slip out of his grasp, but he wouldn't let go. Instead of being annoyed as I normally would have been, I was glad. The gesture showed that I hadn't completely scared him off, that he wouldn't be inventing a cat's surgery in order to flee, and it comforted me.

"Is it okay if I ask why?"

He wasn't the first. "There are a lot of reasons. At first it was religious. What my grandparents taught me. Then when I was old enough to realize how young my mom was when she had me, I decided I wanted to be the opposite of her. And then my best friend had a pregnancy scare when we were sixteen. I didn't want to be a mother at sixteen."

"I totally get that. I didn't want to be a mother at sixteen, either."

I smiled a little. "I'm not really a casual person. I realized it would never not be a big deal to me. And in addition to keeping me not pregnant, it's also made me not diseased. My favorite teacher in high school contracted an STD without knowing it as a teen. It made her sterile, and she wanted a baby more than anything. It was so unbelievably sad."

Chase nodded, not saying anything. It was the most serious expression I'd ever seen on him. My stomach twisted, and I felt queasy. This was it. Now we would break up. Well, it wouldn't really be a breakup, since we hadn't actually dated, but I didn't want this to be the last time I saw him. Spoke to him.

Touched him.

He cleared his throat. "This is why I like making movies. Somebody else always writes the perfect thing for me to say." I squeezed his hand. He hadn't run into the night screaming, so he was already ahead in my book. "I like you and respect you, and I can respect your choice. But there's probably some things I should tell you. Like I don't think I want to get married."

"Ever?" I realized why he'd told me. I was saying "No sex until marriage," and now he was telling me there wouldn't be a marriage.

"My mother's on her ninth husband. It's hard to take marriage seriously when your own mom changes husbands as often as a politician changes their beliefs. Not to mention I work in an industry where I've had colds that have lasted longer than some marriages."

"I guess my perspective is different because I grew up around some really amazing marriages. I know how happy it can make people to find the right partner." But I wasn't going to change his mind. I understood why he felt that way and realized there probably wasn't anything I could say to make him see things differently. He was being a gentleman, letting me down easy. "I guess that means this is it."

"What? That's not what I was saying."

"If I'm waiting until marriage, and you're saying marriage will never happen, then there doesn't really seem to be a point to all this."

"The point is to see if we like each other. What we have right here is supposed to be about having fun and getting to know someone. Maybe even falling in love. And we can experience intimacy that has nothing to do with the physical. It's about you and I feeling safe enough to be open and vulnerable with each other. Being honest and sharing pieces of ourselves. That's what I'm looking for right now. Someone I can connect with on a different level than I have in the past. I'm still in."

Other than the no-marriage thing, everything else out of his mouth was perfect. Like I had ridden a unicorn over a rainbow into a fairyland, and Santa Claus was in charge of showing me around. Magical, fantastical, totally perfect.

I looked down and remembered my cookies. My poor dough was going to get hard if I didn't get the cookies baked. "I'm in, too. But if I don't finish this, it will go stale."

Nodding, he let my hand go, and it was like a part of me had gone missing. I found cookie sheets. The good kind that prevented the bottoms from burning. I started rolling the dough into balls and coating them with granulated sugar. "Don't take this the wrong way, but you're deeper than I thought you would be."

"I am more than just a pretty face," he agreed, going back to his autographing. "Although I can't take credit for my profoundness. That's my therapist talking."

Somehow that didn't surprise me. With all the weirdness that was his life, a therapist sounded like an essential.

He let out a big breath. "And my therapist would say there's something else I should tell you. I'm an alcoholic. Like my father before me. Although unlike him, I went to rehab, and I'm in recovery."

Chase had been so cool about my thing that I wanted to do for him what he had just done for me. I put the cookies in the oven and set a timer on my phone. "That sounds rough. When were you in rehab?"

"I'm two years and ten days sober. I started rehab two years ago. For an entire year."

That year when I thought his tweets didn't sound like him. One-F must have filled in for him.

"At first I stayed away from alcohol because of my dad and his accident. He had filmed the performance of a lifetime and then ran his car into a tree. He won an Academy Award posthumously for that part. I thought he was so stupid, but I got it because Hollywood is all about partying and mind-altering substances. It wasn't easy, but I avoided it. Then there was this director I really, really wanted to work with. Frederic Fontana. We went out to dinner, and he said he didn't trust a man who didn't drink. I wanted to impress him, so I drank. And all it took was that first drink. It was like something chemically changed inside me. Within a few days of hanging out with him, all I wanted to do was be drunk all the time."

"Didn't Frederic Fontana direct *Octavius*?"

"Sure did." He nodded. "That's why it jumped out at me when you talked about how I sucked in that part. I did, because I was wasted the entire production. The day I saw the final cut, I was fairly sober. I saw how bad I was. And I was doing exactly what my dad did. Throwing my entire life and career down the drain. I didn't want to end up wrapped around a tree. I checked myself into rehab that day."

"So you aren't perfect. That's kind of a relief. My roommate warned me that everybody has skeletons in their closet." It probably wasn't the right thing to say, but it sort of fell out of my mouth.

"She's not wrong. Rehab helped me figure out I used to be kind of a douchebag. I was totally full of myself, believing my own hype. I thought I was a lot more important than I actually am." He stared at the autographed pictures in front of him, as if recognizing the irony. "Therapy helped me see that I not only needed to change my behaviors and the people I hung out with, but also that I needed to be a different kind of man. I wanted to be better. Every day I'm trying to be."

Was that all I was to him? "So I'm someone to try out your new personality on?"

"It's not like that. I make these decisions. To think about other people before myself. I stopped being a jerk on set and make sure I show up on time. Which has led to more and better projects to choose from. There are so many jerks in the entertainment industry that people seem to enjoy the novelty of working with someone who tries to be nice."

As far as I knew, no tabloids, bloggers, or entertainment reporters knew any of this. He was telling me things that could totally tarnish his all-American, boy-next-door brand. "Thank you for trusting me with all of that."

"Thank you for trusting *me*."

The timer beeped, and I brought the cookie tray over to the island and laid it on a dishrag. Chase reached for one. "Let them cool off first. You're going to burn your tongue."

"Don't care." The cookie fell apart in his hand, but he dropped it into his mouth anyway. "I'm sorry I ever called your skills into question. These are phenomenal." Then he proved his statement true by grabbing three more.

"Has no one ever baked for you before?"

"My mom wouldn't know what a stove was if it jumped up and bit her," he said after he finished chewing. "My grandma was the ultimate stage mother, and she was far more focused on my career than anything else. The first time I got cookies I was fourteen. There was a guest star on our show. Shayna Rayne. She had an arc as my first girlfriend. She was actually my first kiss. She was a little bit taller than me, and when we tried to—"

"Okay," I said, holding up my hands. "I don't need the details."

He gave me a half smile, like he found my simmering jealousy cute. "Anyway, on her last day of filming, she brought me a plate of cookies, claiming she'd made them herself. I remember being really impressed because they were perfect-looking, and no one had ever baked for me before. When my grandma saw them, she said they were store-bought. I didn't believe her, so she sent out a PA to prove she was right. She was. And then she told me that someday I would find a girl who would make me cookies and not lie about it to impress me. When I saw it in your Twitter posts, it felt like another sign. Like the universe was saying, 'That one.'"

"My grandma said I would know I had the right man when we could wallpaper a room together and not kill each other. Although her frame of reference was definitely different from anyone else's."

At the rate he was going through the cookies, he was going to wolf down the entire dozen before they'd cooled.

"Didn't you say your grandparents were Amish?" he asked.

I used the spatula to take two cookies off the sheet, and I put them on the counter so I could eat them. "They were. My grandmother loved to learn, but once Amish kids turn fourteen, they don't go to school anymore. She asked to go to a regular school, but her parents didn't want her to fill her head with English ideas. They wanted her to meet a boy and get married. But the boy who caught her eye was Zev Miller, the son of her family's sworn enemies. I don't remember what the feud was about. Like, stolen cows or something. He liked her, too, but Hannah Yoder was off-limits."

"Like an Amish Romeo and Juliet."

"Exactly. They started to meet in secret and fell in love. My grandpa was so besotted that he told her he didn't mind if she went to high school and college. And he promised to take her to see the ocean, something she had always dreamed of. When they told their families, there was a lot of yelling and threatening and forbidding. So my grandparents decided to leave. They eloped and ended up in Marabella. My grandpa did woodworking, and my grandma made quilts and cleaned homes. Other than watching *Jeopardy!* with me, I don't have a single memory of her sitting down. She was always moving, always on the go. Eventually she got her degree and went to the beach every chance she got. They wanted a lot of kids, but they didn't have my mom until their early forties. And then, you know, the whole video-vixen-knocked-up-at-fifteen thing happened. So when she left me with them, they didn't let me go to public school because they thought it would be a bad influence on me, like it had apparently been on my mom. I spent my time doing schoolwork or cleaning or baking. Then my mother came and got me because she needed a built-in babysitter, and you know the rest."

"Maybe it didn't have anything to do with babysitting. Maybe once she got her life together, she realized what a mistake she'd made in leaving you behind and wanted you back."

I wanted to believe that, but years of feeling rejected and abandoned made it difficult to consider her motives that way. I ate my cookies, and they were practically perfect. Definitely brag-worthy.

Chase got up and poured two glasses of milk, then handed me one. "To one of the best nights I've had in a long time."

I smiled, clinking my glass against his. I shared the sentiment, but some bitter, unbelieving part of me wondered if he was acting and pretending. Because of his desire to be a better person, he felt like he had to say and do certain things he didn't really mean.

I took a small drink, but he chugged his, leaving behind a white moustache. "You have milk on you."

"Where?" he asked. "Here?" He teased me by rubbing one side of his cheek, completely missing his mouth.

"Not quite."

"Here?" Now he was wiping his forehead.

"Right here," I said with a laugh, stepping forward to rub the milk off with my thumb. It was a reactionary move, and I hadn't allowed myself to think about it first. I rubbed my thumb just above his top lip, and my smile died when I looked up at him.

Because his eyes had the same expression as when I had set the tray of cookies down. Like he didn't care if I had cooled off enough, because he intended to devour me.

For the record, I was the opposite of cooled off. Just one look from him made my blood heat and feel too thick for my veins.

I should have taken my hand away, but I didn't. He had faint stubble that made his skin an intoxicating combination of smooth and prickly. Chase reached out and wrapped his fingers around my wrist, and my pulse there jumped against his touch. He tugged at me gently, and I stopped touching his face.

"I don't know about you, but after all this sharing, I think I'd like to turn my brain off for a while."

He led me into the family room, and my heartbeat got louder with each step he took. His fingers were still around my wrist, causing little waves of heat to travel up my arm. We sat down on the couch, and the only thing I could think of to turn off our brains involved a whole lot of making out. I'd kissed my fair share of guys before, but most of the kisses had been brief and not all that exciting.

I couldn't imagine kissing Chase would feel that way.

And I hoped I wouldn't disappoint him.

But the only person who was disappointed was me when he let go of my arm to pick up a remote from his coffee table. "This is supposed to be a universal remote. You can imagine how sad I was when I realized it didn't control the universe. Not even remotely."

This was not a time for jokes.

"I thought we could watch a movie. And I will even let you choose, as soon as you give me at least one movie from your better-than-*Octavius* list."

My body was so flooded with hormones, anticipation, and want that it made it hard to concentrate on what he was saying. "*Miracle Mile.*" It was about a potential Olympic swimmer who was in a serious car accident and came back to win medals in the Olympics four years later. "Although it has an inaccurate title. It probably should have been called *Miracle Meter.*"

And the fact that he'd spent most of that movie in a Speedo had absolutely nothing to do with my choice.

I mean, maybe a little.

"That character was a drunk, which was what caused the accident. His father and grandfathers were alcoholics, too. I probably should have made that connection before I fell down the rabbit hole myself."

"That addiction runs in your family?"

"It doesn't so much run. Instead, it casually strolls through, taking its time to get to know everybody personally. Anyway, now you get to choose the movie."

This was probably what it was like to date a chef and have him say, "You choose the restaurant." I didn't want to pick one of his, because that would be weird, right? And I didn't want to go total romantic comedy on him, because even though I loved them and thought we were in a place where romance was a possibility, nothing was happening. Did I pick a stuff-blowing-up movie? Depressing one with subtitles? Sci-fi? Fantasy? What if I selected something he thought was terrible and it totally changed his opinion of me?

"Would you like to see the new Brad Pitt movie?" He mentioned the title. I knew for a fact it wasn't available to rent because Lexi had been begging Gavin to take her to see it.

"The one that's still in theaters?"

"Yeah, one of the producers wants to work with me, so she sent this over to show me the kind of work she does."

"That sounds good." His world was so very different from mine.

Chase messed around with his remote and got the movie started. I tried to pay attention. I really did. But all I could think about was our seating arrangement. I was close to him. Close enough that if I leaned sideways, we'd be touching. But we weren't cuddling like Lexi and Gavin always did when they watched TV.

Plus, Chase kept up a running commentary throughout the movie. He commented on the lighting and the costumes and the camera angles. How he would have made different choices as the lead actor. The lines of dialogue that sounded cheesy. Thing was, that's how I normally watched movies. It made Lexi crazy, and she had pretty much stopped watching them with me.

Except Chase's movies. She didn't watch those with Gavin, because they were ours. But I had to promise to keep my mouth shut and not mock bad accents or poor acting choices, and I most definitely could not theorize on foreshadowing and plot twists.

Another thing Chase and I had in common. But I didn't join in. I stayed mute, feeling weird and wondering what exactly was going on. Because I kept thinking of this as a real date. I had built it up in my mind, even though all he'd said was that he liked me as a person and wanted to hang out with me. I reminded myself that he'd said he was interested and that he thought me beautiful, but for all I knew that meant something entirely different in Hollywood. He'd never said he saw me as girlfriend potential, and despite some particularly opportunistic moments, he hadn't kissed me. That was the thing that bothered me the most. Why hadn't he made any kind of move?

Maybe it was like I'd thought earlier—I was just a kindness experiment. Maybe his plan had been *find a pathetic fan, befriend her in real life, and become even more self-actualized as I make her life better.*

He did put his arm across the back of the couch at one point, but he didn't put it around me. He just left it there. Taunting me.

And the longer I stayed, the more pathetic I felt. When the credits began to roll, I stood up and said, "Thanks for inviting me over, but I have class in the morning. I should probably get going."

I went into the kitchen to retrieve my purse, and I was almost to the front door when he called out my name. He jogged over. "Are you sure you have to go?"

So very, very sure. I wanted to escape with whatever remnants of my dignity I still possessed. "I'm sure."

He opened the door before I could, and I had to duck under his arm to get outside. "Okay, bye!" I said over my shoulder, desperate for the sanctuary of my car.

"Wait." He tugged on my arm, turning me around. Then he took both of my hands in his, and I told myself to stop reacting. It didn't mean anything. "You seem tense."

Maybe that's because the guy I'd dreamed about kissing since I was thirteen didn't seem all that interested in it. "I'm not tense. Just, um, alert." And stupid, apparently.

"I had fun tonight."

So had I, until I'd thought he wanted to kiss me, and instead he wanted to sit next to me in a dark room and not kiss me.

He stepped closer, and the air around me forgot how it was supposed to function in providing me oxygen. Either that or my lungs had stopped working. He leaned in, and my entire body cheered, *Yes! Finally!*

And then . . . he kissed me on the forehead. Like I was a child he thought was cute.

Like I was Zia.

"Good night."

Utterly humiliated, I didn't say it back and instead walked away, putting my hands over my cheeks. I functioned on autopilot as I got in my car and drove off.

I couldn't believe he'd kissed me on the forehead. Don't get me wrong, it felt amazing. His lips were warm and firm, and I still had electric tingles shooting through my body from that brief contact.

My phone buzzed, and when I got to a stoplight, I checked it. It was a text from Chase.

> I know I'm not playing it cool, but when can I see you again?

And just like that, all my negativity and doubt dissipated. Like early-morning fog at the beach once the sun started to rise. So what if he hadn't kissed me? He wanted to see me again!

I felt slightly pathetic that I was so easily swayed. I used the speech-to-text feature on my phone to reply.

> Aren't you working twelve hour days all week?

> I'm available Saturday. How about you?

> Possibly.

> What's your favorite place in the whole world?

Without hesitation, I replied:

> Disneyland.

And just as quickly he responded:

> Done.

The smart thing would be to text him back and say *Thanks, but no thanks. I don't want to spend my time trying to figure out what you want because you're sending completely mixed signals.*

Of course I didn't do that.

I was just like Zelda with her chocolate. I should stay away from Chase, but I just wanted to eat him up.

CHAPTER FIFTEEN

Zoe
@zomorezoless

Found out #Disneyland has roaming feral cats who take care of rodents. #watchoutmickey

💬　🔁 0　♡ 1

I received a text from Chase every morning and one every night around bedtime. All innocent and innocuous. Just "Have a good day" and "Sweet dreams." Stuff like that.

He also sent me random questions throughout the week. A couple of days before, he'd asked,

If you could wake up tomorrow with one new quality or ability, what would it be? I would choose a photographic memory. So that I wouldn't have to spend so much time memorizing scripts.

In that moment, despite what I'd said previously, I probably would have chosen mind reading. Just so I could understand what exactly was happening between us.

Instead, I chose:

> The power to clean the oceans in one fell swoop.

> Oh, great. I make mine selfish and yours is about saving the world.

Another day he sent this:

> How do you think you'll die?

> Either in an ice cream factory incident or from Type 2 diabetes. You?

> I suspect either a car accident caused by a paparazzo or getting Misery-ed in some fan's rec room.

My grandmother talked to me a lot about the letters she and my grandpa had exchanged. How they'd used them to get to know each other and how sad it made her that that sort of communication had faded away. But as I sat giggling over my phone, I realized it hadn't. It was different, but we were back to using the written word to see if we liked each other. If we were compatible.

And maybe someday we'd even use it to talk about our feelings.

Or lack thereof, as the case might be.

I went back to looking for work, and on Wednesday evening I got a phone call from a family who lived in the wealthy part of Marabella, not too far from where the Hendersons had lived. Their nanny had up and quit with no notice because she had eloped to Las Vegas with the gardener. The Mendels were desperate for help. They had found a babysitter who could work only mornings, and Mrs. Mendel said she would be willing to work with my schedule. It would involve going to their home a couple of evenings after my internship, which I hadn't done for the Hendersons, but I needed the job. The Mendels had adopted two little girls from China, Lily and Mei-Ling, and I thought watching two girls after my experience with the Henderson boys might be a nice change. They offered me an hourly wage that was a bit higher than the Hendersons had paid me.

It seemed too good to be true.

"I'll have to thank Mrs. Henderson for the referral," I said when we had finalized the arrangements.

"Oh no. You'll have to thank Chase Covington. My husband works as an executive at Daylight Studios, and Chase overheard him talking about losing our nanny and said he'd seen you taking care of kids and gave you an excellent reference."

Once we'd hung up, I wasn't quite sure what to think about what she'd said. Was it okay for Chase to find me a job? Shouldn't that have been my responsibility? Was it too much? It was kind and thoughtful and very much needed. I guessed that if all he wanted was to be friends, he was a good friend to have.

The rest of the week flew by—class, helping my mom, and interning at the Foundation. Before I knew it, it was Saturday morning. Chase said he'd be by to pick me up around nine o'clock.

Knowing Lexi would be passed out until well after noon, I'd agreed to it. I did take the precaution of waiting for him in the parking lot so I could just jump in his car when he arrived.

"This is a really nice car," I said when I got in. He launched into some long explanation of the type of car it was, but I mostly tuned it out. I much preferred watching his profile and how he moved his hands around when he described something he was excited about. It was adorable. He kept pointing out features, and while I liked the cushy seats and the engine that purred like a large cat, my favorite feature of his car was the driver.

Even though he still made me a little nervous, the thing I noticed about hanging out with Chase was that our conversations never stalled. I, Queen of the Socially Inept, Duchess of Awkward Small Talk, enjoyed talking to him. It was like the outside world ceased to exist. Nothing else mattered. It was just me and him, connecting and laughing and joking around.

I didn't think about what Lexi might say if she found out. How fast Stephanie would fire me if she knew Chase and I had become friends and I didn't use our friendship for the Foundation's benefit. How if we weren't just friends, and at some point he pressed his lips against mine, between my celibacy and his no-marriage policy, we had an expiration date. Eventually he would grow tired of nothing happening between us, and I would become frustrated with waiting for him to change his mind about a serious relationship.

Even though it was out of character for me, I decided that just once I would enjoy the here and now. I'd stay on the ride until somebody kicked me off.

Then we were in Anaheim, and I could see Space Mountain, and suddenly I was six years old again, going to Disneyland for the first time with my grandparents.

We didn't go to the main parking lot; he drove around to the opposite side of the park. He spoke to someone at a guard station, giving his name, and we were let in after the guard told us where to park.

"Where are we?" I asked as we got out of the car.

"You're going to love this. Come on."

We came to a nondescript door painted bland green that reminded me of the trash cans in the park. A man with dark hair and wire-rim glasses stood there wearing a red-and-blue plaid vest, a white long-sleeve shirt, and blue pants.

"How are you today? I'm Braden, and I'll be in charge of your VIP tour today. Think of me as your personal concierge. Anything you need, anywhere you want to go, any ride you're in the mood for, just let me know, and I'll take care of everything. So, I already know your name, Mr. Covington."

They shook hands, and Chase said, "Just Chase, please."

"I'm Zoe."

Braden shook my hand as well, his wide grin with perfect teeth never faltering. "A pleasure! This entrance we're using now is the one favored by many of our celebrity guests, both past and present. I shouldn't really name-drop, but let me just say it has been the entrance of choice for people whose names rhyme with Fichael Schmackson and Marbra Smeisand."

We were in a dim hallway, and I saw a light up ahead. When we reached it, I was hit by the smell of seawater and realized we were in the Pirates of the Caribbean ride. We were at the beginning, where the old man in the rocking chair plays his banjo across from the Blue Bayou restaurant just after you've boarded. The tunnel we were in ran along the top of the banjo player's cabin. Patrons were eating and laughing while boats carrying guests launched beneath us. I wondered if people could see us up here. If they would wonder who we were.

I just stood there, totally in awe. "This is the most amazing thing I've ever seen."

"I think I might be offended," Chase teased, not knowing how right he was. Because standing there in the ride wasn't technically the most amazing thing I'd seen. I'd witnessed sweaty Chase partially out of his superhero costume. And lathered-up Chase on the beach. And beach Chase with seawater dripping off him, and . . .

Okay, so this made the top ten of the most amazing things I'd ever seen.

Possibly.

Then we were out on the street in New Orleans Square, and Chase immediately put on his hat and sunglasses, something Braden noted. "Will you be needing extra security today, Mr. Cov—Chase?"

"I'm an actor. If I can't manage to blend in, then I'm not very good at my job, am I?"

I didn't think it had anything to do with whether or not he could act. He had an inborn magnetism you couldn't look away from. Not to mention we were being escorted around by someone in very bright colors, and Braden was sure to draw attention to us. But Chase seemed confident, and I decided to trust his judgment.

"Where to?" Chase asked. "Your wish is our command."

"Since we're here, Pirates and then Haunted Mansion. And then Small World."

Then the best thing in the entire world happened. Braden walked us onto Pirates of the Caribbean. I'd had this brief moment after we arrived where I'd worried about what would happen if Chase waited in line, but now I realized why we had Braden. Because Chase would get mobbed if people recognized him and he stayed in one place for too long.

Deciding to get out in front of my roller-coaster phobia, I explained to Chase that I didn't like the drops on Pirates. I was a serious wuss when it came to fast rides and big drops. When Lexi and I went to Grad Night (once a year, high school seniors go to Disneyland after it closes and spend the whole night), everybody wanted to be on Splash Mountain, the Matterhorn, and Space Mountain. And they'd thought those rides were tame. I could force myself to go on them, but I closed my eyes and didn't like them, which Chase seemed to find amusing.

But rides like Pirates? This was what I loved about Disneyland—it was the best people trap ever set by a mouse. It was the atmosphere, the magic of the surroundings. Not just in the architecture but in the attention to every detail. Hidden outlines of Mickeys everywhere. How clean and beautiful everything was. Even if I didn't go on a single ride, I just loved being there. For me it was like stepping into another world, and if I'd been able to justify spending the money on a year-round pass, I probably would have dedicated a large portion of my free time to being in the park, just hanging out. As a kid I had routinely fantasized about hiding out on a ride and then having the whole place to myself after closing.

Braden pointed out the headboard in the captain's quarters. He said that although all the other bones and skeletons were fake, the skull and crossbones in the headboard were real. Why did that make me want to touch it?

I liked Chase even more when he turned to me and said, "I kind of want to touch that now."

Having been to Disneyland at least twice a year for the past sixteen years, I thought I knew everything there was to know, see, and do in the park. I found out very quickly how wrong my perception was. When we got to the Haunted Mansion, Braden took us around back to show us a pet cemetery I'd never known existed. We also got death certificates when we finished the ride that said, "I survived the Haunted Mansion."

I knew I was going to frame it.

When we rode on It's a Small World, I told Chase about when Lexi and I had gone on the ride on Grad Night. Since it's considered a kid's ride, we were the only ones in line and literally had the place to ourselves. Lexi got out of the boat several times to dance with the animated dolls. At one point she messed around for so long that she missed our boat. She'd had to jump in one behind me, hop over the rows, and climb across the boats until she got back to where I was. I didn't have the guts to run amok like she did, but I was thoroughly convinced that when we got to the end of the ride, we would be kicked out of the park. It didn't happen. The only thing I could figure was that teenage boys were staffing the ride and were either amused or didn't care, and nobody said anything to us.

Even though the song always became an earworm that would burrow deep into my brain, I always thought this ride was romantic. The little gondolas, the water, the darkness. Sitting pressed against Chase only exacerbated it.

The same thing happened on every ride after that. Suddenly they were all magical and romantic, and I wished we were alone and that I had the nerve to rest my head on his shoulder and hold his hand.

I considered it when we were given a ride on a private train car called the Lilly Belle, named after Walt Disney's wife. Braden said she had helped design the car, and it remained just as she'd decorated it. The inside was full of dark hardwoods, red plush armchairs, and Victorian end tables and lamps. It was totally closed in, unlike the other cars, which were open on all sides. It was a nice break, but we couldn't say or do anything because we weren't alone. There were some other people with guides dressed similarly to Braden, and Chase's distinctive voice would have given him away. As it was, we were starting to get some side-eyes and whispers.

When the train returned to the station, Braden seemed aware of what I'd noticed and ushered us out quickly.

We went up Main Street USA and slowed down once we reached the Sleeping Beauty Castle. I veered off to the right, over to the Snow White Grotto. It was an area that people usually just passed through, but it had special meaning to my family.

I dug through my purse and found two quarters, then handed one to Chase. As I stood at the wishing well, for the first time I hesitated before making my wish. I already had so much, it felt selfish to ask for more.

Including the amazing, hot guy next to me reading the sign attached to the well. "They donate the coins to children's charities. Very cool."

He casually flipped his quarter in, and I wondered if he'd even made a wish. I finally made mine, settling on *I wish I knew whether Chase actually likes me.*

"My stepdad sort of proposed to my mom here," I told him.

"Really?"

"Yep. They were right here at this wishing well, watching the swans in the moat and listening to the Snow White music. Duncan was kind of goofy. He dramatically pointed to the castle and said, 'Oh, Zerah, will you come live with me in my castle?' Keep in mind it was only their fourth date. So my mother decided to screw with him and stayed silent for a second, then very seriously answered, 'Yes, I will.' Which freaked Duncan out, although he tried to keep his cool. But instead of scaring him off, it changed things between them, and they went from being casual to seriously dating."

He smiled as he leaned against the well. "So if I ask you to come live with me in my castle, what will you say?"

Yes, yes, yes, yes, yes. And yes.

I didn't say that, though I was surprised by both the immediacy and the intensity of my internal reaction. Not to mention that if I counted hanging out at my mom's, this was our fourth date as well. Chase kept talking about signs and what the universe wanted. I wanted so desperately for this to be one of those signs. Instead, I nudged him with my elbow and laughed.

"What do you want to do next?" Chase asked.

"Shouldn't you pick something?" I didn't want to dominate the entire day by doing only what I chose.

"Nah. I like seeing all this through your eyes."

When I mentioned I liked the Mark Twain riverboat, Braden, who had wisely hung back during our exchange, told us to follow him.

"Do you have to be a movie star to get this kind of treatment?" I asked as he led us into an employee-only area to take a shortcut to Frontierland.

"Anybody can hire a VIP tour guide. Some celebrities choose to; some don't. We recommend that they do because it makes it easier on everyone. A celebrity sighting can really gum up the works for foot traffic in specific areas." Despite the fact that we'd been walking around for hours, Braden remained relentlessly upbeat and professional and knew more about Disneyland than anyone I'd ever met. Like how the purple-flowered teacup on the Mad Tea Party ride spun the fastest. A fact I could now personally attest to, given that I'd nearly puked afterward.

We got to the steamboat landing just as the old-fashioned white boat pulled in and allowed the onboard passengers to disembark. Once they shouted the all clear, Braden took us on ahead of the other people waiting. Jazz music played through the speakers. "I have a surprise for you." We went to the second floor to a wooden door with red curtains marked "Private."

Braden knocked, and a woman wearing a name tag that said "Captain Christy" opened the door. She had on a black vest and pants, a white shirt, and a huge red bow tie. "What have we here?"

"I was told you might be looking for some extra crew members," Braden responded.

"You heard right. Come on up." Captain Christy took us inside the captain's quarters, which was complete with a bed and dresser. She directed us to a set of steps that looked like a ladder, and I followed her up, with Chase right behind me. I tried not to think about the fact that he had a perfect view of my rear end.

"Welcome to the wheelhouse!" the captain said. We were in a tiny white room with windows on every side except the front. "You can sign our guest book, if you'd like."

While Chase signed, using his real name, Braden told us the guest book dated back to the 1950s. I fought off the urge to flip through it and just signed my name instead.

"Who would like to steer?"

"Zoe would," Chase offered, flashing me a grin.

"That puts you in charge of the bell and whistle," the captain told him. She instructed him to ring the bell four times, pull the whistle for five seconds, and then ring the bell again to let the boiler engineer below deck know we were setting off. Chase asked her questions about the other boats in the water, and she told him about their system to slow down or reverse if necessary. I loved how interested he was in everything. Like the whole world just fascinated him. When she mentioned the steamboat being on a track, I realized my steering was largely ceremonial, but I was okay with that.

Finally, it was time for me to "steer," and I could feel Chase watching me. I turned and saw him smiling, and I couldn't help but grin back. This was easily the best date I had ever been on.

Which meant I should have expected everything to go wrong.

"The maiden voyage of the *Mark Twain* was on July 13, 1955. It was four days before the official opening because there was a private party to celebrate Walt and Lillian Disney's thirtieth wedding anniversary. Story goes that Disneyland's construction supervisor found Mrs. Disney sweeping the decks before the party, and he helped her out."

I wondered what would happen if I turned the wheel too hard. "You know so many cool things about this place, Braden. My brain is full of useless information, like which Real Housewives are feuding and which couples from *The Bachelor* are still together."

"Don't let her fool you," Chase interjected. "She knows everything about everything."

He sounded . . . proud of me. Which made my pulse dance. "Obviously not about Disneyland."

"Not yet. But I expect you to be fully briefed soon."

The sound of screams fading in and out echoed off to our left.

"Zoe, that's Splash Mountain. I know what you said about rides like that, but it's my favorite. Would you go on it with me?"

"You mean the one with the five-story drop at the end?" I gulped audibly.

"Fifty-two point five feet," Braden added. Which was so not helpful.

"The ride where people are screaming hysterically. That's the one you want us to go on."

"It'll be fun," Chase said. "Promise."

We had very different ideas about fun. But it was the only thing Chase had asked to do all day. I would be the worst person ever if I said no. I could get on, grit my teeth, and close my eyes. "Sure. Let's do that next."

I got another certificate from the captain, but all I could think about was what I had just agreed to. And before I knew it, we were settling into the Splash Mountain canoes. Which had no seat belts and no straps of any kind. Chase asked if I wanted to sit in the front and laughed when I violently shook my head. The ride operators asked us to put away anything that could fly off—hats, sunglasses, etc. Braden promised to meet us at the exit.

Then it was dark, and we alternated between going slowly and very quickly. I couldn't tell much beyond that, as I screwed my eyelids shut. The worst was going up, up, up to that drop. I held on tightly to the railings on either side of me, my heart beating in my mouth.

"Open your eyes, Zoe! It's awesome!"

"Shut up, Covington!" I yelled back, and even with all the rushing water, I heard him laugh. I didn't open my eyes as we hovered at the very top, then I hyperventilated as we plummeted to our doom.

Okay, not actual doom as we (obviously) survived, but it was terrifying. I did not enjoy it. Chase, on the other hand, was laughing and shaking water off his arms. I forced my limbs to relax, not quite able to breathe yet.

I hoped he realized how much I liked him, given that I was willing to risk premature death to go on a ride he liked.

"See? Not so bad."

"Says you." I put my head down close to my knees, worried I might actually faint even though it was all over.

When we got to the very end, Chase was there to help me out of the canoe. My ankles felt weak, and I leaned against him. "Hey, you seem a little shaky."

"I'll be fine," I told him, feeling much better now that I was back on solid ground.

He put his arm around my shoulders and helped me walk. I didn't know if it was the shock and adrenaline from the ride or just having him touch me, but every nerve ending sparked inside me like fireworks on the Fourth of July.

Which was why I didn't notice all the whispers and stares until it was too late.

"Aren't you Chase Covington? Can I, like, take a picture with you?" A bottle-blonde twenty-something in a tank top so tight it was obviously meant for a toddler stood in front of us, blocking our way.

"My friend's not feeling too well. Not today, sorry." He was polite and kind, but that didn't please his fan.

She wasn't going to take no for an answer.

CHAPTER SIXTEEN

"It's, like, one picture. Are you really that big of a douche?" Miss Too Tight Shirt said, giving us an ugly look and crossing her arms.

"He's not a douche," I retorted, ready to yank out some extensions if necessary.

But our confrontation quickly ended as her actions emboldened the people around us. There were autograph books thrust at Chase, flashes from phones going off, and cell phones being held up, recording us. Girls were screaming and crying, and others started reaching for him, tearing at his shirt. Chase looked panicked. I ducked my head and rummaged through my purse until I found my keys. I yanked them out and blew my rape whistle, hoping Braden would hear. If he didn't, I was going to use the Mace attached to my key ring to get everyone out of our way.

More and more people surrounded us. We were literally being mobbed.

Braden appeared, along with three other cast members, who made an opening for Chase and me. We were led through another employee-only door, which Braden slammed shut.

Chase's shirt was torn in several places. His fans had treated him like a piece of meat, there for them to grab and harass. He leaned against the wall, breathing hard. "Are you okay?" he asked me.

Me? My clothing was intact. "I'm completely fine. Are you okay? That was crazy."

He nodded, trying to catch his breath. It had to have been worse for him. I felt shaky and nauseated, and I wasn't the one they wanted attention from.

Braden kept apologizing, but Chase wouldn't let him. "It wasn't your fault. This could have happened to me anywhere. I should have remembered to put on my hat and sunglasses after the ride finished. I was . . ." His eyes wandered over to me. "Distracted."

Now I felt even worse. "I'm sorry."

"You have nothing to apologize for. That's not what I meant. None of this was your fault, either." Having composed himself, Chase pushed off the wall. "I probably need to buy a new shirt, but do you want to head over to California Adventure?"

That was the Disney park directly across from the Magic Kingdom. My phone started beeping frantically. I had forgotten I had set up a Google Alert with Chase's name. It sent me link after link of pictures and posts on social media about how he was at Disneyland. Everyone in the world knew where he was right then. He wouldn't be able to keep a low profile any longer. I showed him my screen. "Maybe we should go home."

He nodded and took me by the hand. It was amazing how right it felt to hold hands with him. To lace my fingers through his. Like this was how it was supposed to be. Braden escorted us out the way we'd come in, still trying to apologize, but Chase told him, "This is on me. I should have brought security. I was just hoping I could have one normal day." He sounded so sad I wanted to hug him.

Braden walked us all the way back to Chase's car. Chase opened the door for me, and I saw him hand Braden a very big tip. Chase let out a deep breath when he got into the driver's seat, and he took a moment before turning the key and starting the car.

Once we were clear of the parking lot, he reached over and took my hand, and that feeling of rightness, of being where I belonged, returned. "Do you want to come over and hang out?"

"Yes." I didn't even let myself think about it. I didn't want to leave him yet.

Half an hour later, we went through an In-N-Out drive-through, and Chase smiled as the cashier about peed her pants when she saw whose order she had just filled. I tried to give him my debit card, but he wouldn't take it. He pulled his wallet out and passed some cash to the girl. The workers at the second window were expecting us, and they crowded behind the teenager handing us our food. Chase thanked her, and she looked like she was about to start crying.

"Eat now or at home?" he asked, handing me the bags of food.

"Home." I almost started babbling about how I knew he hadn't meant it was *my* home and that I wasn't trying to imply anything or move things along too quickly by thinking of his house as home, but I stopped. He didn't look scared by my answer, so I decided not to make a big deal out of it.

Plus, I didn't want him to let go of my hand, because he probably would have needed it to eat and drive at the same time.

He didn't let go until we got to his place. He excused himself to go upstairs and grab another shirt while I put the bags of food on the kitchen counter. Not even a minute later, Chase came back downstairs, putting his new shirt on and giving me the full visual of his delicious abs before he covered them. I tried not to frown. He grabbed the bags off the counter and took them into the family room, where he set them on the coffee table. He flopped down on his couch and rubbed his eyes. He looked worn out. I figured I should probably let him rest. "Do you want me to call an Uber?"

Chase sat up, giving me a weak smile. "No. I want you to stay."

I couldn't tell if he meant it or if he was just being polite. I decided to take him at his word and handed him his food. We ate in silence, but it was a comfortable one.

He finished way before I did, used a napkin, and threw it in the bag. "Earlier this week they messengered over a movie I filmed a while ago that hasn't been released yet. It's called *The Storm*. Interested?"

That made me sit up straight. "Absolutely."

"Normally I don't like watching myself."

I totally got that. I didn't like hearing myself on somebody else's voice mail.

"But this was the first thing I filmed after rehab. I want to see how it turned out. I've been waiting to watch it with you."

Aw. My heart fluttered. He was seriously the cutest.

He used his universal remote to queue up the movie and turn off the lights. I put my uneaten food back in the bag. I wanted to give this my full attention. I knew a little bit about it already. He played a Maine fisherman who dreamed of going to college but gave it all up to take over his family's fishing business. His character ended up in one of the worst storms on record, and he refused to tell me whether his character survived. "You'll have to wait and see."

Just like last time, Chase made comments and told me anecdotes about filming. Like how he had done all his own underwater stunts and how in each of those scenes he had been surrounded by a team of divers with oxygen, ready to swim in and save him if something bad happened.

On the screen, the first massive wave appeared and knocked him off his ship and into the ocean.

"You're holding your breath," he observed.

I let it out. "Okay, I know it's weird, but whenever I watch a movie like this and someone goes underwater, I hold my breath to see if I would have survived."

"It's not weird. I do that, too. But I almost died watching *Finding Nemo*."

That made me laugh harder than I had all day. He grinned and reached out for my hand, then pulled it to his lap. He didn't put his arm around me, didn't pull me closer, but each circle he rubbed with his thumb on the inside of my palm sent a shiver down my back.

Then he shot me one of those sexy smirks, like he knew exactly what effect he had on me. I tried to focus on the movie.

It ended with his character being the only survivor and deciding to go to college to pursue his dreams, after all, since so many of his friends and family members had permanently lost their chance to do more with their lives.

He paused the credits, and I tried to wipe away tears with my free hand before he noticed.

"Hashtag better than *Octavius*?" he teased.

"Definitely hashtag better than *Octavius*. You were amazing."

He squeezed my hand. "That means more to me than any professional review." He kept the room in the dark, and I wondered if he wanted us to watch another movie. It would have to be something lighter, though. I had been fighting off sobs for the past hour. "Do you regret today?"

What? "Are you kidding me? Today was . . . incredible." I wanted to say more, but I stopped. Until it occurred to me that maybe the reason he was holding back was because I held back. Maybe it was time to break the cycle. "It was easily one of the best days of my life."

He looked surprised. "Even with the crowd chasing us?"

"Even then." Probably because I'd been with him.

"Some women haven't . . . liked that about me."

It wasn't like it was his fault people were crazy. "Everybody's got something, right? Some guys go out to a bar every night. Others play golf all day Saturday. Or have to watch 'the game' all the time. Or participate in *Fight Club*. This is your thing. Being mauled by random strangers."

That got me a half smile. "I was really worried about you getting hurt today."

"I was worried about you. With good reason."

"I think I might have been scratched." He turned the lights on and let go of my hand to yank off his shirt. He turned his back toward me. "Do you see anything?"

Did I see anything? Only the most masculine and magnificent display of broad shoulders and back muscles known to womankind. I reminded myself that I was supposed to be looking for injuries, not fantasizing about leaning forward to press kisses against his tanned skin. I noticed some freckles and a couple of scars but nothing recent. "All clear. Nobody drew blood." My voice sounded small.

He put his shirt back on, and I wanted to pout with disappointment. He grabbed my hand again, like he hadn't wanted to let go in the first place.

"Speaking of today, I realized I did make one mistake. When you asked me where my favorite place was, I should have said London. Or Paris." He was playing with my fingers, sliding his own between them, making my stomach clench and my skin feel too tight.

"Let's go home and get your passport. We'll go right now."

Thing was, he didn't sound like he was teasing. Like if I said yes, I'd be on a private jet in a couple of hours on my way to Europe. "I don't have a passport. I've never really traveled anywhere."

"We'll have to rectify that. After you get your passport."

First thing to do Monday morning: get my freaking passport. Even though I could never let him spend that kind of money and fly me to England or France.

Could I?

There was definitely a part of me that considered it. I kept surprising myself with my reactions to him and the things he said.

"Speaking of travel, I have some not-so-great news. I have to go to Ireland for about three weeks."

"What? Why?" I whined like Zelda did when somebody told her she couldn't have chocolate.

"We have to do some location reshoots. They decided to change a couple of things about the script. Too bad about that passport or you could have come with me."

Little thrill pangs surged through me at the thought of being with him in a place as beautiful as Ireland. Until reality set in. "Even if I had one, I couldn't just . . . I have school. And my family. And I had to start a new job since my last boss was an egomaniacal celebrity unfamiliar with sexual harassment law."

And I'm still not sleeping with you. I kept that last bit to myself.

He grinned and pulled my hand up to his mouth. He kissed the back of it. The contact was brief, but it made my knees melt. I was glad I was sitting down.

"Just promise me you won't go falling in love with some other guy while I'm gone." He said it in a playful tone, but I sensed some seriousness behind it.

"I don't know how that would be possible, given that you basically ruined my last date." I hadn't meant to say that, especially once I saw the wicked gleam in his eyes.

"What happened? Did he take you to see *Octavius* and you realized what a letdown the man next to you was in comparison?" If anybody else had said it, it would have sounded obnoxious. Somehow he was just adorable.

"This guy from work I was sort of crushing on asked me out to dinner. You were tweeting things. And I thought they were about me.

So I kept checking my phone, which I think he didn't like. He's been avoiding me ever since."

Chase didn't say "Good," but it looked like he was thinking it. "Do you mean the day after we talked about *Octavius*? Those tweets were definitely about you."

If he kept making me feel this giddy, at some point my heart was going to give out.

We talked and talked. About everything and nothing. Like whether he preferred going out or staying home. "Socializing and networking is my job. When I'm at a party or a premiere, it's because I have to be. And being surrounded by alcohol is not fun. I've always been a bit of a homebody. And I've been reminded lately just how much fun staying in can be."

Was that another reference to me? Why did I feel like we were swinging back and forth like a pendulum? Even though earlier I'd decided to enjoy the here and now, I couldn't stop obsessing. One second it was like of course he liked me, of course he was interested in me, and then it was back to him just wanting to be friends, and I was blowing everything way out of proportion.

He distracted me from my thoughts by asking me to tell him something he didn't know.

"So, twelve plus one is the same as eleven plus two, right?"

"Right."

"But did you know that when you take the letters in twelve plus one, you can rearrange them to be eleven plus two?"

He got out his phone and typed the words out. "That's cool."

When I answered his request, I knew that wasn't what he'd meant. He wanted me to tell him something personal. But I didn't really have anything like that left. I'd already told him all the important stuff. By our third (maybe fourth) date. I had never done that before with any guy.

Much later on I told him about our family trip to Yellowstone the previous summer and how Zelda had been obsessed with seeing buffalo. How we'd spotted one near a rest stop and Zelda had been thrilled. And the next time we saw a whole herd, we pointed it out to her, but she'd rolled her eyes and said, "I already seen a buffalo," which made him chuckle. Then I looked at my watch.

I realized with a gasp that it was three o'clock in the morning. It was going to take at least forty-five minutes to get to my place. I'd never been so into a conversation with someone that I'd literally lost track of time. "It is so late. I should probably get home."

He flicked on his phone, his eyes widening when he saw the time. "You probably should. But I kind of want you to stay."

I kind of wanted to stay, but I didn't know if that would mean something different to me than it would to him. Would he interpret me staying as some kind of invitation? Not to mention that I didn't normally stay out this late. Lexi had probably called the police. "My roommate most likely has an APB out on me, so I should go."

"You could text her. And stay."

It didn't help matters that he looked so inviting and tempting. I was starting to get that whole Eve–apple thing.

Mind made up, I went to the kitchen and got my purse. "I can call a cab."

"I picked you up; I'm taking you home. Come on."

He held my hand the whole way home. Like this was a thing we did now. We didn't do anything else, but at least it was something.

Unless he held hands with all his female friends. Maybe he was just affectionate and liked the contact.

We chatted for the entire drive, but now there was this underlying current. Because he hadn't wanted me to leave, and I hadn't, either. Did that mean something more? If it did, then what?

When we got to my apartment complex, he insisted on walking me to the door. And my body said, *We are at Defcon 1! This is finally happening!* Because why else would a guy walk you to the door unless he planned to kiss you good night? I had mints in my purse but no easy way to get them or to take one without him noticing. And I knew he would tease me about it.

My heart pounded, my lips tingled, and it was practically impossible to convince oxygen to enter my lungs.

We walked up the three flights of stairs to my apartment. We stood in front of the door, and I fumbled around in my purse, felt the metal mint container, and briefly debated with myself whether I could sneak one out. I decided against it, as I was not known for my manual dexterity. I grabbed my keys instead. "So. Here we are. At my door. Made of wood. Maybe. It could be a wood veneer. Or metal."

Chase leaned against the door frame, and his beauty hit me all over again. How could God have given so many good looks to just one person? "What your front door is made of is definitely important to know."

Was he teasing me? Seriously? When my insides were about to explode?

He gave me a smile and said, "Good night, Zoe."

And now he was leaving? Was he really not going to kiss me? Had he already forgotten our up-all-night conversation and how he wanted me to stay? I had my answer when he turned and walked down a few steps.

I went to the top of the stairs to look at him. "Am I going to see you again?"

He paused on the landing. "If you want to. Why would you ask me that?"

Why would I ask him that? Besides the fact that he was more inscrutable than the freaking Sphinx? "Most of my relationships never go past the third date."

As if he'd heard something important in my voice, he walked back up the stairs, deliberately maintaining eye contact with me. When he got to where I stood, I backed up and pressed into the wall. He stood in front of me, not touching me but so close it almost felt like he was. "Considering that it's four in the morning, I think a new day qualifies as a new date. Which makes it our fourth. And I hear important things happen on fourth dates." His voice dropped to little more than a whisper with his last sentence, and it made my legs and arms tremble.

Was he joking around, or did he mean something else? Was he thinking of me in a different way?

And then . . . he kissed me.

On the forehead.

Again.

"'Night, Zo." He whistled softly as he left this time, and I didn't say anything to stop him. I let myself into my apartment, feeling dazed and thoroughly confused.

As I locked the front door, I wondered whether I needed to invest in a neon sign that I could attach to my forehead that said LIPS DOWN HERE with one of those arrows. I kicked off my shoes and went to the bedroom, fully expecting the third degree from Lexi.

She was in her bed, totally passed out. She hadn't even noticed I was late coming home. I grabbed an oversize shirt to sleep in and angrily took off my clothes.

Why was he so hard to read? I could almost hear Lexi's voice in my head saying, "Duh. He's an actor. You see only what he wants you to see."

Did he not want to kiss me? Why would he talk about taking me to Ireland when he apparently wasn't even attracted to me? He really did treat me like I was his annoying kid sister whom he had to let tag along with him. Thing was—he didn't have to. But he spent time with me anyway.

I considered waking up Lexi to get her advice, but she turned over and started snoring, hugging her pillow with the Chase Covington cover.

I climbed into bed and decided it was beyond sad that my roommate was currently getting more action from Chase than I was.

CHAPTER SEVENTEEN

Chase Covington ✓
@realchasecov

Following

#roughday **turned into** #bestnightever.

💬   🔁 4.7K   ♡ 14K

So of course when I woke up, the very first thing I did was check my phone. No texts from Chase yet, but there was that tweet. *Best night ever.* Ha. Only if his definition of "best night" was "Nobody got kissed."

It was almost noon when I went into the kitchen to get something to eat. Lexi sat on the couch with one of her feet propped up on the coffee table, giving herself a pedicure. "Late night?" she asked with a sly grin.

I growled in response, not ready to talk until I had sustenance. I poured myself a super nutritious bowl of Lucky Charms and sat at our little kitchen table.

She'd lived with me long enough to know that I needed some time in the morning before I turned into a human again. She painted her toenails a bright candy-apple red and hummed a show tune to herself.

I drank the milk right out of the bowl and then put my dishes in the sink. "What does it mean when the guy you're dating hasn't tried to kiss you yet?"

"Gay."

"Just because that happened to you once—"

"Eleven times," she corrected, applying the polish in short, careful strokes.

"Seriously? Eleven times? Okay, just because that's happened to you eleven times doesn't mean that's what's happening here. And maybe you should stop dating fellow theater majors."

She nodded in agreement as I collapsed onto the couch next to her.

"Do you want me to do your nails, too?"

What did it matter? It wasn't like anybody was going to see them. But I was too tired to move. "'Kay."

She put my right foot in her lap and used the file. "He really hasn't kissed you yet? Haven't you been out a bunch of times?"

"Yes. Apparently I'm too hideous to be kissed."

"Stop it. That's not true, and you know it." Lexi pushed my right foot off, and I swung my left one up for her to file. "You're assuming it's because he's not attracted to you. Which has been the case for me eleven times. But maybe that's not what's going on. Maybe it's intentional. You know when somebody says you can't have something, and it makes you want it more? By not kissing you, that's all you're thinking about now, right? Wondering if it will ever happen. Dying of anticipation. So by the time it does happen, it will be the most amazing thing ever, and you'll be head over heels for him. Even if he's not any good at it."

That sounded a little far-fetched, and Chase didn't strike me as the devious type. "Do men actually do that?"

"I saw it in a TV movie once, but other than that, I don't know. Usually they can't wait to get their lips all over you." She realized immediately it was the wrong thing to say and shot me a "sorry" expression. "When are you guys going out again?"

"Not for a while. He has to go to—out of town for business. A couple of weeks."

I switched my foot again, and she applied a base coat of the same red polish she wore. "Maybe that will be good. Give him a chance to miss you. Did he ask you to take him to the airport?"

"No."

"Too bad. Because that's a very girlfriend thing to do," she said, blowing on my nails. She finished my other foot quickly and then separated my toes with those foam inserts. I rested my feet on the coffee table. Lexi picked up her phone, and I felt sorry for myself. "Gavin was supposed to text me. He is my boyfriend, and sometimes I feel like I don't know where we stand, either."

I knew she was trying to be sympathetic, but Gavin clearly adored Lexi. Possibly even loved her. She couldn't have been questioning that.

And I knew from unfortunate firsthand experience that he was definitely attracted to her.

"Well, you know what they say about when life hands you lemons."

"Make lemonade?" I responded.

"No. You throw that crap back and demand chocolate. Hey, have you seen this?" Lexi asked, handing me her phone. "Chase Covington has himself a new skank du jour."

I tried to swallow past the knot in my larynx but couldn't. My ears rang as a metallic taste filled my mouth. Yesterday the potential ramifications of people taking pictures of Chase hadn't even occurred to me. My concern had been only for his well-being.

But now . . . now, with adrenaline skittering and buzzing through me, I realized how very bad this could be for me. If both my mom and Lexi found out.

The headline of the article read, WHO IS CHASE COVINGTON'S MYSTERY GIRL? Had Lexi recognized me? Was this a test I'd already failed? I glanced up at her, but she was packing up her pedicure tools.

I did a quick image search and found multiple pictures of us. I hadn't realized at the time that Chase had been shielding me as best he could with his body. You couldn't see my face in any of the shots. You could see my hands, holding my Mace and ready to spray the crowd down, but that was it.

Because nobody had been trying to take my picture. They'd wanted a picture of him.

"Like Amelia Swan's not bad enough, now he has secret girlfriends?"

Again, I thought I should tell her. This was the perfect opening.

Only I couldn't explain it to her until I understood it myself.

Which I most definitely did not.

Chase texted me routinely and tweeted shots of himself on set and in his costume. Nothing spoiler-y, just stuff that made his fans happy.

Then he'd tweet stuff that left me totally confused.

Was that some kind of cryptic clue? He wanted us to eye-kiss first? That presented a problem, given that most of my flirting consisted of awkward eye contact. We'd never get to eye first base.

Or—

Inappropriate thoughts? What, had he imagined us hugging?

The thing was, I seriously missed him. I was okay being on my own. Introverts are like that. I could go long stretches of time without talking to anyone and be fine. I did what I'd done before we met—went to class, babysat the Mendel girls, worked at the Foundation, helped out with my brothers and sisters. But somehow Chase had wormed his way into my heart.

And I wanted him to come back home to California.

What did you do today?

Went for a run.

Seriously?

Well, an ice cream run. We were all out of Haagen-Dazs.

Ah. There's my girl.

His girl? Just an expression, or did he think of me as his girl?

I probably should have just womanned up and asked him outright. But frustrated as I was, I didn't want to lose whatever we had. And some part of me feared that if I pressed him, tried to force him to define the relationship, he'd define it as a friendship, and we'd be done.

I also did tweet some posts that were meant for him.

Zoe
@zomorezoless

I say I'd like to travel and my checking account's response is, "To your mom's house?" #ErinGoBragh #IWish

♡ ⟳ 0 ♡ 1

He liked that tweet, and I noticed I had, like, forty new followers. All Chasers. Probably because of how often he liked what I tweeted.

About a week in, I had plans to go to my mother's for Sunday dinner. As I got ready, he sent me a text that made my heart slam against my rib cage.

> Did you know you're on my To Do list today?

It was hard to type a reply as my fingers kept fumbling.

> What is that supposed to mean????

> Things to do: Text Zoe. What did you think I meant?

My phone rang a second later. It was him.

"You're super funny," I told him.

"I know."

"It's all fun and games until somebody doesn't pick up on the sarcasm," I said while slipping on my shoes.

"I'm sending you something. It should be there tomorrow or the day after."

"It better not be a car."

I could almost hear him rolling his eyes. "It's not a car. It's a script. My agent sent it over. It's about a high-functioning teenage boy with autism whose parents die in an accident, and he's sent to the East Coast to live with his aunt. He wants to go home, so he walks back to Idaho. It's about how he survives, the people he comes into contact with, having his first kiss, that sort of thing. I want your opinion on it."

I shut my front door and hurried down the stairs. "Why? I don't know anything about scripts."

"But you like movies, and you're familiar with my acting."

"That doesn't make me qualified." I put my car into reverse and tried to steer while talking to him. Realizing I wasn't being safe, I put the phone on speaker and set it down.

"It does. They're considering Ryan Hofstead for the role."

Ryan Hofstead was one of those beef hunks who had risen to fame in a franchise based on a YA vampire book. To say he was a talentless hack would be insulting to talentless hacks. He literally had two expressions but somehow kept being cast as the lead in movies.

"He would butcher this part."

"Probably. After you've read it, give me a call and tell me if you think I should do it."

Didn't he have a manager and a publicist and an agent for this kind of stuff? Even One-F was probably far more qualified to give Chase professional advice. Honestly, I didn't even need to read the script. I couldn't let Ryan Hofstead stink up another movie, given that his relationship with subtlety was strained at best.

"When it comes, I'll read it. And let you know what I think. Anyway, I need to go. I'm heading over to my mom's for dinner."

"Cool. Be sure to give Zia a kiss from me."

Oh, sure. Zia got kisses. And I got scripts.

"I will." I gripped the steering wheel tightly, willing myself to be strong and tell him something true and honest, like he wanted. Put myself out there. Maybe he'd return the favor. "And Chase? I miss you."

I hung up the phone before he could reply, too scared of his reaction. My phone buzzed. I didn't know if it was a tweet or a message. I didn't check until I got to my mother's.

Zia tumbled out of the front door, holding out her arms for me. I picked her up and gave her a big kiss on her baby cheek. "That's from Chase."

"I love Cheese," she said, hugging my neck.

"I know you do."

"He comes sees me?"

I carried her inside and put her down on the hall floor. "Maybe. I want him to come see me, too."

That seemed to satisfy her, and she toddled off. I got out my phone. I had a new text.

Although I hadn't had the chance to hear his reply, I got to read it.

I miss you, too.

Chase Covington
@realchasecov

Following

Ireland has a million castles. I wonder if she'll live in my castle zomeday. #Chasers

13K   67K

The next day was Gavin's birthday. He and Lexi had made plans to go to the fanciest restaurant in town, La Bella Vita. It was only three o'clock in the afternoon, but Lexi had started getting ready.

"It's so unfair. He'll take a shower and shave while I have to do all this." She gestured to her body, then went back to putting her hair in curlers.

"At least he'll appreciate it."

"He will. Hey, did I tell you I ran into Ron on campus today?" Ron was this cheating jerk Lexi had dated for about three weeks until she'd caught him on a date with another girl. "He had the audacity to tell me I'd made a mistake breaking up with him because I'd never find anyone like him again. I was all, 'That's the point, moron!'"

Before I could agree with her, the doorbell rang. I knew it couldn't be Gavin yet, and we weren't expecting anyone else. I looked through the peephole and saw a huge bouquet of flowers. "Lexi! I think there's a present for you!"

I opened the door, and the delivery man smiled at me. "I'm looking for Zoe Miller."

"That's me," I said in shock because he was holding a vase of white roses bigger than our TV.

"Can you sign for these?" He handed me a pad, and I gave him my signature. He had a manila envelope clamped under his arm and gave that to me. I was surprised at how heavy the vase was when he put it in my hands.

"Thanks!" I said. I'd never gotten flowers before.

"That's not all. I'll be right back."

If that delivery dude came back with car keys, Chase was in trouble. I set the flowers down on the kitchen table just as Lexi entered the room. "Are those for me? Gavin's not supposed to send me gifts on his birthday!"

"Actually, they're for me." I opened the card with my name on it and read.

I didn't know what you liked.

There was a soft knock at the door, and the delivery man carried in two more giant bouquets of flowers. One was purple tiger lilies, and the other was bright-yellow sunflowers. I told him to put them in the kitchen and noticed he wasn't alone. Two other men followed behind him, carrying tulips and daffodils and daisies and other flowers I didn't recognize but were beautiful.

They had to make one more trip to bring all the flowers inside. We were running out of places to put them.

"Does your man have a trust fund?" Lexi asked in awe, deeply breathing in the scent of the roses.

"He could." Not technically a lie. Chase could have family money beyond his acting earnings.

"Why can't more men be romantic like this?"

I was only half paying attention, overwhelmed at the gesture. "Mormons can't be romantic?"

"No, I said more men. Not Mormons."

"Your boyfriend is very romantic."

"I know." There was a wistfulness in her tone. "But nobody's ever bought out a flower shop for me."

Nobody ever had for me, either. But Lexi already knew that.

"Don't get me wrong," she said, catching my expression. "I'm super happy for you. But a tiny bit jealous, too."

"Makes sense." It was how I'd felt about Lexi for most of our lives. "I've got some reading I need to do."

"And I've got some painful waxing I need to do."

I took the manila envelope into our room and slid the script out. The front said *Spectrum*. The pages were the color of goldenrod, and I opened it and began to read. At first it took some getting used to, with phrases like INT.—RICK'S ROOM and camera directions, but once I understood it, it was almost like reading a book. I could see all of it in my head.

The second I finished, I jumped up and shut the bedroom door so Lexi wouldn't hear me call Chase.

He answered on the second ring. "Hey." His voice was warm and so clear it made me miss him all over again.

"Thank you for the flowers. They're amazing, and I absolutely love them, and nobody's ever done anything like that for me before. And you have to make this movie. You are going to kill it and win every award in the entire universe."

"Even the Martian Academy Awards?"

"Especially that one."

"You liked the flowers?"

"Liked them? Cartwheels might have been involved."

"I wish I'd been there to see that." I could hear the smile in his voice. "I didn't know which ones were your favorite."

I lay back on my bed. "Pink tulips are my favorite. My grandmother always had them at the house. She said they reminded her of Pennsylvania. They took a lot of work. Like, she had to keep them in the fridge before she planted them. But she thought it was worth it. So did I."

"Noted. Speaking of things we weren't talking about, a good friend of mine is getting married this Saturday. Would you like to go with me?"

"To a wedding?" My question ended in a squeak. "Isn't that more of a girlfriend kind of event? For people who are dating?"

He stayed quiet for so long I thought we'd lost the connection. "What do you think we've been doing here?"

"You keep calling it *hanging out*. I thought that's all it was. If you feel differently, that's news to me."

He let out a frustrated sigh. "This is more of an in-person conversation. I've been putting in extra hours so we can finish early. We should be done shooting by Friday evening, and I plan on being home by Saturday afternoon. I can send a car to pick you up. What do you say?"

A whole week earlier than I'd thought? My heart twirled around inside my chest, deliriously happy. "Okay. I'll see you on Saturday."

My first fizzy, thrilled thought after we hung up was, *Yes! Chase thinks we're dating!*

And my second overwhelming, intimidating thought was, *Oh no! Chase thinks we're dating.*

He would have expectations.

I was seriously out of my depth.

CHAPTER EIGHTEEN

Chase tweeted that early this morning and then followed it with a text to me that said:

I burn.

After my heart stopped racing and all my goose bumps went away, I realized what the problem was. His words didn't match his actions. He flirted, said hot things, claimed he was interested.

But everything in his body language, how he kept me at a distance physically, told me the exact opposite.

It wasn't a problem I could have solved right then, so I just focused on getting ready for his friend's wedding. Chase's text had settled deep in my stomach, causing an ache and light-headedness that made me more than a bit accident prone.

I'd told Lexi I had a date for a wedding, and she practically shook with excitement. "That is huge! He's claiming you in front of the entire world!"

I wanted to believe her, but her optimism only made things worse. I dropped makeup brushes more than once and almost burned Lexi with a curling iron when she was helping me put up my hair.

"Careful! Don't brand me with that thing. You must really like this guy. I've never seen you so clumsy. You are completely and totally twitterpated."

If only she knew how on the nose her proclamation was, given that Chase and I had met on Twitter.

Because I didn't own anything fancy enough to wear to a formal wedding with a movie star, I enlisted Lexi's help. She got on the phone to every single female friend she'd ever had and tracked down the perfect dress for me. It was pale silvery-gray chiffon, and the bodice and three-quarter sleeves were made out of sheer fabric with matching gray lace overlay to cover everything important. The skirt swished when I moved. The bodice was a bit too big for me, but Lexi used her years spent in theaters to discreetly stitch it into place. "This color makes your eyes pop. I can take the stitches out when you get home, and Joslyn will never even notice. Just don't take it off."

Ha. Fat chance of that.

She went through my shoes until she found a pair of fancy high heels with delicate silver straps I'd never even worn. Shoes she'd practically forced me to buy two years ago because they were on clearance and in my size, a rare occurrence. "Aha! I knew I hadn't imagined these beauties."

"These are going to kill my feet. I've never worn them before."

"Didn't anybody teach you that you have to suffer to be beautiful? That's what Epsom salts and warm water are for."

Lexi insisted on helping me pick the perfect lipstick shade from her vast collection of pink tackle boxes. And then she touched up my mascara. And added a bit more blush. Until I got annoyed, and she backed off. "Okay, okay. I'm done. And might I just add, you are smoking hot."

The only way I'd ever be smoking hot is if I were cremated, but I loved her for saying it.

At least somebody thought I was hot.

"I have a cute silver clutch you can borrow, if you want. I'll be right back."

There was a knock at the front door, and for a brief moment I panicked, thinking it was Chase. But he said he'd send a car for me. The driver? I rushed to the front door, determined to get there before Lexi.

It turned out to be Gavin. He let out a low whistle. "You clean up nice, Miller. You are going to give that guy from work a heart attack."

Lexi ran into the room and leaped into Gavin's arms to shower his face with kisses. "What are you doing here?"

"I was hungry, and I remembered you also sometimes eat food, and I thought we could check out that new Brazilian steakhouse."

Her mood shifted from happy and excited to annoyed and let down. Probably because of her new cleanse that didn't allow protein. "Ugh, you know I'm not eating anything with a face for the next two weeks."

"They cut that off before they bring it to you," he said, taking his customary spot on the couch and getting out his phone. He and Lexi went back and forth, suggesting names of restaurants, but they couldn't decide on a good compromise.

Lexi got on my laptop, which I'd left on the kitchen counter, and opened a browser window. I expected her to look for more restaurants, but instead she did a search for "Chase Covington."

"Hey, look at that." She pointed at the screen. "Chase's friend Austin Adams is getting married today, too. Chase is supposed to be one of his groomsmen. I hope somebody publishes the pictures. Because, seriously, how hot is Chase?" Her voice rose with the last sentence, making it obvious that her observation was for Gavin's benefit.

"Depends on what you use to ignite him with," Gavin replied, not the least bit fazed.

"It's good to make them a little jealous," she whispered to me. "You don't want them to forget how good they have it." Given her boyfriend's lack of response, I didn't think her plan had worked.

My phone buzzed, and it was a text from an unknown number. "Looks like my ride is here."

"Here's the clutch. Take this lip gloss so you can reapply, and I want to lend you these." She held out a pair of diamond solitaire earrings that had once belonged to her mother.

"Lexi, I can't. What if I lose them?"

"You won't. Every girl needs a little bit of sparkle when she gets dressed up."

Knowing Lexi would not take no for an answer, I accepted and put them on. Then I transferred everything I needed from my regular purse—keys, tissues, lip gloss, a couple of credit cards, driver's license, some cash, and my cell phone.

And a tin of mints. Because apparently I was a glutton for disappointment.

I said my goodbyes and headed downstairs, where a chauffeur in a suit waited for me. He opened the rear door of the black town car to let me in. After he greeted me, he said, "There's been a change of plans, and I'm going to drive you directly to the wedding."

"Oh. Okay. Thanks." The driver shut the door behind me after I'd carefully climbed in.

Chase had said he'd have the driver take me to his house and we'd head to the wedding together. I got my phone out, intending to text him and ask what was going on, and I saw his last text again.

I burn.

That same shivery, warm, delicious ache started all over again.

I so wanted him to be serious. For this to be a real thing and not something I'd blown way out of proportion.

Although the thought of making him burn scared me just a little.

Because if Chase burned, I knew I'd be consumed.

I knew some details about the wedding because I'd looked it up. Austin Adams had met Chase on *No More, No Less*, where he'd played Chase's next-door neighbor. His part got bigger and bigger as the showrunners realized how much talent he had and how much the audience loved him. He had stayed on television, easily transitioning from child to adult actor.

His bride to be, Marisol, was a makeup artist on his most recent show, a medical drama that had been on the air for about five years. The entertainment magazines kept calling this a "Cinderella wedding" because the bride wasn't famous.

The wedding and reception were being held at Austin's Malibu estate. I had to pass through several checkpoints before I arrived at his home, a classic Spanish revival with white stucco walls and a red tile roof. We inched our way through the line until it was my turn to get out. My driver (whose name was Jeff with two *F*s) opened my door, and I was immediately inside a canvas tunnel that led from the driveway to the front door. It dawned on me that they had constructed it so nobody could see who the guests were. I hadn't seen any paparazzi, but I knew what long-range lenses could do.

At the end of the tunnel, I had to give my name again and show my ID, and then I was inside, surrounded by so many celebrities it felt like

I was playing a game of Movie Star Whack-A-Mole. They kept popping up all over the place. It was like I'd accidentally crashed the high school cool kids' party, and they all knew one another, but nobody knew who I was or why I was there. I kind of wanted to call my mom and ask her to pick me up.

A waiter in a tuxedo with a white jacket offered me a glass of champagne, and I took it so I would have something to do with my hands. I'd never really liked alcohol, and in high school I'd observed that getting blackout drunk wasn't very conducive to staying celibate.

Austin's family room had French doors leading out to a terrace and a backyard the size of a football field. Everything was covered in big white tents. Over piano music and conversation, I heard a metallic buzzing sound. I followed the strange sound outside, where I finally spotted Chase. My heart tripped over itself when I saw him sporting a well-tailored black suit with a bright-yellow tie. He paced back and forth near a silver van, gesturing wildly as he talked on his phone.

I didn't know whether I should stay put and let him finish his call, but he saw me and stopped speaking. His mouth dropped slightly, and he blinked several times as his gaze raked over me. I couldn't tell if his reaction was good or bad.

"What? Yeah, I'm still here, Mom." He waved me over. "Okay. I will see what I can do. I know it's important to you. I understand. Okay. Bye. Love you. Bye." He hung up and paused for a moment before he said, "You look amazing."

Then he enfolded me in a hug, enveloping me in his strength and his tasty scent. I sighed, loving how it felt to be in his arms. His breath danced against my skin. "I'm so glad you're here." He kissed me on the cheek, and my blood rushed up to meet his lips.

Well, at least it wasn't my forehead. He released me, and it took me a second longer than it should have to step back. I didn't want him to stop holding me.

"Talking to your mom?" I fought the urge to touch the spot where he'd just kissed me. I wondered if I'd be able to feel the warmth from his lips against my fingertips.

"She wants me to come to this charity event she's hosting. Baby seals or something."

"But you support ocean conservation."

He sighed. "I know. And I'm sure it's a good cause. I'm going to have to rearrange my schedule. I guess it bugs me that she calls only when she wants something. Just like every other person in my life. Except you."

I had thought he might be open to the idea of coming to the Foundation benefit, but now I was fervently glad I'd never asked him.

"What's with the tie?" I asked as I ran a finger down the length of it. Silk. "You kind of look like a bumblebee."

"Have a thing for bumblebees, do you?"

"Buzz, buzz."

That made him laugh, and he hugged me again.

Only this time he didn't quite let go of me. Just pulled his head back slightly while still holding me tight. Every cell in my body zoomed around with delight at his proximity, the feel of him. "Zoe, there's something I wanted—"

"Mr. Covington, you're needed up front. It's almost time to begin." A woman wearing a headset and carrying a tablet interrupted him.

Nodding, Chase let his arms drop, and I experienced that same sense of loss all over again. "I'll be right there."

What had he almost said? It sounded important. Stupid wedding minion. Especially since she stood there, waiting, tapping her foot.

"Time to stand up for my friend. Even though he's marrying a woman who is far too good for him."

He followed the headset lady, and I went to the groom's side and sat in the back row. I felt like a fraud sitting there as all these famous people and their equally famous spouses filed into the tent.

There was a beautiful gazebo at the front, decorated with sunflowers. The chairs were soft and draped in white organza, and all the flowers were bright yellow with gray ribbons. Austin Adams came in with his groomsmen, and I thought it was a shame that Chase was so much prettier than the groom.

A string quartet played classical music as I tried to stargaze without being noticed.

Something whirred past my head. At first I suspected a bird, but I'd heard the same sound earlier. A metallic whirring. It was a drone.

And it flew level with another drone. They darted at each other, like some kind of aerial Battle Bots match. I wasn't sure, but it seemed like the paparazzi were trying to sneak some pictures with their drones, and somebody here had their own drones to block the shots.

Clever.

The music changed, and everyone stood as bridesmaids in yellow gowns that matched Chase's tie walked down the aisle, followed by Austin's fiancée, Marisol.

Instead of watching the bride, I watched the groom. The look on his face—the openness, the love evident in his eyes—made me a little weepy. It was like he couldn't wait to marry her.

The officiant began the service, and admittedly Marisol surprised me. Austin had been a bit of a player and tended to date lanky, overly thin, supermodel-perfect types. Of course Marisol had flawless makeup and perfect hair and a gorgeous wedding dress, but she looked normal. Pretty, but normal.

Maybe there was hope for us regular girls, after all.

Chase caught my eye and winked, and I couldn't help but grin back.

I hadn't been to many weddings, but this one seemed to fly by. I wondered if that was partly because I was able to spend so much time admiring Chase in his expensive suit. The officiant pronounced the couple husband and wife, and they kissed as everyone cheered.

Music from the reception area started before the kiss had even finished. "Let's party!" Austin called out to more cheers. There wasn't an orderly procession out, just people standing up and making their way to the other tents.

"Are you hungry?" Chase asked when he'd jostled through the crowd.

I nodded. "Starving, actually."

He told me Marisol had insisted on an informal buffet so guests could serve themselves (or not eat at all, as was the case for many of the actresses). But this was no regular buffet. It was a five-star restaurant version of comfort food, and there was enough of it to feed a small nation.

"What's with all the yellow?" I asked Chase as he filled his plate with chicken wings and Kobe beef sliders.

"It's Marisol's favorite color. And Austin calls her his sunshine."

Aw. "That is so sweet."

"Yeah, he's head over heels for her. They didn't even sign a prenup." He added some garlic potatoes to his plate. "Dessert now or later?"

"Look at that," I breathed. There was an entire table filled with candy and desserts in shades of yellow. Lemon macaroons on silver trays, mini lemon meringue pies in little shot glasses, an apothecary jar full of yellow M&Ms.

And in the center of it all stood their five-tier *gray* wedding cake. "Why is it gray?" I whispered.

"Trendy?" he guessed.

"It looks like it died a hundred years ago and came back to haunt the reception." Food was not supposed to be that color.

"Says the woman in the gray dress."

"But I'm not supposed to be delicious."

"Says who?" His lazy, predatory expression sent sparks skittering across my already sensitive nerves.

I shook my head as though he was silly, even though my heart was pounding louder than the bass from the speakers. He led me to an empty table, and I was glad. I didn't really want to make small talk with people I'd watched on big and small screens my entire life.

"I'm going to have to run an extra mile tomorrow," he said with a sigh as he looked over the mountain of food he'd piled on his plate.

"And I'm going to have to feel bad for you that you're running an extra mile tomorrow."

He laughed. "Hey, did you see who's here?" Chase asked after he ate a slider in a single bite.

"Um, everybody in Hollywood?"

"There." He pointed with his fork, and I followed it to . . .

"No way."

Alex Trebek, host of *Jeopardy!*, was here.

"Do you want to meet him?"

"What? No!" What would I say to Alex Trebek? "Maybe later." After I'd built up some courage. I looked away, wanting to distract myself. I noticed a sign on the table and picked it up. It talked about how everything was sustainable, organic, farm-friendly, etc. "It says the confetti on the table was handcrafted from Austin and Marisol's favorite books. Do you think anyone here knows you can actually buy confetti and not destroy books?"

"You mean the people who have a live wedding painter in the corner? They may not know."

"A wedding painter?" I'd never even heard of such a thing. "How does that work? Does everyone just hold super still for four hours straight?"

"Come on. It's just like having a photographer. Only more pretentious."

We laughed and watched as Marisol shared the first dance with her father. Austin came to claim her as soon as the song ended. As they swayed to the music, I realized it had been a long time since I'd seen two people so blissfully in love.

"They look so happy," I remarked.

"Too bad it won't last."

"Why would you say that?" I leaned over to smack him on the arm. "Don't be such a cynic."

"It's not cynicism. It's reality. The majority of marriages end in divorce. It's a fact."

"Nobody gets married thinking it won't work. They get married because they have hope that it will."

I could tell I hadn't convinced him. Other couples began to join Austin and Marisol.

Chase stood up and held out his hand. "Dance with me."

I didn't have much experience dancing, Especially not the slow variety. "I'm not very coordinated. I would probably trip over your feet."

"Zoe. I'd never let you fall."

As I slipped my hand in his, I knew he was wrong. It was too late. I was already falling.

CHAPTER NINETEEN

Zoe
@zomorezoless

Kissing burns 2-5 calories per minute. First time I've wanted to exercise. #Trivia

💬   ↻ 0   ♡ 2

Chase took me out on the dance floor and wrapped my arms around his neck. He slid his hands around my waist, squeezing me gently as he did so. I took advantage of the situation, pressing myself tightly against him as we swayed to the music.

He didn't seem to mind.

His mouth stirred the hair next to my ear, and the sensation on my earlobe nearly made my eyes roll to the back of my head. "Do you know," he murmured, a dark roughness edging his voice as he spoke, "that you're the most beautiful woman in here?"

As if. "I thought we were going to tell each other only the truth." It was somehow easier to talk to him when our eyes didn't meet.

"That is the truth." I felt his lips brush against the top of my ear, and my stomach did flips as my knees went hollow.

I struggled to speak. "You, uh, probably shouldn't say that in front of Austin or Marisol."

"If they ask, I'm not going to lie." One of his hands slid up to the top of my back, and he held me close against his chest.

Feeling inspired by his declaration, I said, "The actual truth is that you're the most handsome man here."

"Even better than James Cruz?"

His touch, his voice, mesmerized me, putting me into a foggy haze. The name James Cruz sounded familiar, but I was having a hard time remembering who he was. "He's the short, dark-haired one who looks like a jerk, right?"

Chase's hands pressed into me as he chuckled. "You could have pretended you didn't know who I was talking about."

I didn't. The only man I saw was Chase.

Right then, right there, I had to know if he felt the way I did. "Are you attracted to me?"

"What?"

I was afraid, so I'd said the words too softly. I cleared my throat. "Are you attracted to me?"

He went completely still but said nothing.

Oh no, I'd done it. I'd ruined everything. I couldn't have just waited to see where things went. No, I had to have explanations and definitions, and now I'd freaked him out. "I get it if you just want to be friends. That's fine. I just don't have very much experience with things like this. I haven't dated all that much. No, I've dated a lot, just not the same person more than a few times. So I'm not an expert and . . ."

Just shut up, my brain told me. *Shut up!*

Without a word, Chase took me by the wrist and led me into the mansion, away from the dance floor and the other guests. He walked so quickly that I almost tripped a couple of times in my stupid high heels. He took me upstairs, and I ignored the people giving us a mixture of strange and knowing looks.

He pulled me into a slightly darkened room, stopping to close the door behind us. Then in one smooth and sure motion, he whirled me around and pressed my back against the door. He stood directly in front of me, almost as close as we'd been just a few minutes earlier on the dance floor. He put his hands on either side of my head, pinning me into place. He looked angry, and though I probably should have felt a bit worried, it was strangely thrilling instead.

"Why would you think I'm not attracted to you?" His voice sounded deeper, rougher.

My heart pounded so hard I could barely breathe. "You . . . you don't act like it. You've never even tried to kiss me."

I saw his Adam's apple bob slowly, and he stayed silent, not moving, not speaking. When he finally did say something, I almost jumped out of my oversensitized skin. "Do you know what I want to do right now?"

His voice had a rawness to it, a rasp I didn't recognize.

"What?"

"What I want is to lock this door. I want to tear this very nice dress off you. I want to throw you on that bed, and I want, more than I have ever wanted anything, to spend the rest of the night showing you over and over just how attracted I am to you."

Heat bloomed in my chest, and my lower abdomen tightened at his words. "Oh."

The right side of his mouth pulled up in a rueful half smirk. "But I can't. Because I like you and care about you, and I respect you. And your decisions. Even if I'm going to be personally responsible for California's next water shortage, thanks to all the cold showers." He moved closer, trapping me between him and the door, and my breath knotted in my lungs. "I haven't kissed you yet because I was afraid if I started, I wouldn't be able to stop."

There was nothing I could say. Mainly because I now shared his concern. If I was this excited just by standing close together, I didn't know how I could handle it if he kissed me.

Chase brought his right hand down, running his fingers along the side of my face, leaving trails of fire. He moved his hand to the back of my head, massaging my scalp while his palm pressed against my cheek. Our noses grazed against each other as his lips hovered above mine, mingling our breath. It made my lungs constrict and my legs threaten to give out.

"Zoe . . ." He said my name as both a plea and a warning.

I realized he was offering me the chance to say no. To move away. I didn't.

"Tell me I shouldn't. Tell me to stop."

Still, I stayed quiet.

"I put an entire ocean between us so I wouldn't do this. I'm not known for my restraint. I don't trust myself." He used his other hand to rub this thumb across my jawline and over my tingling lips, sending shivers cascading down my spine.

Somehow I reached up and slid my hands to his chest. I could feel how fast his heart was beating. Just as quickly as mine. The air around us felt charged, like the feeling you get when you stand outside just before lightning strikes. "I trust you."

With a growl of both disbelief and need, his lips crashed into mine, like waves against a cliff in a storm. Which sent me into shock because of a total system overload. So many sensations overwhelmed me at once that I didn't know what I was feeling. Every part of me, including parts I didn't know I had, responded to his passionate kiss.

Forget the butterflies. He had unleashed the entire zoo.

"Kiss" felt like a poor description of the way he ravaged my mouth. I thought I understood what kissing should be like. I was seriously mistaken. Because no one had ever kissed me like this before. Not with this hot, hungry intensity. Not with this confidence, this surety, this level of skill. Like somebody would be grading him later on how well he kissed me, and he planned on getting an *A*.

And going for extra credit.

His lips glided over mine in a rhythmic frenzy that had me tilting against him, holding on for dear life. His insistent, wild, bruising kiss made me dizzy, and I concentrated on the taste of his mouth. The feel of his muscles underneath my hands. The sound of his labored breathing. The delicious heat from his body pressing against mine. The intoxicating, masculine scent of his expensive cologne.

The pleasure of it all flooded through me.

My hair came undone as he ran his unsteady fingers through it, tugging and soothing, those sensations balanced by the pressure of his firm lips moving on mine, igniting sparks with each touch. He devoured me, making my body shudder from all the waiting, all the pent-up frustration and denial he let go with his kiss.

I'd been right. I knew that if Chase burned, I'd be consumed. We were like two bonfires edging closer together, merging into one super fire, glowing hotter and brighter in the night.

He moved from my lips to nipping and pressing hot kisses against the side of my throat. I dug my fingers into his shoulders, trying to pull him closer, wanting this feeling to last for eternity.

Because this was more than just physical. The reason I'd never been kissed like this before was because I'd never had feelings like this for any man. My brain was too woozy to understand those emotions. I only knew I wanted to be near him and didn't want to lose him.

And I never wanted to stop kissing him.

"Zoe." His harsh whisper against my skin felt like a branding. I turned my head, intent on bringing his lips back to mine, but he pulled back slightly, just out of reach. I wanted to whimper in protest. It sounded like he said my name again, but I was having a hard time hearing. Because I didn't know which was louder: my desperate, shallow breathing or my thundering heart.

"Tell me I can lock the door."

That shot a bolt of clarity through my fuzzy mind. I knew what he was asking. What he'd just told me he wanted. And it all began with a locked door.

He started nibbling on the bottom of my ear, and I slumped down as my bones turned liquid. He put one of his strong, muscled arms around me and kept me upright. He was not fighting fair.

I wanted to say yes. The word *yes* pounded quickly inside my brain, keeping time with my throbbing pulse. I'd never felt so tempted. It would be so easy. And feel so amazing.

But something inside me whispered that I'd regret it. It was like dumping a bucket of ice water over my head.

"Chase." I pushed softly against his chest so he'd stop burning my skin with kisses. "I'm sorry. We should stop."

He leaned his forehead against mine and let out a sigh of regret. "Don't be. You set your boundaries and made them clear. I just really want to cross them."

Now that I'd had a small taste of what it would be like between us, I kind of wanted to cross them, too. "We should go back to where there are other people."

He kissed me one last time, fierce and quick, and it was over far too fast. Then he leaned across me and turned the knob to let us out of the room. He laced his fingers through mine, and we walked down the hallway, my legs totally unstable beneath me.

We passed a mirror, and I said, "What?" when I saw my reflection. It wasn't because my cheeks were flushed or my lips looked swollen and well kissed. My hair looked as if it had been attacked by a dray of crazy squirrels. "Why didn't you tell me how bad my hair looked?"

He twisted a lock of it around his finger. "Because I like how it looks right now. Like somebody was running their fingers through it. And very much enjoying it."

Hearing him say that made me feel it all over again. Like we were still in that bedroom, and he was drugging me with his magic touch.

But if I walked downstairs like this, everybody would know what we'd been up to.

And nobody would believe we'd stopped at just kissing.

We were next to a bathroom, and I ducked in, looking for something to help. I found an elastic band, quickly took out the bobby pins Lexi had used, and pulled my hair into a messy bun. It wasn't as cute, but it would have to do.

I studied myself in the mirror. I looked different. Maybe because I felt different. I felt . . . beautiful. Wanted. Desired.

Even a little adored.

Chase came up behind me, slipped his arms around my waist, and kissed the top of my ear. "I liked your hair better before."

I gulped, hard. I loved the feeling of being held against him. "We really need to go back downstairs."

Before I forgot about my morals and choices and stuff.

He seemed to find that funny, and he kissed my hand once before turning toward the stairs.

When we reached the bottom step, he asked, "Do you understand now how attracted I am to you?"

Now that we weren't alone, it felt safe to tease him. "Almost. I may need more convincing."

"Careful, woman," he growled playfully, and I giggled in a way I didn't know I could.

I felt light and free and just . . . really happy.

Which sent a jolt of worry through me. The only times in my life when I'd felt this way, truly happy and contented, something had always happened to ruin it. I'd suffered some truly terrible losses.

I'd grown so attached to Chase in such a short amount of time, I didn't think my heart could take it if I lost him, too.

CHAPTER TWENTY

Chase Covington @realchasecov

Following

Congratulations to Austin and Marisol! Wishing you all the happiness in the world.

🗨   ↻ 89K   ♡ 126K

"So where's your second favorite place?" Chase asked. We were in the parking lot of my apartment complex. When we left the reception, we'd been chased by the paparazzi for about half an hour, but Chase finally lost them on the freeway. I thought he would just drop me off, but we'd been sitting in his car for hours, talking and carefully kissing. Neither of us felt ready to push our boundaries again, so his kisses were soft and playful and tender.

Which turned out to be almost as dangerous as his passionate kisses, given what they were doing to my heart.

"Paris, France," I promptly responded, making him laugh.

"Well, Miss No Passport, that's not a possibility. But I will take you there someday. We'll climb the Eiffel Tower, walk next to the River Seine at twilight . . ." He laced his fingers through mine, and I sighed. Both at the imagery of us being together in the most romantic city in the world and because I didn't think I'd ever get over the electricity that sizzled through my blood every time he touched me. "But what about Vegas?" His eyes didn't quite meet mine.

"Vegas?"

"We could fly there, get married in one of those little white chapels on the Strip, spend a week in a suite, and get it annulled when we get back."

My stomach sank at his words. He didn't get it. It wasn't about a technicality. It was about being committed to someone so thoroughly that I knew I would love and trust him for forever. I got that he couldn't understand my perspective, since it would be so foreign to someone like him. He thought he'd found a loophole that would allow us to be together. He'd already let me know he thought marriage was disposable and unimportant.

"My grandparents were married for over fifty years. My mother and stepfather had the most incredible marriage before he died. I've been surrounded by good examples that showed me how important marriage and those vows are. I could never treat them so lightly."

"Worth a shot, right?" He winked at me, and I felt better. Even if I'd disappointed him, he wasn't sulking or getting angry with me, like some other guys had when they'd realized I was serious about this celibacy thing. "But you didn't answer my question. Where else do you love to go?"

"The Marabella aquarium. My grandma had season passes, and we went there almost as often as we went to the beach. It made me love the ocean."

"How did she die?"

"She got breast cancer and didn't find out until it was too late. She waited until she'd been admitted to the hospital to tell us. It all happened so fast. My grandpa died a year later. I know dying of a broken heart's not supposed to be a real thing, but I believe it." Especially now that I'd had a little taste of what it felt like to have serious feelings about someone. "And my mom and Duncan moved into their little bungalow after my grandparents died. Sometimes I think they did it for me. So I would miss them less by being where they'd raised me."

"I'm sorry." He breathed the words against my lips just before he kissed me and made me forget what I was talking about. He broke away to add, "I can't believe you thought I wasn't interested in you. I thought I'd made myself pretty clear."

"Muddier than swamp water in Louisiana," I told him.

"Not wanting to push things too far wasn't the only reason I waited," he said as he reached up behind my head to undo my bun and let my hair fall loose. He started massaging my scalp, and it took all my willpower not to purr in response. "In the program they tell you to wait a year before you start dating. I met you online at exactly the one-year mark. My therapist and my sponsor thought I could start dating again."

"You thought your best bet was to find a fan and date her? What if I'd been psychotic?"

"Then I wouldn't still be here."

"Oh, you would be. Tied up in my basement."

He laughed and pressed a kiss against my eyelid that made my stomach go all fluttery. "But my therapist warned me to go slowly and to date like it was 1955."

I opened my eyes to give him a pointed, teasing look. "You've totally failed. We haven't been to a single sock hop or drive-in, and we haven't shared even one milk shake."

"That wasn't what she meant." He shook his head, smiling at me tenderly. "She wanted me to go glacier slow. To not trade one addiction for another. Problem is, I think I was already addicted to you long before I kissed you."

Another gentle, quick kiss. "Does that mean you'll have to go to Zoe rehab?"

"I don't ever want to get you out of my system."

My heart started to race not only from what he'd said but also because I wanted to ask him something. "So, are we dating? Are we exclusive?" Because the thought of another woman touching him filled me with a slightly murderous rage.

He studied me seriously, tracing my jawbone with his thumb. "I haven't been with any other woman for a very long time. I can't even imagine wanting to. But that's going to come down to you trusting me. To not believing tabloids or online gossip. I'm not the cheating type, no matter what they say to sell content. If you ever have any doubts, please talk to me first."

"I will. And I already told you. I do trust you."

OMG, Chase Covington was my *boyfriend*. The fourteen-year-old girl in me fainted with delight. A much older-sounding voice reminded me that he hadn't committed to anything. He'd only said he didn't cheat and "couldn't imagine" being with anyone else. That didn't mean he wouldn't.

I told her to shut up and stop ruining this for us.

"Yeah, you're the first person I've ever been with who didn't text me forty times a day when I was off on location."

I leaned forward, feeling bold now that I'd decided he was my boyfriend, and pressed a kiss at the base of his throat. I heard his breath catch. "I'm not really the clingy type."

"It wasn't about that. I mean, it might have partially been." He stopped talking and closed his eyes when I kissed his neck again, softly. "It was about checking up on me, and they wanted me to know how much they hated that I was gone. They were angry I had to be away on a regular basis."

"I didn't like you being gone, either. I missed you. But I'm good being on my own. And why would I get mad? You were working. It couldn't be helped."

I kissed him again right below his ear, and he groaned softly and then put his hands on my shoulders to push me back. "It is much too late, and you are much too beautiful, and that feels much too good for me to keep my hands to myself. You should probably go inside. My lack of self-control is what landed me in rehab in the first place." I loved the rough timbre in his voice.

"You're not going to walk me to the door?" I protested, leaning forward slightly to see if he'd let me.

He didn't. "I'll watch you from here, and then you can text me when you get inside safely."

I knew I should listen to him and stop acting like the Tease-manian Devil. "Okay. Good night." He released me, and I got out of the car but stopped before shutting the door. "Before I go, I want you to know that what happened tonight between us at Austin's house . . . that was even better than meeting Alex Trebek."

He flashed me his most charming grin, and it was all I could do not to climb back inside and throw myself at him. "You're only saying that because when I introduced you, you yelled out 'Who is Alex Trebek?'"

Embarrassment rippled through me, turning my cheeks bright red. "When are you going to stop teasing me about that?"

"I was planning on never."

I sighed. "Good night, Chase." I ran up the three flights of stairs, my feet feeling light and carefree. Even with multiple blisters from my new shoes. When I was inside, I texted him that I had made it through the gauntlet safely and then took off my annoying heels. He texted back to tell me to lock the door. I liked that he was protective.

> But if I lock up won't that make it harder for the serial killers and rapists to get inside?

> You're not funny.

> I'm hilarious. Maybe you should come up here and lock it yourself.

> Also not funny.

I really should have stopped provoking him. I think I was just so happy and thrilled that Chase Covington not only liked me, not only wanted to kiss me (and more), but also was my protective, gorgeous, amazing boyfriend. I couldn't help myself. I saw dots on my screen, indicating that he was typing to me.

> Maybe I just need to build up a tolerance to you. See you as often as I can and then I won't keep having improper but fun thoughts about you.

I was glad he couldn't see me blushing.

> So what you're saying is I'm like poison.

> The opposite. I think you might be the cure. I'll call you tomorrow. Night.

I heard an engine rev and a car pull out of the parking lot, and I assumed it was Chase leaving. I didn't want to text him while he was driving, but the cure? The cure for what? Boredom? Alcoholism? Having to date women whose IQs were lower than their BMIs?

I padded into the kitchen and saw a bag from CVS on the counter. Lexi had made a snack run!

I opened the bag, but the only thing inside was an empty pregnancy-test box. Oh no. A second later I heard her sniffling.

I ran to the bathroom and knocked on the door. "Lex? What's going on? Are you okay?"

"It's open." I found her on the floor next to the sink with trails of black mascara running down her cheeks. She'd been crying for a while. "I'm okay. The tests were negative."

Hadn't we already déjà-ed this vu? "What happened? You told me you're always careful." I sat on the floor next to her and put my arm around her shoulders.

"Remember when I was sick last month and I took those antibiotics? Apparently those can interfere with birth control pills. Which I feel like somebody should have told me."

"Lexi, how many times do I have to tell you that the only one hundred percent effective form of birth control is having my social skills?"

That got her laughing. "I thought you were going to say abstinence."

"That, too." The horse was kind of out of the barn on that one. "If you had been?"

"I don't know. I think I might love Gavin." She laid her head against my shoulder.

"Seriously? I've never heard you say that about anyone." Other than Chase, but she didn't even know him. Not the way I did.

"I can't tell."

"My mom always says go with your gut."

"My gut is really small and easily distracted." She sighed, and I squeezed her.

"Yeah, mine just demands food, and then my butt says, 'Shut up!'"

Another laugh, and she started wiping mascara with the backs of her hands. "Okay. Enough crying. How was the wedding?"

"*Incredible* doesn't seem like a strong enough word." I stood up and grabbed some tissues for her. She cleaned up her face and followed me to our bedroom. She lay down in bed while I got changed.

"You didn't tell me Noah has money." Hearing her use the wrong name made me cringe, but I didn't say anything.

"Why do you think he has money?"

"Because even with my stuffy nose, I can smell his cologne on you. And that did not come from a drugstore."

For a moment I panicked and wondered if she would place the scent from the day she'd worked with Chase on the movie set.

"He does have money."

"We should double-date sometime. And let him pay," she teased, but I kept my back to her as I pulled out a soft T-shirt to wear to bed. "That is, if this thing is serious between you guys. Do you see a future?"

Oh, I saw a future all right. And it included a Labrador retriever, and blonde, blue-eyed babies, and me standing up to applaud him for winning another Academy Award while we crusaded to save the ocean in our free time.

But since it wasn't normal to say that about someone you'd been out on only a few dates with, I settled for, "Right now we're just living in the moment."

I put on thin-cotton pajama bottoms and pulled the shirt over my head.

"Did he knock on the door of the Fortress of Solitude?"

"He knocked, but I didn't answer." Just thinking of the word *door* made me feel the phantom pressure of Chase against me, holding me and kissing me hotly. "And before you ask, yes, there was finally a pretty serious kiss."

She sat straight up in bed. "How was it?"

How could I explain that he'd made me feel like I had molten lava pumping through my veins? "It was like my birthday, Christmas, frolicking puppies, and rainbow-colored unicorns had a baby."

"I love magical kisses."

So did I. "Let's go have ice cream and *Jeopardy!*" It was our go-to pick-me-up when we were sad. I didn't think Lexi even liked the show that much, but she watched it because it always made me feel better.

"Okay." She shuffled out of the room, and I leaned in to smell my dress. Lexi was right. I could smell his cologne. I wished I didn't have to get it cleaned and give it back.

We opened some Ben & Jerry's and sat on our couch. Lexi queued up the show. She settled in with her pint and smiled at me. "Just so you know, you're the friend I'd feel the worst about killing in a postapocalyptic death match."

"Right back at ya. I'm always here for you. Like a celebrity apology after a sexist comment," I said, the guilt inundating me. She was my best friend. NDA or no NDA, I should tell her. My deception ate away at me, making me lose my appetite. I set the ice cream on the coffee table.

I would tell Lexi. Later. When she knew whether or not she loved Gavin and wouldn't take Chase from me, accidentally or otherwise. When I knew whether or not what Chase and I had was serious. When I figured out where this was going and how he felt about me.

Soon. I would tell her soon.

CHAPTER TWENTY-ONE

Chase Covington ✔
@realchasecov
Following

Scientists say it takes 224 tweetz, 163 text messages
& 24 days to fall in love. #trueorfalse?

💬   🔁 15K   ♡ 44K

The next morning, I made lemon squares, inspired by Austin and
Marisol's wedding. I checked my laptop, and Chase had sent me an
e-mail with an attachment. Pictures. Of me and him at Disneyland.

But not the ones the tabloids had used. These were all personal
pictures of us throughout our day. Sitting close together, smiling at each
other, laughing together. As I flipped through each one, I wondered
how I could have ever questioned his feelings for me. They were all
over his face.

And mine.

> Where did these come from?

> I gave Braden my phone and asked him to take some pictures. I wanted you to have them, too.

I liked that we were the only two people who had these pictures, and they weren't splashed across some magazine cover.

> What are you up to? Anything interesting? And how much clothing is/is not involved? And should there be more pictures exchanged?

> Just finishing my last batch of lemon squares. While fully dressed.

My phone rang. It was Chase. Wanting both the lemon squares and for me to go with him to the Marabella aquarium.

The completely people-free aquarium. On one of their busiest days of the week, he had rented out the whole thing for just us. I brought the requested lemon squares, and he finished the entire plate before we'd even reached the first exhibit.

"I wish you'd mentioned beforehand that we'd be the only people. And I don't think you're supposed to eat in here," I told him in a hushed voice. I probably shouldn't have been complaining, as I preferred not having other people around so I wouldn't have to make small talk, but it was strange being in this darkened place without anyone around but the fish. Beautiful, but odd.

"They can add it to my bill," he said, throwing his plate into a trash bin. "You know I'm never going to pass up the opportunity to eat something you baked." He kissed my right temple, making me sigh.

"I can't believe you rented the entire aquarium," I said as we approached the sea-horse tank. They were such weird-looking creatures, like underwater aliens. I loved watching them swim with their little fins and hang on to tall blades of seaweed with their curly tails.

"If there were other people here, I couldn't do this." Before I could catch my breath, Chase spun me in his arms and held me tightly while his warm, strong mouth kissed mine thoroughly and completely. Some still-functioning part of my brain registered that he tasted like lemon and sugar as I collapsed against him.

"You could, but they would probably ask us to leave," I whispered when we came up for air, making him smile.

We made out for a while longer. When he started nuzzling my neck, I had to make him stop because I wasn't sure how much more of that sweet torture I could take.

"So what about the staff?" I asked as we entered the jellyfish room.

"There are some people in the back. They gave me a number to call if I needed to, but why would I?"

"What if there's an emergency?"

"And what kind of emergency are you envisioning?"

I shrugged my shoulders. "I don't know. I've seen those videos of octopi escaping their tanks. That's probably worth a phone call."

"If I see an octopus escaping, I plan on standing clear, and he can do whatever he wants."

I loved how he could make me laugh. "I shouldn't let you do this kind of stuff."

"What do you mean? Like kiss you?" He punctuated his sentence with another bone-melting kiss.

"No," I said, breathless when he let me go. "That's, um, good. I meant the extravagant gestures. Like renting an entire aquarium."

There was a round white-leather seat in the middle of the round room, meant to mimic the jellyfish. He pulled me over to it, and we sat down. "The last woman I seriously dated used to leave catalogs lying around with things circled. She also sent me links to her wish list on Amazon. Took me into jewelry stores to show me her favorite pieces. In every other relationship I've had, there's always this expectation that I'll spend all this money and go to all these extravagant places. But with you I never feel that way. I never feel like you expect anything from me. And it makes me enjoy doing things for you. I love experiencing things you love and seeing how excited you are."

Wow. I didn't love hearing about the last girlfriend, but he was seriously so sweet that it made my soul ache. I looked over at the translucent-moon jellyfish directly across from us, fluttering around the tank the way he made my heart flutter in my chest. "I still feel like I should say it's too much."

He pressed my fingertips against his lips and kissed each one softly, drawing all my attention to his clever mouth. "Why would you deny me the pleasure of doing things for you? I didn't get upset when you brought me lemon bars."

"That's different," I said, my voice shaky because he had turned my hand into Jell-O.

"Not to me. If our financial situations were reversed, would you still think that?"

Think? He wanted me to think? How was I supposed to think when he made everything inside me quiver? He probably had a point. Possibly. Had someone infused his lips with magic so that every time he touched me with them I was put under a spell? One that made me mindless and so full of need for him that it shut everything else out?

As if he knew exactly what was happening to me, he flashed me a knowing grin and pulled me into a kiss that made me very glad jellyfish don't have eyes.

After spending the afternoon in the aquarium, where we had occasionally looked at fish, he took me back to his place. The sun had begun to set, but he didn't let me relax on the deck and enjoy it. Instead, he led me to the kitchen, where a big beige rectangular box sat on the counter. "That's for you. Open it," he encouraged, looking pleased with himself.

A present? I carefully undid the pink ribbon, pulled off the lid, and moved the tissue paper to find a pink skirt and a collared white shirt. "I don't get it."

"Look at the bottom of the skirt."

There was a black poodle with a leash at the bottom.

"We're going on our 1950s date. But we have to go upstairs and get changed. What do you say?"

Did he just sit around and think of adorable things for us to do? "I say that sounds like a lot of fun. What did you have in mind?"

"It's another surprise," he said as he came over and wrapped his arms around me. "All the guest bedrooms upstairs have en suite bathrooms, so you can choose whichever one you want. Or . . . you could join me in my room, and we could get changed together." My brain knew he was joking, but apparently the rest of my body did not get the message.

"Which room is yours?" I asked in a breathy voice, and I felt him go still. "So that I can avoid it."

He nipped my neck in response to my teasing, then led me upstairs and pointed out his room. I chose the guest room farthest from it.

"Go put those bobby socks on, because I plan on knocking them off!" he said just before I closed the door, laughing.

It looked like a hotel room. Big, fluffy white comforter with huge pillows, everything perfectly clean and expensive-looking. Like someone had cut out a page from a decorating magazine and copied it exactly.

The bathroom was more of the same. Gleaming granite and tile, everything sparkling. And all the drawers were full. There were brand-new toothbrushes and toothpaste and hairbrushes and rubber bands and deodorant and mouthwash—every drawer I opened had more still-packaged toiletries.

I got into my 1950s outfit and put my hair up in a ponytail. I didn't even want to know how he'd managed to get me clothing without knowing my size, but everything fit. Even the white canvas tennis shoes I'd worn today matched.

I brushed my teeth and wasn't sure what to do with the toothbrush now that I'd used it, so I just left everything on the counter. I made my way downstairs and found Chase standing in the living room, and my heart stopped.

Now, I was never one of those women who fangirled over Elvis Presley or James Dean. But looking at Chase with his hair combed up, wearing a white T-shirt and blue jeans with a black leather jacket, I totally got it.

"There you are, gorgeous. I had dinner delivered. Including one milk shake with two straws. You ready to go to the drive-in?"

"Drive-in?" I repeated, forcing my feet to move forward and telling myself to stop gawking at him. I didn't think there were any drive-ins nearby.

"Just follow me." We walked out the front door. Chase carried the food. I offered to help, but he wouldn't let me. We went around to the side of his house where there was a huge movie screen set up in front of his garage door and an old black fifties convertible in the driveway. He must have had someone do this while we were upstairs.

"How?" was all I could ask.

Chase put the food in the middle of the front seat and opened the door for me. Then he ran around to his side and jumped in without using his door. "That's how the cool cats do it," he informed me, grinning at my laughter.

"This is an awesome car. But if we're using this, then how are Danny and Sandy going to get to heaven?"

Chase handed me a burger with one of his soul-stealing smiles. "Tonight we'll be watching *Rebel Without a Cause*."

He pushed a button on the projector set up on the hood. The movie started, and I took a big bite of my food. After I swallowed, I said, "I can't believe you had someone set all this up for us."

"I pay the salary of the guy who set all this up, so in a way it's like I did it."

It wasn't like that at all, but he seemed so proud of himself. "Tell One-F thank you for me."

We watched the movie, eating our dinner, sharing our chocolate milk shake. Which might not have been all that sanitary, but considering the amount of spit already swapped between us, it was not a big deal.

When we finished eating, I slid across the seat, and he put his arm around my shoulders and held me tight. I laid my head against his shoulder. The smell of leather filled my nose. There was just something about being with him that felt right. Made me feel safe.

As if I had figured out where I really belonged.

Watching the movie, I had to revise my earlier opinion about James Dean fangirling. Because Chase was a thousand times hotter and would have performed the role a thousand times better. I might also have been distracted because Chase was drawing patterns on my arm just below my sleeve, making me crazy.

The movie ended, and Chase had to let go of me to lean over and turn the digital projector off. "What did you think?"

I knew he meant the movie, but I asked him something else. "When did you know you were interested in me?"

He went back to where he'd been sitting and put his arm around me again. He kissed the top of my head before answering. "When you didn't send me any ungrammatical declarations of physical interest on

Twitter. Although a few might have been nice." He yelped when I hit his arm, then laughed. "And you weren't an Emoji Wan Kenobi. I also appreciated the fact that you didn't proposition me five minutes after meeting me in person. I didn't know whether to find it refreshing or worry I was losing my touch."

"You haven't lost your . . ." I let my words trail off when I saw his self-satisfied smirk.

"What about you? When did you know you were interested in me?"

"I was fourteen the first time you made me blush." I put my hand over his heart and felt the steady thump-thump under my palm.

He took my hand from his chest, lifted it, and kissed the inside of my wrist, making me gasp. "Interesting. Explain."

That wasn't going to happen. "You'll have to get it out of me," I said, pulling my hand free and lifting his arm off my shoulders.

"And just where do you keep your answers? Because I'm happy to search for them."

I smiled, then climbed into the back. "I have another movie for you. It's called *Zoe and Chase Make Out in the Back Seat of a 1950 Chevy Convertible.*"

He got up on his knees and slid off his leather jacket. "I don't know. Doesn't seem very 1950s appropriate to me. The making out, not the car."

"I've seen *Grease.* Very era appropriate." I crooked my index finger, beckoning him to join me.

A second later he was sitting next to me in the back seat. "Okay. You convinced me. Even though they made that movie in the 1970s."

I giggled, sliding my arms around his neck as he pulled me close. "Here's a preview." I leaned in to kiss him and fell into the delicious heat and taste of him, loving the way he made my pulse thump and my spine melt.

"Nice trailer," he murmured against my lips. "I'm very much looking forward to the feature-length version."

With a smile, I showed him the whole movie.

CHAPTER TWENTY-TWO

Zoe
@zomorezoless

Scientists say dogs experience jealousy the same way humans do. #Trivia

Life proceeded as normal over the following weeks. Well, as normal as it could be when your boyfriend starred in major motion pictures. I went to school, did my job, volunteered at the Foundation, and spent whatever free time I had with Chase. He had an unpredictable schedule, so we squeezed in time together whenever we could. We stayed in mostly. Played video games, watched movies and TV (especially *Jeopardy!*, although as soon as the theme music played, Chase would call out "Who is Alex Trebek?" every time we watched), and spent a lot of time kissing until we were breathless.

I didn't spend as much time with Lexi or my family as I normally did, but they seemed to understand. Especially Lexi.

The one serious problem I had was that I didn't want our nights to end. I hated leaving him. And Chase didn't make things better by telling me how much he wanted me to stay. Not to fool around or take things further than I wanted but just because we loved being together.

If this was how addiction worked, I was beginning to understand how hard it had been for him. I had teased him about going to Zoe rehab, but I might seriously need Chase Covington rehab.

One morning after another late night with my boyfriend, Lexi pulled me out of bed. "Come on, Chase Covington is on *The Helen Show*."

"Yeah, I . . ." My voice trailed off as I realized what I had almost admitted to. That I knew he had already filmed the interview that aired that day. He had started a press tour for his newly released movie, *Shadow of Time*, and would have to leave for Europe soon. I was dreading it.

I grabbed my bowl of Lucky Charms while Lexi commanded the commercials to hurry up. "They had Amelia Swan on earlier, and you should be glad the TV is still in one piece. Skank. They're doing the press tour for that new time-traveling movie where he comes from the present to the 1940s to stop World War II, and she's the stupid tramp he falls in love with."

They showed a clip from the movie, with Chase looking extraordinarily dashing in a mid-twentieth-century army uniform, saying goodbye to Amelia Swan's character. Then he crushed her against his mouth and kissed her desperately.

I dropped my spoon. It was like somebody had punched me in the gut. Hard.

Lexi muttered some unkind things under her breath. I was starting to share in her hatred of Amelia.

"Please welcome Chase Covington to the show!"

Chase walked in, and the audience went bonkers. Like, I expected underwear to start flying through the air given how they screamed. He flashed them my favorite charming grin, waving as he went over to Helen and hugged her hello.

"So it must be rough to be so unattractive that nobody can stand to look at you," Helen teased, and Chase laughed as the audience of women started screaming all over again.

"How are things? How are you?" the hostess asked once the hysterics died down.

"Good. Good. And you?"

"Nobody is watching right now to find out what's going on in my life. They want to know about this." Helen pointed at the screen behind them, and I stopped breathing when I saw the picture. It was one of the Disneyland photos. Not our private ones, but one taken by somebody in the crowd.

"About Disneyland? I highly recommend it," Chase said.

"That's not what I meant. Is it?" she asked the audience, and they all started screaming again. Helen waved her hands, trying to get them to calm down. "I mean, is this your girlfriend? Are you seeing someone? Do you have a significant other? Is there someone special in your life? If I knew another language, I would ask you in that."

The audience chuckled, and Chase didn't hesitate. The genuine smile never left his face. "I'm not seeing anyone. I don't have a girlfriend or a significant other. There's no one special in my life. Sorry to disappoint you."

That earned him more screams, whistles, and catcalls. A concrete brick settled in the pit of my stomach, and it was like someone had sucked all the oxygen from the room, making it impossible to breathe.

"If you don't mind me asking, since that's kind of my job, who is the girl in the pictures?"

"Just someone who used to work for me." He sounded so nonchalant.

My brain reminded me, *Chase lies about personal things in interviews.* But my heart said, *He doesn't feel about you the way you feel about him.*

He talked more about the movie and waved off rumors about him and Amelia by saying, "We're just friends. She's a talented actress I admire and respect, but there's nothing else going on." Then they went to commercial, ending Chase's segment. Lexi clicked off the TV.

"I've got to get ready for my improv class," she said, standing up. "Come talk to me while I do. Tell me how things with you and Noah are going. I feel like I hardly see you anymore. Which means things must be going good."

I was so distracted by Chase's announcement that he didn't have a girlfriend that it took me a second to remember she wasn't actually talking about Noah from work. "Things are good." This morning notwithstanding. I stopped by our room to grab my cell phone. Somebody had some explaining to do.

Lexi headed for the bathroom, and I saw her plug in her flat iron. "And have you had the talk?"

"Birds and bees?" I asked, sitting on the side of the bathtub and turning on my phone. "Had it when I was twelve."

"I meant the talk where you define the relationship. You mentioned he's commitment shy. Is that still the situation?"

The guy who just announced on national television that I wasn't his girlfriend? "The only thing he's committed to right now are his commitment issues," I muttered, opening my messaging app. I texted Chase.

> I need you to call me ASAP.

She grabbed a lock of her hair and clamped the iron around it. "He must be serious about you."

"Right now I feel like I'm in this alone. Like his feelings aren't as strong as mine."

Lexi met my eyes in the mirror. "Zoe, don't. Don't go there."

Problem was, I already lived there. It wasn't like it was a long commute. "We're in this, like, bubble situation. Everything's good when we're together, but we don't really discuss the future or where things are going."

"Things can't stay that way forever," she said and put down her iron to turn and face me. "Like on that shark show you made me watch. You have to keep moving forward or you die."

My phone buzzed with Chase's response.

> In a production meeting. Will
> call you later.

I knew that, because One-F always copied me on Chase's schedule. I still felt frustrated, though. I had just seen him kiss someone else and deny my existence. I felt vulnerable and needy and insecure, and I didn't like it, and it ended up making me upset. I mumbled something to Lexi about needing to get dressed.

And once I was dressed, I decided to bake something, as that was the only thing that could calm me down when I was mad. The more time passed, the more pissed off I got.

Lexi left but not before giving me a hug and saying it would all work out. I made chocolate-chip cookies and root beer–float cookies and snickerdoodles. I was too angry to even eat them.

By the time my phone rang, I was like a volcano, ready to erupt.

"Hey, babe. What's up?"

"What's up?" I repeated, seething. "What's up? Why would you even care? I don't mean anything to you!"

There was a long pause. "I don't know what's happening right now."

"I saw you this morning. Telling Helen you don't have anybody you care about. No girlfriend. No one special. Did you stop and think how that would make me feel?"

"Hang on." There were some muffled sounds like wind, and then I heard a car door slam. "Did it ever occur to you that I was protecting you? The second I give the press any hint that I'm dating someone, your private life is over. They will find out everything. They will camp out at your apartment and go through your trash. They'll bribe anyone who might possibly know you into telling them stories. They will follow you everywhere you go. Do you think I want that to happen to you? It's bad enough it happens to me. Do you really think I want it to happen to someone that I . . ." His voice trailed off, and he let out a huge sigh.

That took some of the righteous indignation out of my sails, but I was still upset and still wanted to fight.

"Even if that was your reason, I had to watch you kissing that Amelia Swan."

"What? When?"

"On that clip today!" I said, stirring snickerdoodle dough harder than I needed to. "From your movie!"

"Are you serious?" Now he sounded mad, which for some reason I found satisfying. "I didn't kiss Amelia. Hank kissed Lorraine. The character I was pretending to be kissed the character she was pretending to be."

"Yeah, but he did it with your lips."

"I can't even tell you how unsexy those scenes actually are. They're so technical. It's all choreographed beforehand, done over and over again, and there are thirty people watching you do it. I wish I could explain it better, but what it comes down to is this is my job."

While I logically understood his argument and knew it was his profession, how many other women had boyfriends with jobs that required them to kiss and have pretend love scenes with beautiful actresses?

"I know it's your job," I said in a resigned tone, recognizing my own irrationality.

"Where is all this coming from? You've seen me kiss other people before."

"Yeah, but that was different. That was before . . ." I didn't finish my sentence. *Before you were mine.* "It's just hard."

"I know it is, babe. And I'm sorry. It's weird. But I love my job, and I'm good at it, and I want to keep doing it."

Did he think I wanted him to quit? "I would never ask you to give it up."

"I know you wouldn't. I just hope you can find a way to be okay with it."

With a sigh, I sat down at the kitchen table, holding my forehead in my hands. "I'm sorry I overreacted."

"It's kind of nice. The jealousy thing."

"You won't think it's nice when I'm boiling Amelia Swan's bunny."

He laughed, and I knew things were okay again. "You still planning on coming over tonight?"

Chase had mentioned yesterday he had a big date planned for us, along with some surprises. "Of course."

"Good. Because now that we've had our first fight, you know what that means. The make-up hug is going to be amazing."

I brought Chase some of my anger-induced cookies, and he showed me his surprise. He'd hired a famous television chef who was known for his love of swearing to give us a private cooking class. The chef turned out to be a total sweetheart and attempted to teach us how to make pan-seared chicken breasts, rosemary mashed potatoes, and green beans with almond slices. We didn't get cussed out once, and there were only two minor mishaps involving fire, so I counted that as a win.

Chase walked the chef out, and when he came back into the kitchen, I wrapped my arms around his shoulders and hugged him. "You don't have to keep doing stuff like this. It's so sweet and thoughtful, but being with you is impressive enough for me."

His arms were around my waist. "I'm just trying to . . ."

"What?"

"I told you, this is why actors have writers," he said with a self-deprecating smile. "You're different. And special to me. I want to show you that."

My heart grew ten sizes bigger. "You don't need a writer. That was pretty perfect. So, what else do you have on the agenda for this evening?"

He twisted his mouth to the side and raised his eyebrows as if thinking hard. "Strip poker?"

I just shook my head. "I don't even know how to play regular poker."

Chase shot me his best leer. "Then most definitely strip poker."

He laughed when I smacked his arm, then he gave me that blinding grin that always made my knees buckle. "I do have something planned. But I have to give you something first. Stay here."

He ran upstairs, and I put some of the dishes in the sink and filled the burned pans with water. Next time I saw Sofia, I would ask her the best way to clean them, because I hoped there were more burned pans in our future.

"Close your eyes."

I put my hands over my eyes and turned toward the sound of his voice. "So . . . I don't know how you're going to take this . . . uh . . . the thing is . . . .see? I do need a writer." He let out a little laugh before continuing. "But I don't want you to think this means something it doesn't . . . and . . . I . . ."

Now he was starting to make me nervous. "Consider the suspense built! Can I open my eyes?"

"Okay."

I blinked a couple of times in confusion. "You're giving me a board?"

CHAPTER TWENTY-THREE

 Zoe
@zomorezoless

It is thought the tradition of bundling comes from the Old Testament story of Ruth & Boaz. #Trivia

 ♡ ⟲ 0 ♡ 1

The board was about six feet tall and had grooves on one end, like the edge of a saw blade. Chase seemed so excited about it that I realized how rude I was being. "Oh. Thank you?" I hadn't intended for it to sound like a question.

"It's probably not what you think."

"I think you're giving me a piece of wood."

"It's a bundling board." He looked at me expectantly, like I should know what that was. "Like what the Amish do. When you told me about your grandparents, I did a little research. When a couple is courting, they are allowed to stay up all night talking. The girl's family puts this board down the middle of a bed, and the girl gets under the covers, but the guy doesn't. It was something about conserving fuel in the winter. I'm going to be leaving tomorrow afternoon. At the end of every evening we're together, saying good night to you is the worst part of my day. I thought maybe this way you could stay."

My mouth hung open in shock. I didn't know what to say.

He put his free hand in his jeans pocket, a gesture I knew meant he felt anxious or nervous about something, which was so endearing. "I don't expect anything. I know nothing's going to happen between us. I just want to spend as much time with you as I can before I go."

It was . . . incredibly sweet. And thoughtful. And respectful. And I'd never had anyone do anything like this for me before.

My silence made him keep talking. "I considered emptying one of the guest rooms so we could wallpaper it. Isn't that what your grandmother said? If we could wallpaper a room without killing each other, we had a promising future?"

I finally found my voice. "I can't believe you remember that."

"I pay attention to things you say, Zoe. Anyway, I thought bundling was a much better idea. I wouldn't want you to get all dirty and tired."

"So it had nothing to do with getting me to stay all night in your room. You were only thinking of me," I teased. I rested my hand on the top of the bundling board.

"I'm very selfless like that."

"But I don't have anything to sleep in." I knew I didn't have to worry about brushing my teeth given his well-stocked guest rooms.

And I would most definitely be brushing my teeth.

"I actually have something for you to sleep in. I asked One-F to go pick out a nightgown. Or I can lend you something of mine."

He always thought about the little things. I loved the idea of sleeping in his clothes, surrounded by his scent, next to him in his bed (even if a board was between us). But he had made the effort to get me something, and it would be rude not to accept. "I'll take what your assistant picked out. You're very detail oriented."

His eyes flashed hot, and he raked them up and down my body, sending shivers racing across my skin. "You should remember that. For a possible someday."

There was no way I would ever forget.

I gulped and asked, "So where's this nightgown?"

"Does that mean you'll stay?" His eyes were big and hopeful.

"You know I want to stay."

Chase reached out and hugged me with his free arm, then kissed my cheek. "It's up in the guest room you used last time. Get changed, and join me when you're done."

We parted at the top of the stairs, where I went to the guest room, and he went to his. I took out my phone and thought about calling Lexi. Getting her advice. Which would probably be useless, because she would just tell me to toss the board and see where things went. I settled on texting her that I'd be home really late and not to worry. If I said I'd be out all night, she'd never stop bugging me for information.

She responded quickly.

squee HAVE FUN!!!!

A paper bag sat on the bed, and I had a moment of apprehension. What had One-F bought? I reached in and pulled out the most old-fashioned nightgown I'd ever seen. I actually laughed. It was made out of light-blue cotton, long-sleeve with lace ruffles, and when I held it against me, I saw it would go to midcalf. It had dumb little pink bows on it and lace that went up to my neck. I hadn't needed to worry. There was nothing immodest or appealing about it at all. I wondered what kind of instructions Chase had given his assistant.

I decided to have a quick shower, and I put my hair up so it wouldn't get wet. I locked the door behind me, but I knew I didn't need to. Chase wouldn't come in here. As I'd told him more than once, I trusted him.

The hot water beat against my back, and I leaned my forehead against the shower wall. Was I making a mistake? Would this be too much temptation? Were we just playing with fire? The problem with fire-playing is that it ends when people got burned. Then again, if it was an Amish tradition, how risqué could it actually be?

Deciding I trusted him and myself, I turned off the shower, toweled off, and put on the ridiculous nightgown. I tried not to laugh at my reflection. I looked like I had just wandered off the set of *Little House on the Prairie*.

After I had brushed my teeth and put my clothes in the bag on the bed, I walked down the hall to Chase's room, feeling nervous excitement bubbling in my stomach.

I hesitated and then knocked on his door. He yelled out, "Come in!" His words sounded garbled, like he was brushing his teeth. I opened the door, and the first thing that hit me was that specific, amazing Chase scent. His room was decorated in dark blues and different shades of brown. His bed was enormous; it looked bigger than a king. It had a quilted cream-colored headboard, and behind it were planks of wood in different sizes and colors. I heard Chase turn off the faucet and felt a new wave of anxiety. I distracted myself by looking at the opposite end of the room. There were two window seats with pillows that matched the ones on his bed and a bookshelf between the windows that I wanted to check out.

But Chase chose that moment to walk out of the bathroom, his hair still damp from his shower. He wore drawstring cotton pajama bottoms, and I put my hand over my stomach when I saw his chest. *Have mercy on my ovaries.*

He muttered things that sounded suspiciously like swear words. "I should have told him to get you a burlap sack."

He had a problem with this ridiculous thing? Seriously? He was the one sporting abs of steel that probably set off metal detectors in airports.

Chase was still complaining. "I told him to get the least sexy thing he could find."

Holding out my arms, I said, "Mission accomplished."

"No, not mission accomplished. This is worse."

"What? Why?"

"Because now that I can't see anything, I'm imagining it all instead."

I thought about teasing him, suggesting I could take it off, but things felt edgy enough already, and I didn't want to push him too far. "I could sleep in the guest room."

"No." He crossed over to me and held my hands. "No. I want you here with me."

"This is where I want to be, so that works out well."

Even though I knew nothing would happen, I couldn't quite shake my anxious feeling. I wondered if it was obvious.

"Do you need anything?" he asked, looking concerned.

Yep. Obvious.

"Some water?"

And a defibrillator.

He squeezed my hands and kissed me briefly. I crossed my arms and watched while he grabbed a couple of bottles of water from a built-in minifridge. He handed me one, but I didn't open it. Instead, I just stared at his chest, wanting to run my fingers across his skin. It was like a topographical map to Hot Guy's Chest, and I wanted to explore.

Then I realized my hand had made an independent decision, and that's exactly what it was doing—running my fingertips across his abs, feeling the muscles contract and his breath catch when I made contact. I curled my fingers inward and pulled my rebel hand away.

He raised one eyebrow at me, looking amused. "You don't have to stop on my account." I wondered how much I was blushing when he added, "I don't normally sleep with a shirt. Should I put one on?"

"*Yes!* I mean, whatever you want."

With a knowing smirk, he went back into his bathroom. I guessed his closet was in there because I didn't see a dresser.

I decided to get into bed, but then I didn't know what side he slept on. I had a twin mattress in my apartment, so my regular side was everywhere. Chase returned, pulling on a T-shirt that bore the name of a band I'd never heard of. I put my water on one of the nightstands, not really wanting to drink it. He grabbed the bundling board and placed it in the middle of the bed, but we both quickly realized we didn't have any way of making it stay put. It kept leaning to one side. We tried stacking pillows against it, but that didn't work.

"The bed frames they used with this probably had some kind of slot or something," I offered. "We could just put pillows between us."

"That could work." He put the board on the floor, and we piled up pillows, which stayed this time. "Climb in, and I'll get the lights."

I chose the side of the bed I was closest to, pulling back the covers and settling in. Chase plunged the room into darkness, and the mattress sank under his weight. He didn't move the covers, though. He stayed on top of them. My eyes adjusted after a few seconds, and he removed the pillows that blocked us from seeing each other. We turned on our sides, our faces just a pillow width apart.

"Hey."

"Hey," I whispered back.

We lay in silence for a few minutes, just looking at each other. I couldn't believe how much I loved this. Being here with him.

I wished I could do it every night.

"Yeah, I can't do this." Chase started tossing pillows to the floor.

My throat felt tight. Was he going to send me away? "Do what?"

"Have you here and not touch you." He pulled me against him, and I rested my head in the hollow between his neck and shoulder, laying my hand over his chest. My whole body let out a sigh of relief, saying, *This is where we belong.*

"I don't think this is how the Amish do it."

"Well, I don't shun electricity or travel by horse, so I'm taking some liberties. I can put the pillows back later. For now, I want to hold you. It's been a long day, my girlfriend picked a fight with me earlier, and I'd just like to relax."

My heart beat so hard I was sure he could feel it against his rib cage. "Girlfriend? You've never called me that before."

He kissed the top of my head. "I haven't? You are." He said it so matter-of-factly that it calmed any doubts I might have been harboring.

His breaths started becoming longer and deeper.

I touched his neck. "Chase, I thought we were supposed to stay up and talk all night."

"In a minute," he mumbled.

His breathing grew slower, more rhythmic. I should have let go of him and moved back to my side of the bed. But I wasn't willing to give up this warmth that had spread through me. This contented, happy, peaceful feeling was because of the man whose strong arms held me tightly.

I'd move back to my side. Like he'd said. In a minute.

CHAPTER TWENTY-FOUR

Chase Covington ✓
@realchasecov

Following

You know I love you guys, but seriously, call first before stopping by.

💬   ↻ 97K   ♡ 278K

I woke up to the sensation of butterfly kisses on my face. Chase kissed my eyelids, my cheeks, my forehead, the tip of my nose. I opened my eyes, and he smiled at me. "Good morning."

"Morning," I said with a yawn. I became aware of the fact that at some point during the night I had kicked off my covers, and I was now seriously intertwined and entangled with my boyfriend (which I could now officially call him).

It sent heat careening around my body, making me super aware of how good it felt to be so close.

He studied my face as he ran the back of his hand along my cheek.

"What?" I asked in a panic. Had I drooled, and there was some physical evidence of it near my mouth? I reached up to check.

"I was just wondering how I got so lucky."

"It helps that you're really hot."

He laughed and kissed me but not for too long. Which was probably a good idea, given our current situation.

His blue eyes looked so bright in the early-morning sun. I stroked his face, a mixture of smooth and rough where his stubble had started growing in.

"I was also wondering if this is what marriage is like."

My hand stilled. The only time he ever talked about marriage was to disparage it. "What do you mean?"

He turned his head to kiss my palm. "Marriage always seemed so big. Such a commitment. But maybe it's not about the big things but the little day-to-day, mundane, real-life stuff. About being together like this. Waking up together. Wanting to be with you and missing you when you're not here. Maybe it's about meeting the right person." He paused. "And lots of sex."

I laughed as my heart leaped up in my chest, causing me to hope in a way that I hadn't for a long time. I'd just ignore the fact that he had possibly called me mundane. "I think that is what it's about. Finding someone you want to be with. Someone you're willing to make a commitment to and fight for, no matter what. And I'm sorry."

"For what?" His arms tightened around me as he rubbed one of his bare feet against mine.

"For asking you to be a monk. I know this can't be easy for you."

"You don't have to apologize for your choices. I was a monk long before we met. I needed to focus solely on my sobriety, and that's all I've done for the past couple of years. Besides," he added with another kiss, "you're worth the wait."

In that moment I realized something I never had before.

I loved him.

I was completely head-over-heels, buck-wild, madly in love with Chase Covington. My breath rushed out of me, my cheeks felt hot, and it was a struggle to keep the words inside.

Because I would not say it before he did. I'd already spent most of our time together hoping our feelings were equal. I wasn't willing to risk it, especially not with my heart on the line.

"Definitely worth it—even if you drive me insane," he said in that low, rough voice that put all my nerve endings on edge with anticipation.

"You're not alone in that, you know." I couldn't meet his gaze, worried he would see all the love and want I had for him. And that was what had become harder over time. I'd fallen in love with him, and I wanted to show him. I wanted to express those feelings physically. Even though I knew I wouldn't.

"Obviously. Of course you want to get with all this," he said, making me giggle and snuggle closer. "Despite what I want, I would never want you to regret anything that happens between us."

I sort of hated that he was right. I would regret it. Regardless of how very much I would enjoy it up to that point.

Chase started kissing me then—soft, intoxicating, unhurried kisses that had me tightening my arms, wanting to melt into him. My heart thudded firmly and slowly, keeping time with his mouth.

He broke off the kiss suddenly. He turned me and pressed me flat on my back while he hovered above me, bracing himself on his elbows.

"What are you doing?" I asked, both alarmed and thrilled.

"That depends on what you let me do," he teased, but I watched as the amusement faded from his eyes, replaced by a look of so much heartrending tenderness and longing that it made me feel like I was breaking apart. Then he used his lips to put me back together piece by piece.

I ran my hands over his upper arms, stroking the tensed muscles there, and made my way up to his shoulders and then to his thick, silky golden hair. I lightly dragged my fingertips along his scalp. I knew how much he liked that.

He made a sound of pleasure in the back of his throat that made every bit of me tingle. But he resisted deepening the kiss, keeping it featherlight but still tantalizing. It made me want to drown in his loving sweetness. Some part of my brain registered that I hadn't brushed my teeth yet, but I completely did not care.

Especially once Chase trailed a column of velvet warmth down my throat that started a hot ache in my core. I arched my back, wanting to feel his edges and planes against my curves. My newly discovered feelings for him made it imperative that we get closer.

"This is going to get out of control if you keep doing that," he murmured at the hollow at the base of my neck, but I couldn't stay still. My entire body throbbed with need, and I tugged at him. Still too far away.

I sighed with relief and pleasure when he lowered his body to mine, but just as he did so, a siren started to shrill, loudly.

"What's that?" I asked.

"The somebody's-virtue-is-in-peril alarm," he said, then pulled at my earlobe with his lips.

I pushed against him, and he pushed himself up. "Seriously, what is that?"

He rolled away from me and reached for his phone, then flicked through a couple of screens. "It's the perimeter security alarm. Somebody's on the grounds."

I sat straight up. "Isn't that a big deal?"

"My security company has an excellent response time. They'll be here in a couple of minutes with dogs and big guns." He put one hand behind his head, and he looked so comfortable and at ease that I wanted to hit him.

"Does this happen a lot?"

He frowned for a second. "It's usually just some overzealous fan who figured out where I live. As soon as the alarm sounds, they take off. It's one of the reasons I don't want my fans knowing where I am all the time and knowing when I'm not home. They tend to get bolder when they think no one's here to stop them. But you're safe. Don't worry about it."

I pulled my knees to my chest and wrapped my arms around them. It bothered me that anyone would try to sneak into his home. "And you're leaving today. I could house-sit for you."

He propped himself up on one elbow, his eyes serious. "No way.

"You just said it was safe." I hated the idea of some crazy person breaking in to lie in wait and then take a sledgehammer to Chase's ankles when he got back. I had my Mace. I could take her down.

"I don't want you here alone. At least at your apartment you have Lexi with you."

"Not always."

He put his hand on my foot. "But no insane people are trying to break into your apartment. And if you stay here and something happens, I don't want to have to go to jail for permanently maiming the person who hurts you."

The doorbell rang, making me jump. "It's just the security team," he reassured me as he got up to answer it.

While he was downstairs, I went into the guest room and grabbed my stuff. I used the bathroom and got ready for the day as best I could. I didn't want to wear the same clothes I had yesterday, so I planned to stop by my apartment and get changed before going to class.

When I got to the front door, Chase was shaking hands with a man dressed all in black carrying a massive gun. A buzz-cut, thick-neck kind of guy who looked like he could snap me in half without blinking.

Chase thanked the man and closed the door. "They didn't find anyone. They're going to review the security footage and let me know if there's anything on it. Why are you down here and not up in bed waiting for me?"

The heat rushed to my skin at his words, making me want to turn around and go back upstairs. "I have to go."

He pulled me against his chest, rendering me weak-kneed and powerless. "I can't convince you to stay?"

"You probably could, but I have class, and you have a flight to catch."

"Stupid real-life responsibilities," he said and then lavished more soft and all-too-brief kisses on me.

"I really do have to go." It was getting late, and my nerves felt a little shot from the scary siren and the kiss in his room.

Chase walked me to my car. "I'll call you and text you whenever I get the chance."

"Have fun in Europe. I'll miss you." I wished I had the courage to tell him I loved him, but I hoped the opportunity would present itself soon. Like, after he said it to me first.

And with one last lip-searing, soul-shattering kiss, I was finally on my way. I passed the guard station and realized I was in dire need of gas. My phone's GPS guided me to a gas station about four blocks away.

I got out, started the pump, and then decided to wash my windshield. In the middle of doing that, I felt someone come up behind me. I turned to see an older balding man with a bit of a paunch and a nose that had been broken more than once. He wore a red, white, and blue denim jacket that looked like the Fourth of July had thrown up on it.

"I'm sorry, but do you know how to get to the 405 from here?" He held up his phone, smiling. "Mine died. I forgot my charger, and I'm a little lost."

Although he appeared friendly and nonthreatening, something about him gave me the creeps, and I was glad we were in a public place. I gave him the quickest directions possible, put the squeegee back in the cleaning solution, and took the nozzle out of my car.

"Thanks," the man said, and I nodded to him, wanting to get away.

I was just about to get in when I heard him say, "Hey, by the way, haven't I seen you before? Are you dating someone famous?"

It was such a bizarre (and truth-based) question that at first I didn't know how to respond. I blurted out, "You have me mistaken for someone else." Hoping I'd misled him, I got in my car and drove off, going fifteen miles per hour over the speed limit. I kept checking my rearview mirror to make sure he hadn't followed me.

Despite my paranoia, I wasn't being tailed. I thought about calling Chase to tell him what had happened, but I had probably overreacted. He was most likely some lost tourist who thought everybody in Los Angeles was either famous or dating someone famous. I was just jumpy because of the alarm earlier.

When I got home, I found Lexi sitting on the couch, watching TV. Her eyes went big when she saw me, and she used the remote to turn the TV off.

"Out all night! Did you let him scale the walls of the Fortress? I am looking for vivid, electrifying details here."

She knew I wasn't the kiss-and-tell type, but she kept hope alive. "Still no wall breaches," I told her. I headed to our room to quickly change before class. She followed me. I set the shopping bag on the bed. "Although I kind of wanted to throw him a grappling hook, because he is the most amazing kisser ever."

"You don't have to provide any climbing instruments. Only Superman can get into the Fortress of Solitude. And it sounds like you've found him."

"He is kind of perfect. But I think we may have overused this metaphor." I kicked off my jeans and looked in my drawers for a clean pair. I realized I was running out of clothes. I desperately needed to do laundry.

"What's in the bag?" Before I could stop her, she'd pulled out the nightgown. "Did he buy you this? Because if this is his idea of lingerie, I can see why nothing's happening."

I grabbed a shirt off a hanger and put it on. "He didn't want me to be too alluring so he could resist my womanly charms," I said in a joking tone.

Lexi stayed deadly serious. "Well, this would make sure he had no problem resisting. It's like man repellent. We should burn this. It's an affront to nightwear everywhere."

"No!" I grabbed it out of her hands. This was something I'd always keep, even if Chase and I broke up. I folded it and put it on the top shelf of my closet. "I think he kind of liked it."

"So what you're saying is he's a hopeless romantic. Because he obviously has no hope of being romantic if he actually bought you this. Although, if he didn't run off screaming when you wore it, I guess that's good."

"Sometimes I worry he will. Run away screaming. Because of my celibacy."

"I'd wager that if you haven't lost him by now because of it, the odds are pretty good that you won't." Lexi lay down on her bed and did something on her phone. "Hey, random question, but do you think Gavin has good abs?"

She flashed her phone at me, but I wasn't interested in checking out her boyfriend's chest. "I've never seen them and don't really want to now."

"I'm trying to decide if his abs are as good as Chase's." Her eyes flicked up to one of her posters. "Although Chase's are probably Photoshopped."

They were so not. And they were better in real life. But I couldn't tell her that.

"While you're figuring out that deep mystery, I've got to get to class. See you later." I grabbed my book bag, took my laptop from the kitchen, and headed out. On my way to school, my phone buzzed.

Chase had sent me a text with a photo. It was a picture of me sleeping.

> Wish I could pack you up and take you with me to Europe.

> I don't know what's more disturbing - that you're taking pictures of me while I'm asleep or that you want to stuff me in a suitcase.

SALTS

That made me smile a little. I thought about Lexi saying I needed Superman to break down my walls. Which made me think of Chase and how he didn't want me to stay in his house without him being there to protect me. How he'd threatened bodily harm if someone hurt me. That he thought of me as his girlfriend.

I didn't need Superman. I had Captain Sparta.

CHAPTER TWENTY-FIVE

Zoe
@zomorezoless

Some animals who mate for life: gray wolves, turtle doves, French angelfish, swans, gibbons, beavers, barn owls, etc. #Trivia

 🔁 0 ♡ 0

Although I missed Chase when he was away on his European press tour, it couldn't have come at a better time. It allowed me to study for and finish my finals so that when he got back, the only thing I'd have to do was find a grown-up job. I still had my fingers crossed that the Foundation would hire me on full-time, but I worried on days like today when everything was so slow that I had nothing to do.

I should have used the time to study, but instead I went through some of the texts and e-mails Chase had sent me while he'd been gone. Like the picture of the back of a minivan with one of those stick families on it.

I'm so glad this guy thought it important to inform the world that he has a stick figure family of six. His minivan gave me the impression he was wild and single.

It reminded me of Chase's disdain for marriage, something I hoped had started to change, given our last conversation.

Then there was the black-and-white photo he'd taken of himself lying in his hotel bed. To say he was photogenic would be an understatement. He was lying on a bed on fluffy white pillows with an arm behind his head, surrounded by a massive comforter. His shirt was off, and he wore that sly, sexy smirk I loved.

I'm in my bed, you're in yours...one of us is in the wrong place.

Instead of drooling all over the photo and letting him know I'd only barely retained consciousness after I'd seen it, I texted back:

I'm in California, you're in Europe. One of us is in the wrong place.

(Hint: It's not me.)

Not much longer until I'm done. I might have left an amazing kiss at your place. Do you mind if I come by and get it when I get back?

We talked on the phone when we got the chance. He'd called last night, and I had gone out on our tiny balcony to talk to him.

"What have you learned about this week?" Chase hadn't had traditional schooling or gone to college, but one of the things I loved about him was that he read about subjects that interested him all the time. He thought it was because his on-set tutors let him choose which things he wanted to study. Sometimes to do research for a movie role, other times because the topic of the book appealed to him.

"In women's studies I learned men suck." I had told him many a tale about our discussion topics in that class.

"Present company excluded, of course. I meant other than that."

I had this ancient–American civilization class to fulfill a world-civ requirement, and we'd ended the semester with a guest lecturer who taught us about the Mayans. I told Chase some of the things the professor had said. "I'm kind of fascinated. I went out and bought the book he brought to class, and I've been reading it when I should be studying for other classes."

"Who is it by?" His voice had a strange quality I didn't quite recognize.

"Michael D. Coe."

"Hang on."

I got an alert that he had sent me a picture. It was of his nightstand. At the top of a pile of books was the very same one I'd been telling him about. It had a different cover but the same title, same author. I was pretty sure I hadn't tweeted about it or told him about it before. "How is that possible?"

"I don't know. I was in a used bookstore in Dublin a couple of days ago and came across it. I thought it looked interesting. I guess you and I are on the same wavelength."

Or it was another one of those signs Chase was always looking for. Although reading the same book at the same time was probably just a coincidence and not a message from the universe saying that Chase and I were meant to be.

"You really should get a tablet. You're going to strain your back carrying around all those books."

"It's okay. I'm strong." Then he sent me a picture of himself flexing, and I had to use my notebook to fan my face. He had the best arms. I did think it was adorable that he insisted on reading only paper books because he liked the feel and smell of them. I loved that he read because he enjoyed it and not because some professor forced him to or because he was a random hipster hoping to show up on some girl's Instagram reading paperbacks in public (and yes, I once went out with a guy like that).

My phone beeped, interrupting my daydreams about Chase's arms. He had put out a new tweet.

Every time Chase deliberately substituted a *Z* for an *S*, it was a special tweet meant just for me.

But it didn't help my blood pressure when stupid Amelia Swan, who was on the press tour with him, tweeted back:

Grr. Stupid Amelia Swan. Why wouldn't she leave Chase alone? Were you allowed to punch movie stars? Or was that reserved for politicians and scary clowns?

My grandma always told me not to hate people, so I knew I shouldn't hate Amelia Swan, but if she were on fire and I had a glass of water, I would drink it.

Things only got worse when Lexi sent me an urgent e-mail with the subject line of "When will this girl get a clue?" telling me I had to look at a link. It led to an article entitled, "Old Flames Reignite!" It had a bunch of pictures of what looked like Chase and Amelia walking down a sidewalk, heads close (and she was wearing a skirt so short I could see her tonsils). There were pictures of them eating at a café. Smiling and laughing. One where she had her hand on his arm.

And then one where they were about to kiss.

With my heart in my throat, I read the article. It talked about how these pictures had been taken in London yesterday on their press tour and said the website's source revealed, "When they got away from all the cameras, Chase remembered why he fell for Amelia in the first place. They've been inseparable and are definitely dating again. It's serious. They have plans to move in together when they return to the States."

It's not true, I told myself over and over, ignoring the shards of ice that had solidified my veins. *It's not true. Chase wouldn't cheat on me. He said he wouldn't.*

My nasty, insecure voice raised her ugly head. *But she's gorgeous and would sleep with him in a heartbeat. She can give him what you won't.*

Even if they weren't on the verge of getting back together, had they dated? Chase had never mentioned that before. Not that I'd pushed him very hard about his past. From what I'd gathered, it was more colorful than a Vincent van Gogh painting, and I didn't need the details.

Now I wondered if that had been a mistake.

I texted Lexi.

> Do you think they're hooking up?

I wanted her to talk me down. To tell me like she normally did that of course they weren't and Chase had much better taste than that. Instead what I got back was,

> If they aren't doing the mattress mambo yet, it looks like they've at least put on their dancing shoes and turned the music on.

So not what I needed to hear. I decided to call Chase right then and there. He was supposed to be in Berlin today, and I was about to look up the time difference when Miriam stuck her head in the door. "They need you in the conference room."

With a heavy sigh, I shut my laptop and followed her out. I wondered if it would be another rah-rah/bragging meeting. Within the last few weeks, staff members had managed to secure a former Vine star, a stand-up comedian I'd never heard of, and an actor from a seventies sci-fi show who currently made his living going to Comic Cons and charging fans to take pictures with him (Stephanie almost spontaneously combusted at that last one).

But it wasn't a staff meeting. Just a handful of people, including Francisco. Francisco glanced at me when I walked in. "Thanks for finally joining us, Zoe. This is the committee to redesign the solicitation letter and our brochure, and Stephanie asked that you be included."

Design and graphics weren't really my thing, being a math kind of girl, but I was excited that Stephanie had requested I be included.

That sounded like it would bode well for my future here. I was all for anything that would tip the scales in my favor when I applied for a paying job.

But two hours later I wasn't sure why she wanted me on that committee. Nobody listened to anything I suggested, and after two attempts I gave up and stayed silent, wondering about Chase. Where he was and what he was doing. If he remembered to dead-bolt his hotel room to keep that opportunistic succubus out.

The meeting ended, my shift was over, and I just wanted to get out of there. My phone rang, and I couldn't answer fast enough when I saw it was him. "Hey!"

"Hey, babe. What's going on?"

I gathered my stuff and had a momentary pang of weirdness when I noticed that my laptop was open. I could have sworn I'd shut it before the meeting. I swept it into my bag and headed for the front door. "The aliens have invaded and demanded our top movie stars be turned over. It's a good thing you're out of the country."

"Not so good." He sounded tired. "Amelia's terrorizing everyone."

I was so happy he was the one who'd brought her up so I wouldn't sound jealous and psycho. I would be smooth and subtle. "What's she doing?"

"Apparently they brought her poached eggs with yolks instead of scrambled egg whites, and she's refusing to come out of her room. The producers want me to convince her to do our scheduled interview and photo shoot."

"Did you have a thing with Amelia in the past?" So much for smooth and subtle.

"A thing?" he repeated, which made me nervous. It seemed like he was being evasive.

"Did you and Amelia date?" Couldn't be plainer than that.

My stomach flipped repeatedly while I waited for him to answer.

"For, like, five minutes a very long time ago. It wasn't serious. At all."

Oh. Somehow that made it worse. Obviously I didn't know from personal experience, but I'd heard that casual flings were easy to fall back into. Although, on the plus side, he must have been the one to break it off, since she was the one still publicly pursuing him. I hated the fact that she was there with him and I was here without him.

I had to get hold of myself. Not overreact. Smooth and subtle. "Maybe you shouldn't be the one to convince her to do the interview and photo shoot, considering that the last time you asked her to do something, it was to stop being your girlfriend."

"You say girlfriend; I say angel of darkness. For the record, she was never my girlfriend."

The insecure voice was back. *Do you know who goes on the record? People with something to prove.*

Shut up, I hissed back. "That sounds rough."

"And now all the people from the magazine are mad, and you know nothing good comes from a bunch of angry Germans." He let out a tired sigh. "I have to go and see if we can salvage this. Knowing I get to see you soon is the only thing getting me through this. I should be home by nine tomorrow night. Will you come over?"

I'd be able to get more information out of him in person than I could when he was trying to work. "Absolutely. Good luck. I lo—bye." I hung up in a hurry, stunned at what I'd almost just done. I'd almost told him I loved him, when for all I knew he was using his lips to convince Amelia to do the interview.

The entire drive home I convinced myself I was fine. That I could trust Chase and he wasn't cheating on me. But when I was in the safety of my own bedroom, I opened my laptop and started searching for the pictures of him with Amelia. A half hour in and I was sobbing.

Which is how Lexi found me. "Are you—are you crying?"

I was never much of a crier, so I understood her surprise. "No. A twig covered in dust fell in my eye while I was chopping onions."

She sat on my bed. "Well, that's not true. You would never chop onions."

That made me laugh-cry and sniffle. She went to the bathroom and got me a box of Kleenex. "Do you want to talk about it?"

Sucking in a deep breath, I tried to calm down. "I think he might be cheating on me."

"Why?"

I blew my nose and threw the wadded-up tissue into our trash bin. "There's this woman from work who's after him. She's just like Amelia Swan." Not just like. The actual Amelia Swan.

Lexi nodded. "I hate her already. And she's going after Noah?"

I nodded, my throat feeling so thick. "I told you he was on that business trip, and she's with him."

She crinkled her nose. "I would hope he would have more integrity than that."

"You and me both." My breath was shaky when I tried to inflate my lungs. "The thing is . . . the thing is, I keep wondering if he's messing around with her because I won't."

"If you have to sleep with a guy to hold on to him, you never had him in the first place. Don't doubt yourself or your decisions."

She was right, but some part of me kept insisting I had to do something to secure Chase. To make sure he didn't start looking around for someone who would give him what he wanted.

"Isn't he coming home soon?"

"Yeah." I sniffled again.

"Then you need to get in there and mark your territory when he gets back."

I knit my eyebrows in confusion. "You want me to pee on him?"

"What? Ew. No. When you see her, you let her know he's your man and she needs to back off."

That wouldn't be possible. "I've never even met her."

Now it was Lexi's turn to look confused. "I thought you said she was from the Foundation."

That was the problem with lying. You started to lose track. "Right. I mean, I don't really hang out with her or talk to her." I pulled a thread on my blanket, unable to look my best friend in the eye thanks to the shame and guilt. So I deflected. "Shouldn't you be telling me to ignore her and take the high road?"

"Meh. That road's too high. We could fall off."

I sat up and hugged her. I felt like the worst person in the world. After telling me everything would work out, she went to the kitchen to make dinner. She offered to cook me something, but I'd been crying for so long that eating was the last thing I wanted to do.

Plus, I didn't deserve her food or her kindness. I had all these reasons, all these excuses, one even legal, for why I hadn't told anyone I cared about that I had been dating Chase. But that's all they were. Excuses.

And all I had done was lie. Over and over again. To the people I loved. Sometimes by omission, sometimes deliberately.

Maybe this was karma trying to teach me a lesson about being dishonest with my best friend.

Chase was my boyfriend. There was no reason not to tell Lexi. Even if he did cheat on me with Amelia, and twenty-four hours from now we'd be broken up, it didn't matter. I needed to tell her. Once Chase was home. Then I would bring him over and explain the whole thing to her. If he was sitting with me when it happened, hopefully that would lessen the chance of her leaping across the room and choking me for stealing her lifelong crush.

To make myself accountable, I sent Chase a text.

> Are you ready to be formally
> introduced to Lexi as my
> significant other?

He had asked me on a couple of occasions why I hadn't officially introduced him to my friends or my mom. He'd wanted me to meet *his* mom, but she was with Husband No. 9 in Zanzibar. Although I was thrilled he'd thought we were at the meet-the-family stage, I'd told him my concerns. That Lexi would be hurt. That my mom would freak out and go off the deep end. And I'd said, "You are the only thing that's ever been just mine. If I tell them, then I have to share you. I like not having to share you."

He'd kissed my temple. "That's why I didn't tell Helen and all of America about you." Which made me feel worse that I'd been upset at him for denying he had someone special in his life in that interview.

Chase texted me back.

> I would love to hang out with Lexi. Let's figure something out when I get home.

There. Now I had to do it. Because it was time to tell my loved ones about Chase.

I just hoped Lexi wouldn't hate me.

CHAPTER TWENTY-SIX

Now that I had a countdown and a mission, I was driving myself nuts. I tried all kinds of distractions. I kept rereading the same sentence in one of my all-time-favorite books. Missed entire plot points in the romantic comedy I streamed. Not even *Jeopardy!* could hold my attention. In desperation I drove out to Marabella, thinking housework and small siblings would help take my mind off things, but all Zia talked about was how much she loved and missed her Cheese.

Which I totally got.

I was relieved when Mrs. Mendel called and asked if I had a couple of hours free to watch Lily and Mei-Ling. Finally, somewhere Chase-free. Until I got there and saw one of Mr. Mendel's movie posters on the wall and remembered the reason I even had this job was because of Chase.

After I returned home, I got a text from him.

> My flight's been delayed. I should tell you I'll see you tomorrow. I'd hate for you to drive out here so late just to turn around and go back.

> No! The thought of not seeing you makes me feel sick.

It was probably more than I should have admitted, but it was true. I needed him. To reassure me and get this Amelia garbage out of my head.

> I'll send a car and then I won't have to worry about you driving home late.

The arrangements were made, and the driver picked me up a little earlier than I'd thought he would. Which was fine, because I could let myself into Chase's house. But when I got there, Chase sent me another text saying the flight had been delayed again. I told him I was at his house and would see him when he arrived.

I hated how quiet it was without his laughter and his presence. I wanted to feel close to him.

So I went upstairs to the last place we'd been together. The place where I'd realized I was in love with him. When I got to his room, I kicked off my shoes and climbed into his bed. His pillows and sheets smelled like his laundry detergent, and the faint scent of his cologne surrounded me. I planned on staying there for just a few minutes because I didn't want to lie in wait like a creepy stalker. But I had underestimated my emotional exhaustion, because next thing I knew, Chase was shaking me awake.

"Hey, Goldilocks."

"Chase!" For a second I thought I had dreamed him up, but the feeling of his strong hand against my shoulder was very real. I sat up and threw my arms around his neck, so relieved he was here. I almost knocked him off the bed.

He laughed and then kissed the side of my neck. "I missed you, too."

I started planting kisses on the side of his face, then moved around to his mouth. He offered me a gentle and easy kiss, and I met it with desperation and intensity. I pulled him down with me, opening my mouth under his, crushing him against me. I needed to know he was mine. Not Amelia's. That I was the only person who mattered to him.

Chase quickly responded, a groan of pleasure sounding in his chest as his hands went around my waist, pressing and kneading. My heart jackhammered against my rib cage as the heat sizzled and snapped between us. That heat made my body languid and pliant, and I sank into the sensation of his expert kisses and touches.

He teased me with his mouth until I was gasping and frantic. It was like he was using his lips to stoke a growing fire, one that threatened to rage out of control. It sent all my senses spinning until he was the only thing that kept me anchored to reality. I wrapped one of my legs around his, as if that would tether me. I wanted more. I was so greedy for him, for all of him. To feel him and kiss him and have the warmth of his skin against me.

Without thinking, I reached down and grabbed the bottom of his T-shirt, intending to pull it off. I moved it up his torso, luxuriating in the feel of each taut ridge and muscle in his back. He lifted up slightly and helped me yank it off, then returned to me. I reveled in the feeling of his smooth skin under my shaky hands as I explored his back, shoulders, and chest. I wondered how it would feel against my own skin. But then, as if suddenly realizing what had happened, he grabbed one of my wrists.

"Zoe," he panted. "Zoe, wait."

I shook my head. I didn't want to wait. I couldn't remember a good reason for it.

But he lifted his head so I couldn't kiss him. "Wait," he repeated. "Not that I don't very much want to keep going, but what are you doing?"

Breathing hard, I tried to coax him back with the hand he wasn't holding, but he was like an immovable stone. I whimpered in frustration. I was throwing myself at him, and he was telling me to wait?

"Have you been crying? Your eyes are all red."

It had been hours since I'd last cried, but he sounded so tender, so concerned, that it made the tears well up again.

"Babe? Talk to me." His touch became soothing and sweet, and he turned onto his back and pulled me against his bare chest, then stroked my hair. And even though my face burned with electric heat from his tantalizing skin, he calmed my erratic pulse and made the tears go away.

I again reminded myself to be smooth and subtle and not jealous, but what I said was, "Are you sleeping with Amelia Swan?"

His hand went still against my hair. "What? Why would you ask that?"

Not a denial. "Because I saw the pictures from London. Where you two were about to kiss."

"That didn't happen." I felt him move and realized he was digging around in his jeans pocket for his cell phone. A minute later he turned the screen toward me. "Are you talking about this?"

It was the right picture. I nodded.

"We were doing an interview at a café during lunch. These photos were taken by the photographer the interviewer brought with her. At this point Amelia had dropped her napkin and was leaning over to pick it up. They just have to catch you at the right moment and angle, and it looks like something it's not."

"But there was an article with it saying you guys had reunited and were going to move in together."

"And who am I with right now? It might be a little awkward if I'm supposedly going to live with Amelia, but here I am with you like this."

"Oh." It was all I could think to say because I felt so stupid.

"We've talked about this. I told you how the tabloids are. It's probably the studio's publicity department trying to manufacture a relationship between me and Amelia to sell more tickets." He put his fingers under my chin and drew my gaze up to his. "I have to say I'm kind of disappointed you thought any of this could be true."

"You didn't have to say it," I grumbled. "You could have just thought it." I already felt bad enough that I had doubted him.

He repositioned himself so we were lying side by side, looking into each other's eyes. "You have nothing to worry about. I would never give you any reason to doubt or distrust me. I would never want to hurt you like that. Because I'm in love with you."

My heart stopped, the air in my lungs turned to ice, and there was a definite ringing sound in my ears. This was not real. This was not happening. I was still asleep and needed to wake up.

"Ow!" he yelped. "Did you just pinch me for saying I love you?"

"No, I thought I was dreaming and meant to pinch myself."

A satisfied grin spread across his perfect face. "This isn't a dream. If it was, there'd be a lot less clothes involved."

But I couldn't play along with his teasing. This was too serious, too important. "You love me?"

"I love you," he repeated, punctuating his declaration with a kiss that made me melt, like chocolate chips in cookies fresh from the oven. "When I was gone, I wanted to call and tell you about everything that happened. I realized you're the most important person in the world to me."

"I love you, too," I told him, but before I'd finished the last syllable, his lips were parting mine. As we kissed, everything felt different because he loved me. There was so much emotion behind his embrace I'd never registered before. He showed me with his sugary, addicting kisses that his words were true.

"Um, I should probably go home," I managed as he showered feathery kisses along my jawline. I didn't want to, but I wasn't sure I could remain strong if I stayed.

"You probably should," he agreed. He kissed me soundly one last time before sitting up. He put his discarded shirt back on and grabbed his phone. "I'll call the car service."

"Or I could stay." The words were out of my mouth before I could tamp them down. "If we can keep it PG."

His back was to me, and his shoulders hunched, like he was tense. I reached over to trace the bit of his spine he'd exposed with his actions.

"Your mom's event is tomorrow, and the movie premiere the night after that. This way we wouldn't have to drive back and forth to everything."

He turned toward me, one eyebrow raised. "Does that mean you're planning on spending the night tomorrow night, too?"

I looked down at his comforter. "I guess I'm feeling a little vulnerable and needy. I just want to be with you."

Chase sighed. "I want that, too. I'm trying to decide if I can handle it. Do you have any idea how many times I've had to leave the room when we're together because I've wanted so badly to rip off all your clothes and have my way with you?"

His words started a pulse throbbing in my stomach, low and hard. "I've wanted that, too."

At that, he let out a groan and covered his face with his hands. "You can't say stuff like that. I'm barely keeping myself in check here."

"I promise I'll behave," I said with a smile.

He dropped his hands in his lap. "It's not you I'm worried about."

With what I was feeling right then, maybe he should have worried about me a little.

"Come on. I'll find you something to wear."

Giddy that I didn't have to go, I followed him into his bathroom and then his walk-in closet, which was probably the size of my entire apartment.

"Here." He handed me a T-shirt and the kind of drawstring pajama bottoms he'd worn last time. "Hopefully this will be easier on my vivid imagination than that nightgown of yours. I'll let you get changed."

He turned around, yanked off his shirt, and threw it into a laundry basket near the door. I watched, fascinated by the play of muscle as he moved, and it took me a second to realize he'd done it just to mess with me. The smirk on his face as he walked out with his own set of pajamas tipped me off.

Knowing I had already tiptoed along the line I'd set for myself, I got changed quickly and waited a few heartbeats, not wanting to walk in on him. Well, I wanted to, but I knew I shouldn't. His shirt was oversize but soft and comfortable. I tightened the drawstring in the pants, tying it so they wouldn't slide off. I caught my reflection in a full-length mirror. Not my best look.

I texted Lexi to let her know I wouldn't be home anytime soon. Her response?

> So, what you're saying is he's faster than a speeding bullet and leaps buildings in a single bound?

I was about to send her a withering text when I heard the sound of pillows hitting the floor. I went into Chase's room. He stopped midthrow and stared at me. He shook his head. "That's not any better."

"Sorry I don't have anything more hideous to wear," I said as I helped him with the pillows. We pulled the blankets back together, like we'd done it a million times before, and the promise in his smile made me hope we'd do it a million times more.

I climbed in, and he hit the lights. As soon as the mattress sank with his weight, I scooted closer so he could hold me. He was so warm. It was like cuddling a cozy fire that wouldn't burn you. "You're like a furnace."

"Are you saying I'm hot?"

Even though it was dark and he couldn't see me, I rolled my eyes. He knew he was hot. "I meant you give off heat like a furnace."

"Given that you have ice blocks for feet, I'd say that makes us a good match."

Last time he'd fallen asleep quickly and easily, but now his breathing remained normal, and his chest felt tight under my hand, as did the arm wrapped around me. "What are you thinking?" I asked.

"I'm running the RBI stats of last year's Padres lineup as a way to distract myself from the lovely, lush, but untouchable softness in my bed right now."

That made me giggle and burrow closer to him, which he didn't seem to appreciate. "Do you do that a lot? Think about sports when you're with me?"

"Hush, woman. You've ruined baseball for me. Now whenever I watch a game, I have illicit thoughts about you."

I giggled again, and this seemed to relieve some of his tension.

"I still can't believe I'm the one who stopped," he murmured, his voice sleepy.

"Neither can I. You must really love me."

"I really must."

This time we didn't try to build a wall between us in the bed. This time I drifted off feeling safe, secure, and totally loved. Happier than I ever remembered feeling.

As if part of me had been missing and I'd finally been made whole.

CHAPTER TWENTY-SEVEN

Zoe
@zomorezoless

Dreamt is the only English word that ends in "mt."
#Trivia

○ ⇄ 0   ♡ 1

Chase woke me around noon by kissing the back of my neck, getting me all hot and bothered before I'd even regained consciousness. "Stop that." I swatted at him, and he laughed and nipped the spot he'd just kissed before he released me and got out of bed. I heard a zipping sound that I guessed was his suitcase.

The mattress tugged to one side when he sat. "I got you a present."

"Last night was the best present ever," I told him, stretching like a sunned and well-rested cat. His eyes roved over me and then snapped up to my face. Getting to be with him all night, having him say he loved me . . . what could be better?

As if he could read my thoughts, he said with a smile, "I promise you someday I'll show you the best present ever." As I flushed, he handed me a wrapped package. "But for now, there's this."

It was a heavy, wrapped rectangle. The words Debauve & Gallais were printed on royal blue-and-gold wrapping paper. I pulled off the paper and found a leather-bound book inside. It was the same royal-blue color with gold embossing around the edges and an elaborate design in the middle. I started to thank him for the book, but when I opened it, I realized it wasn't an actual book. It was a box of expensive-looking chocolates.

"I heard the way to a woman's heart is with chocolate."

Excited, I gobbled up one of the truffles, and it melted in my mouth with a smoothness that American chocolate seemed to lack. "Mmm. This is so rich it should have its own trophy wife."

"You shouldn't make sounds like that. When you do, I want to finish what we started." He kissed me, tasting the chocolate on my lips and mouth, leaving me dizzy. "But we have a lot to do today."

"I've been so focused on school for the past couple of weeks that I honestly forgot about the party and premiere. I don't have anything to wear." I assumed one did not show up to a Hollywood movie premiere in a dress she had bought from Walmart.

"Don't worry about it. One-F is sending over a stylist and people to do hair and makeup. I can just buy whatever dresses you choose."

"I can buy my own dresses," I told him. I ate chocolate between sentences. "Or buy one and wear it to both events."

"You should probably let me pick up the tab on this," he said. "Your picture will be taken, and you'll want to be in the same kind of expensive clothes as everybody else."

I paused, a piece of chocolate hovering in front of my mouth. "Are we going to take pictures together?"

He shrugged one shoulder. "We can if you want, but I'd prefer not to, just because I want you to keep your privacy for as long as possible. And don't fight me on this dress thing. Just let me do it."

"Fine. But you should know I'm financially independent. I make over four figures a year."

Chase grinned. "So what you're saying is, I'll be a kept man."

"I'll keep you for as long as you'll let me."

His blue eyes danced just before he kissed me, and his kiss was better than any French chocolate.

"I have a phone meeting scheduled with my agent in half an hour. I'm going to take a shower, and then we can have lunch and get ready for my mom's fund-raiser. And before you say anything, I know, standard introvert rules apply. You don't have to talk to anyone but me. I just don't want to be there without you."

"Okay. I guess I can go because I love you. I'll even take a shower so I don't stink."

"Awfully considerate of you." He kissed me quickly and then headed into his bathroom. He paused. "Were you planning on taking one now? Or did you want to join me?"

I hoped he couldn't see my cheeks flush from there. "I thought I'd wait until you're done and use yours." I didn't want to get out of his bed and stop eating my delicious chocolates until I absolutely had to.

His hand gripped the door frame. "You should probably use the guest room to shower and change. Because I can't be held responsible for my actions if you wander around my room in nothing but a towel."

Gulping, I nodded and skittered off the bed. I grabbed my clothes from the previous night and went to a different bathroom. Where I refused to let my imagination run wild and instead just focused on what we had to do that day.

And how I could hardly wait for his mom's fund-raiser to be over so I could end up right back here, in his arms.

When we had both showered and dressed, he defrosted a lasagna Sofia had made and entertained me with stories from his press tour. Most of them involved Amelia acting like a moron, and I felt silly that I'd ever thought him capable of cheating with her.

An hour later the stylist and her beauty team showed up with boxes of makeup and hair products, a rack of dresses, and loads of shoes in a variety of sizes and styles. Lexi would freak. No wonder she wanted to work in Hollywood so badly.

I ended up gravitating toward a royal-blue cocktail dress for the party, which reminded me of the box of chocolates Chase had given me, and a red formal-length one for the premiere, which I chose only because of how it made Chase's eyes light up when he saw me in it. It was a little bold for my taste, with a high leg slit and a neckline a tad lower than I'd normally wear, but he'd made me feel beautiful in it. There were no price tags, which concerned me, because I had learned that meant "more than a normal person can afford." But I'd said I wouldn't fight him, so I just smiled and thanked him instead.

Chase got a phone call and excused himself as they started getting me ready. He didn't come back into the room, and I heard him go upstairs to get ready. He came down in a gorgeous, perfectly fitted dark suit. My heart did a tiny flip when I saw he had chosen a metallic royal-blue tie that matched my dress.

But something was off. He seemed frustrated and was uncharacteristically quiet. "What's wrong?"

"That movie? *Spectrum*? It's falling apart. I invested some of my own money in it. It's a mess. But I don't want to think about it. Let's just go and have a good time." He kissed the back of my hand and forced a smile.

When we arrived at the venue, Chase directed the driver to drop me off at a back entrance. His mother would expect him to walk the red carpet and have his picture taken for publicity. "I'd much prefer to sneak in with you, but my mom is miserable when she doesn't get her own way."

While waiting for the security guard to look up my name, I heard someone call out, "Zoe!" I turned to see One-F walking toward me. It was funny. I hadn't seen him in person since I'd dropped a bowling ball on his foot, but given how often we'd corresponded via e-mail, I felt like I'd just talked to him.

"One-F! How's the foot?"

He held it out in front of him. "Much better. How's the boyfriend?"

"Amazing." It was such a relief to be able to talk to someone who knew Chase and I were together.

It's your fault that nobody else does, that voice whispered. I knew that. Which was why I had already planned to sit Lexi down tomorrow and confess.

One-F presented his arm. "Will you allow me to escort you inside? My boss would not be happy if I let anything happen to his favorite person."

His favorite person. I let those words light me up like the massive Christmas tree in Marabella's main square.

The guard found both of our names, and I slipped my arm through One-F's. "I'm glad your foot is better. Sorry about that again, by the way."

"You know, I think it might have been worth sacrificing a foot to see Chase so happy."

The benefit was being held at a club on the beach that was constructed almost entirely out of glass. I could see Chase on the red carpet, smiling and waving, turning and posing. I couldn't believe someone so wonderful and beautiful could actually be mine. I noticed his publicist behind him, urging him on every few feet. The one Lexi had flirted with to meet Chase. What was his name? Oh. Right. Aaron.

"Can the people outside see us?" I asked.

"No, it's reflective glass. We can see out, but nobody can see in."

Which meant Chase and I didn't have to pretend we weren't together once he came in.

One-F offered to grab us something to eat and drink, and I told him I was fine. He said he'd be back, leaving me to watch Chase. He was so good at what he did. Every reporter he talked to wore a huge smile after he finished speaking to them.

Chase finally made it inside, and I saw his face flatten into a look of exhaustion for a second before we made eye contact. Then the sparkle was back in his eye. "Good. You're still here. I was worried you'd meet somebody else and run off with him."

"There's nobody here who compares to you."

"Not even James Cruz?"

I blinked. "Who?"

That made him grin, pull me toward him, and kiss me so thoroughly that I forgot we were in a room full of people. He finally stopped, remembering himself, but he kept his arm around my waist, holding me close.

Many people came up to say hello to us. Well, to Chase. People looked at me curiously, but Chase didn't introduce me, and I didn't offer any explanation. It was nobody else's business.

"Mom! I want you to meet my girlfriend, Zoe."

Chase's mother had to be in her early sixties, but she looked twenty years younger. She wore a champagne-colored dress and a delicate floral scent. She had the same bright blonde hair as Chase, the same blue eyes.

"It's a pleasure to meet you!" I held out my hand, and she took it gingerly. She nodded to me but focused all her attention on her son.

"I wanted to let you know that Richard and I are getting divorced. It's going to be announced in a press release tomorrow. My publicist has hopes of getting some morning talk shows as well."

"Did you cheat on him?" Chase's words were measured, angry.

"It's nothing to concern yourself with." She kissed Chase's cheek, leaving a lip print behind. "I shouldn't neglect my guests."

She walked away, and I reached up to rub off her lipstick. His jaw was tight, and the veins in his neck were popping. I'd never seen him mad like this before.

"She uses my fame to get those talk shows. She thinks if she gives me a heads-up that everything is fine, and it doesn't matter that she uses my name to get herself on television. That she exploits every divorce as a way to grab more publicity. She acts like we have the best relationship in the world when she barely even speaks to me. Unless she wants something."

I hugged him, not sure what to say or do. A second later I felt his arms circle around me.

"My mother makes me want to drink."

"But you won't."

"I won't," he agreed in a gruff voice. "But I really want to."

A glass broke behind him, and I peered over his shoulder to see a waiter trying to pick up the large shards. Chase released me, and I turned around. My stomach sank, and sweat broke out along my hairline when I saw who was standing in front of us.

It was Stephanie. Hair done, makeup on, wearing a sophisticated little black dress.

Please don't let her say anything stupid, I begged. *Please.*

But apparently no one heard my plea.

Hoping I could get her away from Chase and explain the situation to her, I said, "Stephanie! I didn't know you'd be here. Have you tried the dessert bar yet? It's supposed to be amazing."

She ignored the last part. "The SSLF was kind enough to invite several heads of ocean-related charities to the event. It's been an excellent way to network."

When she said that, I knew I was done for.

"Mr. Covington? I'm so glad to meet you. I'm Stephanie Barber. I'm Zoe's boss." She offered him her hand, and not realizing what was about to happen, he shook it enthusiastically. I felt like an extra in a zombie movie. Where the zombie was slowly shuffling toward me, but instead of running away, I just stood there in dread, waiting for my life to be over. "I heard about your relationship with our Zoe, and I'm so hopeful you'll be able to attend the Ocean Life Foundation fund-raiser next month. I'm sure she's told you all about it."

My mouth dropped, and my insides constricted. Heard about our relationship? How? No one knew.

And I most definitely had not told him anything about the fund-raiser.

"Zoe?" Chase asked, looking confused.

"Chase, it's not—"

Stephanie interrupted me before I could explain. "We're having a bit of a competition at our organization to see which intern can land the biggest celebrity. And I think Zoe might win that, don't you?" She had a laugh that reminded me of a hyena mixed with a donkey, but all I could think about was how she was destroying everything, given the way Chase's face had fallen. "I mean, who's a bigger star than you? I told Zoe we could assure her a place at the Foundation after graduation if she could help us nab a big name. And here you two are."

"It's not like that," I tried to tell him. She'd made it sound like I'd been scheming and plotting and using him.

Stephanie handed him her business card and said, "I'll have Zoe give you all the details, but please don't hesitate to call me anytime if you have any questions."

As if she didn't care about the nuclear bomb she'd just lobbed into my life, she walked away blissfully unaware, stalking her next victim.

"Is it true?" Chase asked, his face cold and impassive.

"No! I mean, yes, the things she said were true, but that is not why I—"

"Chase, you need to see what just popped up in my alerts." Aaron approached with his phone out and showed it to Chase. Aaron shot me a dirty look, which bewildered me. What had I ever done to him? "I thought One-F had her sign an NDA. I warned you about dating someone we hadn't thoroughly vetted."

What now?

Before I could ask what was going on, Chase turned the phone toward me. "Care to explain?"

CHAPTER TWENTY-EIGHT

HOMEWRECKING WHORE DESTROYS CHAMELIA!

ENZ can exclusively report that Chase Covington, 25, has been carrying on an affair with college student Zoe Miller from Marabella, California. The 22-year-old vixen has been seen coming and going at all hours from Covington's Hollywood Hills home. A source states, "Obviously Amelia's beside herself. Totally devastated and inconsolable. She doesn't know how Chase could have done this to her." Recently leaked photos show Covington and Miller at Disneyland and in other private moments.

My hands shook as I stopped reading the article and scrolled down. And there were the photos Braden had taken on Chase's phone. Along with the pictures Chase had texted me, like the one of him in his hotel bed, the one of his arm.

There was even a picture of my driver's license, with my personal information blacked out.

"I don't know how this happened. I didn't share these with anyone."

The expression on Chase's face filled my stomach with shards of ice. He plucked the cell phone out of my hand and gave it back to Aaron. Then Chase took me by the elbow and steered me away from the ballroom. He found a small conference room with the door unlocked. `

Once he shut the door, he released my arm, like he couldn't bear to touch me. "How could you do this?"

"I didn't do this. I swear to you." My knees felt weak, my pulse frantic and irregular. It was one thing to have my privacy completely invaded but quite another to have Chase accuse me of being responsible for it.

A muscle ticked in his jaw. "The only two people in the entire world who have these pictures are you and me. And I know I didn't sell these to ENZ."

"I didn't, either."

"They have your driver's license! How did that happen?" he yelled, his voice echoing off the walls around us.

"Just because I can't explain it doesn't make me responsible for it. I don't know. Maybe I was hacked? Maybe you were?" I felt desperate. I wanted to erase the rage from his eyes and have my Chase back. I tried to take his hand, but he stepped backward, out of arm's reach.

That hurt me more than anything he'd said.

"Were you trying to get your fifteen minutes of fame? Did you think you'd make yourself infamous and that would bring people to your fund-raiser and get you a job? Was this all just some scheme? Is that why you wouldn't let me touch you?" Every word felt like a staccato punch to my stomach. Before I could respond, he raked his fingers through his hair and continued. "I am so stupid. I've been so concerned about your privacy and protecting you, and you couldn't care less about mine. You are just like everyone else. You used me."

My fear and hurt had started to warp into anger. "That's not true! I've done nothing but protect you from the moment we met! No one in my life knows about you. Meanwhile, everybody in your life seems to know about me. How do you know it wasn't Aaron or One-F?"

"Because I trust them." His eyes were so cold and dark, it was like he was a different person.

And there it was. I could actually feel my heart shattering into tiny little slivers, so small they would never be put back together "You told me over and over again to trust you. And I have. I've done nothing but trust you, even when I've been afraid to. Even when I thought you might be cheating on me, I chose to take your word. But the one time I need you to put everything aside and trust me, you're not capable of it?"

He crossed his arms and said nothing.

"I'm the stupid one. I won't be with someone who doesn't trust me. I don't lie to you. You're always telling me what a terrible liar I am. Look at me. Am I lying to you? I've never given you a single reason not to trust me."

His jaw clenched tightly before he spoke. "You've done nothing but lie to your friends and family about me from day one."

I felt that devastating barb go straight to my gut. He was right. I had been lying. But never to him.

As I stood there looking at him, I realized there was nothing I could say. He'd made up his mind, decided me unworthy of his trust, and there was no longer a future between us.

It was over.

And I was over being accused of something I didn't do.

"You couldn't possibly love me if you think me capable of this." I put my hand on the doorknob, knowing I was about to walk out of his life and never see him again. "You said once that you'd permanently maim anyone who tried to hurt me. But I can't imagine anybody in the world hurting me more than you just did."

Tears blinded my eyes as I went out into the ballroom. I thought I heard him call my name, but I didn't look back. I felt the stares and whispers of everyone around me. The story had obviously spread. I took the only exit I saw, the one leading to the front. It wasn't until I was halfway down the red carpet that I realized what a mistake I'd made. I should have gone out the back entrance.

The paparazzi and entertainment reporters lining the carpet had obviously seen the same article and photos. They started screaming my name, asking me about my relationship with Chase, if I felt any guilt over hurting Amelia. Some even called me names to get my attention. I held my hands in front of my face and risked only a single glance at them. There, in the middle of the crowd, was the man from the gas station. The one wearing the red, white, and blue denim jacket. He had a knowing smirk on his face. Was he involved in this somehow? I had to get out of there. And away from all this. I hurried to the valet station. "I need an Uber or a taxi, please."

"Right away, miss."

Chase would probably think I'd chosen this exit on purpose. That I wanted my picture taken. Sadly, I realized it no longer mattered what Chase thought.

Then I had to just stand there, with raw and primitive grief choking me, tears pouring down my face, my arms wrapped around myself, ducking my head so they couldn't see me. The paparazzi kept screaming questions and insults, but I ignored them.

Finally, a car arrived, and the valets helped me get in. They blocked the photographers as best they could. As we drove off, I thought about that morning. How it had been the happiest I'd ever felt. My life had been perfect.

And now it lay in smoking ruins all around me.

I had lost the man I loved.

When I got back to my apartment, having cried myself out, I had to pay the driver a week's worth of babysitting money. The worst part?

There were a handful of paparazzi already standing around in front of my stairs. How had they found me so fast?

"Do you need help getting inside?" the Uber driver asked when he caught sight of my face in his rearview mirror.

"I'll be okay. Thanks." It hurt to speak. My throat felt shredded, worn out.

I rushed past the cameras, refusing to look at them or answer their questions. This was life when you dated a movie star. We had been living in this little cocoon of bliss and safety where nobody else in the world mattered. This being hounded and harassed, this was the price of dating him.

They took pictures of me struggling with my keys, trying to get inside. Their shouted questions made me so anxious. I finally managed to open the lock, and I collapsed against the door once I'd shut it. I heard my neighbors across the landing threatening to call the cops on the paparazzi because they were studying for finals. I'd have to bring Jill and Teena some cookies as a thank-you.

Baking cookies immediately made me think of Chase, and the tears I thought I'd used up sprang back to life.

In the bedroom Lexi sat on her bed with resting murder face. Every poster of Chase in our room had been torn down. Her pillowcase had been removed.

She had seen the article.

My shoulders drooped. "Lexi, please. Let me explain. This has all been really painful."

"Oh, I'm sorry. Did my back hurt your knife?"

I sat on my bed, letting my purse fall to the floor. Lexi eyed my expensive dress, my shoes. "Did he buy those for you? Is he your sugar daddy or something?"

I gasped. "I can't believe you just said that to me." She knew me better than that.

"You're offended?" she hissed. "Just think about the stuff I'm holding back! You've been dating Chase Covington for months. You've been lying to me for months. Which part of that is okay? Which part of that do you think you can explain?"

I put a hand over my queasy stomach. "Technically I didn't lie. You just assumed I was dating Noah, and I let—" Even as I said it, I knew it was no excuse.

"Technically? Seriously? You think I'm going to stop being mad because of a technicality?" She stood up and started pacing, something she did only when she was really upset. "We've been fans of Chase our whole lives. And you were dating him. How could you not tell me?"

"I wanted to protect what we had. His privacy is really important to him."

"So you were doing this all for Chase. Awesome. That makes you a martyr." She flung her arms wide. "I hear churches keep a special spot in heaven for people just like you."

"You're right. I'm sorry. I'm so sorry I lied to you. I shouldn't have. I was just afraid you would take him from me. That he would like you better than me. And I . . . I love him, Lexi. I didn't want to lose him."

Now that I had told her the most important reason, I hoped she would forgive me. Hoped I could tell her everything that had happened. I needed my friend.

"I can't do this with you. I'm going to stay at Gavin's." She grabbed a bag that she'd already packed.

Tears burned at the corners of my eyes. "Lexi, wait. Please don't go. Let's talk about this. You're my best friend."

That made her pause in the doorway. "I hope he was worth our friendship, Zoe. I hope the two of you are really happy together."

"We broke up," I told her in a strangled voice.

She blinked a few times before responding. "Then it sounds like you got exactly what you deserved."

When the front door slammed shut, my tears started all over again. It was painful to cry; my throat was already sore, my eyes burned, and my chest ached. In one day I'd managed to lose my boyfriend and my best friend.

I wanted my mom.

Once the tears subsided, I took a shower, washed my face, brushed my teeth, and changed my clothes. I looked at the expensive designer dress lying in a puddle on the floor in my room. I wondered if I should return it to Chase.

Deciding he could eat the cost as a jerk tax, I kicked it into my closet. I checked outside my bedroom window and saw the same paparazzi smoking and talking to each other as they waited in the parking lot.

I wasn't going to let people like that make decisions for me. I wasn't going to allow them to turn me into a cowering hermit. I grabbed a pair of sunglasses and held my head high as I ignored them again. They got in their cars to chase after me, but I didn't know what they were hoping for.

Once they realized that I wasn't driving toward the Hollywood Hills, they gave up. They probably wanted an updated photo of Chase and me together. Too bad none of them would be getting that.

I arrived at my mother's house. I had half expected to see more paparazzi on the street or in her driveway, but the neighborhood was quiet, as always.

As I opened the front door, I called out for my mom. She didn't answer. I wondered if she'd seen the article. If she would be angry with me, too. I didn't know if I could bear it.

"Mom!" I was panicked as I called for her again. It was almost the little ones' bedtime, but they might not be home. Maybe they'd gone out to eat.

She walked out of her bedroom, still in her scrubs, Zia trailing behind her. "I'm here. What's going on?"

My mother didn't know. She didn't hate me like the rest of the world.

I began to sob, and she opened her arms and hugged me tight. "Oh, baby, what is it? What's wrong?"

I nearly choked when I tried to speak. "Everything."

CHAPTER TWENTY-NINE

My mom took me into the living room and sat on the couch. When I collapsed next to her, she put my head in her lap and stroked my hair, the way she had when I was younger. I poured my heart out, telling her everything that had happened, including how Chase and I had met online and the events of earlier today. How he had accused me of leaking photos. How betrayed Lexi felt.

She just listened quietly, not saying anything. Zia stood next to me and kept patting my cheek with her pudgy hand. "Poor Zo-Zo. My poor Zo-Zo." She even gave me a couple of kisses, something she did not bestow lightly.

When I ran out of words and tears, my mom finally spoke. "I'm so sorry you're going through this. I wish I could take the pain from you."

I had seen this pain before in other people. I'd watched as my grandpa faded away without my grandma. I'd walked in on my mother sobbing over Duncan more than once. I didn't know a worse pain than heartbreak. And I'd suffered loss before. I should have been used to it by now. But somehow this deep, sharp pain in my heart felt unbearable.

Grief and loss were the cost of love, and I didn't want to pay it.

But the bill had come due, and I didn't have a choice.

"I hope you know you could have come to me sooner. You could have told me about Chase." Although she sounded calm and loving, I detected a note of pain in her voice. Another person I'd hurt with my selfishness.

"I'm sorry. I know. I was just afraid."

My mom's hand stilled on my hair. "Afraid of what?"

"I know how much you wanted to be famous. And I guess I thought . . ."

"What? That seeing Chase Covington in real life would make me run off and leave you guys behind so I could try to be famous?" It sounded stupid when she said it out loud. "I'm not a rebellious teenager anymore, Zoe. I'm a grown woman with grown-woman responsibilities. If I had to do it all over again, of course I wouldn't leave you behind. But I can't undo what's done. And to be honest, you were better off with your grandparents. I never could have taken care of you the way you deserved. I was still a kid myself. But I love you. I have loved you from the very first moment I laid eyes on you. I'll never leave you again."

That made the tears start up again. I knew my mom loved me, but we'd never really talked about her leaving me with my grandparents. It healed my heart a little to know that she'd take it back if she could.

At some point my siblings had all filed in to the living room and quietly listened to us. The older ones smelled of sunshine and grass, as if they'd been playing outside in the backyard.

Zia crouched down so we were eye level. "Cheese makes Zo-Zo sad?"

"Yeah, Chase made me sad."

Her eyes narrowed. "Then I hits Cheese."

"We don't hit people, Zia," my mom reminded her for the millionth time, but Zia wasn't having it.

She nodded and whispered dramatically, "I hits him."

"Captain Sparta sucks," Zane contributed from behind his Spider-Man mask. Zelda nodded. Zander didn't say anything, but given the lack of sound from his tablet, it seemed that he had paused his game, which was the equivalent of him agreeing.

"Today he kind of does," I agreed.

"He forgot to be a hero."

Yep. He'd put the damsel in distress instead of trying to rescue her.

At that, my mom told everyone to get ready for bed. There was a lot of whining and complaining, but eventually they left.

"The Lexi situation is easy. She will come around. This isn't the first big blowout fight the two of you have had, and I'm sure it won't be the last."

"This felt different." My mom hadn't been there. She didn't know.

"It isn't any different. It feels that way because for the first time you're in love and you've had your heart broken. It's coloring your perspective. I give her forty-eight hours before she's apologizing. But with Chase . . . I don't know what to say. I think I'm supposed to give you some cliché about fish in the sea or time healing. But I know from personal experience that none of that helps."

"You could always go with when one door closes, a window opens."

"That's not usually helpful, either. Because sometimes when a door closes, you should get some big boards and nail it shut. And sometimes you should open that door back up because people deserve second chances. You don't think Duncan and I fought? That sometimes we accused each other of things that weren't true? We did. But I loved him and our relationship more than my own pride. Something to think about."

I did think about it. A lot. I spent the entire weekend in Marabella with my phone turned off. I wanted to forget about my real life and just be with my family.

Feel like myself again.

Early Monday morning I had to go to school. I got up in enough time to beat the traffic, but my mom was already in the kitchen, packing school lunches.

"There are some reporters on the front lawn," she offered.

"What?" I went into the living room and peeked through the blinds. Sure enough, there were three guys standing outside, waiting for me. "That's probably going to happen for a while," I said apologetically.

"The only exciting thing they'll see around here is Zia's rear end when she takes off her diaper to run in the sprinklers. Don't worry about us. We won't say a word. School's almost done. Take your finals. Look for a job. Get all your ducks in a row."

I didn't know if I could get my ducks in a row, but I could probably manage to herd them into the same pond. Because I didn't want to blow it, either. I was so close to graduating that this was not the time to drop the ball. I gave my two-week notice to Mrs. Mendel via e-mail, because I didn't want to work a job that Chase had found for me. I had some savings and just had to hope it'd be enough for living expenses until I found a full-time salaried job.

I went back to my apartment, not knowing if Lexi would be there. She wasn't, and I didn't see a note or any sign that she'd been there since she'd stormed out.

I wondered whether my mom was right about Lexi.

Turned out she wasn't. Lexi didn't come around in forty-eight hours.

It took seventy-two.

My day felt so dark and awful that it should have come with Swedish subtitles. I was getting ready to go to class when I heard Lexi's key in the front door. I stood, stomach roiling, not knowing what would happen when I saw her.

What happened was she threw herself in my arms and hugged me tightly, begging for my forgiveness. "I am the worst friend ever. I never should have said those things to you. Can you ever forgive me?"

"No, I'm the worst. I shouldn't have lied to you. I should have told you about Chase!"

We cried and talked over each other and apologized and then finally sat at the kitchen table to work things out.

"Why didn't you tell me?"

I'd done nothing for the past three days but think about why I had lied to the people I loved. "I had all these reasons why I couldn't tell you. But they weren't reasons. They were excuses. Rationalizations. I think part of me couldn't believe someone like Chase could really love me. I was just always waiting for the other shoe to drop." My chest constricted, and I could feel tears coming on. "Because deep down I knew I wasn't worthy of him, and telling other people about it would have reminded me of all my shortcomings and flaws. I knew we wouldn't last. I just didn't want everybody to remind me of how hopeless it all was."

Lexi got up to hug me. "You stop that right now. You are absolutely worthy of him. If anything, he doesn't deserve you. But I wish you'd told me. I wish you'd let me help you."

"You know how hard it is for me to trust people. Even you."

She nodded. Her arms were wrapped around me, and I felt guilty for not being more confident in our friendship. For letting my insecurities and doubt rule my life.

"And you trusted him."

I could only nod, knowing if I spoke right then, I would cry. Her arms tightened around me like she understood. We stayed that way until my shoulders relaxed, and she finally let go and sat down in her chair.

"Now that I've had a chance to mull it over, I'm not mad that you dated Chase."

That surprised me. "You're not?"

"Maybe a teensy bit jealous. But if he wasn't interested in me, don't you think the best thing in the world was him dating my best friend?

Don't you know I want only amazing things for you? I'm not upset about him. I was upset you lied. It's so unlike you."

"Some part of me was also afraid he would love you instead of me." I didn't need to remind her about all my high school crushes who had liked her more. "I convinced myself that at first what was happening between me and him was nothing and wasn't even worth talking about."

"And now?"

"And now . . . he became everything to me." And he was out of my life for good.

Lexi gave me a sad smile. "I totally overreacted. And I was melo-dramatic. But that's kind of my brand," she said with a teasing shrug.

"It's why everybody loves you."

She suddenly burst into tears, and I reached across the table to put my hand on top of hers. "What did I say? What's wrong?"

"Not everybody loves me. Gavin broke up with me."

What? "Why?"

"He thinks I'm in love with Chase, and that's why I was mad at you. I kept trying to explain it to him, but he's so stubborn. It's like he decided this was reality, and there was nothing I could say to make him see things differently."

Boy, did I know how that felt.

"But it's okay. There are lots of other guys to date. Maybe we should go out and find some." She smiled and said the things she always said after a breakup. But she wasn't okay. Gavin was special. She loved him.

"Maybe. We can talk about it later. I've got to get to my women's studies class. It's our last one. We're having a discussion on the true meaning of feminism."

Lexi wished me luck. I ignored the reporters waiting downstairs for me, who followed me all the way to campus. Fortunately, security stopped them from coming onto school grounds, but they couldn't stop them from yelling and snapping pictures and making everybody in the area stare at me.

I felt like an animal in a zoo.

When I got to my women's studies class, I avoided eye contact with every other student in the discussion circle. I was so tired of being scrutinized and not being able to go through my breakup in private.

Professor Gonzales came in and took her seat. "So, let's get into it. What is the true meaning of feminism?"

"Equality."

"What kind of equality?" the professor asked.

"All kinds. Social, economic, political, religious."

"It should mean we stop telling girls to not be too smart or too ambitious because men won't like them," someone to my left offered.

"It means we fight for our causes and our rights."

Then the sweater-set sorority girl said, "I'm sorry, but are we really not going to talk about what happened to Zoe?"

My head snapped up. "That's none of your business."

"The fact that the media is portraying you as a whore and a home-wrecker when you told us you're celibate? It's untrue and reiterates the whole virgin–whore paradigm."

At some point I had to run out of tears, right? "I don't want to be recorded and have anything I say end up online."

"Not a problem." She stood up and grabbed her bag. "Everybody give me your cell phones. And if you can't keep your mouth shut, leave now." She looked specifically at me. "And by the way, my name is Tiffany." No one left, and they all turned over their cell phones.

They asked me questions that didn't venture into anything too personal, just the true facts of the situation I had experienced. And that led to a discussion of how I was being vilified in the media even though I'd done nothing wrong. How Amelia Swan had gained sympathy and popularity on the back of another woman—me.

Every comment made after that was complimentary and supportive. They were all on my side, even the guys, and it made me feel understood and heard in a way that healed another piece of my heart.

"This is feminism," I told my professor. "A sisterhood of women who stand up for one another, support one another, and know that they're stronger together."

Professor Gonzales smiled and nodded. She announced that class was over, and Tiffany redistributed our phones. I realized that although I'd carried it with me and charged it, I hadn't yet turned it on. I was almost afraid to.

"If you need to talk to someone, you can call me," Tiffany said as we went into the hall. She handed me a piece of notebook paper with her phone number. I felt bad that I had dismissed her and judged her when she was obviously a kind person.

"Thanks."

That class discussion had made me think of Lexi and how my breakup with Chase was more bearable because now I knew she was there for me.

She needed her own happy ending, and as her "sister," it was my job to help her get it. I had my girl's back.

Gavin's apartment was north of campus. When they'd first started dating, Lexi wanted to set me up with one of his roommates. She'd taken me to his place, but we were not interested in each other. I banged on the front door. If Gavin wasn't home, I would wait until he got back.

I hoped somebody answered before the paparazzi found me.

The door opened, and I'd obviously woken up one of the roommates. I couldn't remember his name. "Is Gavin here?"

He didn't say anything. I heard muffled voices before Gavin came into the living room. "What do you want, Zoe?"

"I want to tell you you're an idiot."

"Thanks for that. Bye." He moved to close the door.

I stuck my foot in the frame. He wasn't going to get rid of me that easily. "Lexi is not in love with Chase. He was a childhood crush. She met him. Twice. And she didn't go after him. In fact, after she met him, she pretty much stopped talking about him other than to make you jealous. If you haven't noticed, Lexi can be insecure and needs constant reassurance. You are the only guy I've ever seen her serious about. I think she might even love you. She was mad because I lied to her. And she had every right to be mad. I shouldn't have done it."

"Did she tell you to come and plead her case?"

I resisted the urge to shove him in his stupid chest. "Of course not. You know she wouldn't. She'll just move on and pretend like she's over you, even if she's not. You're perfect together. Don't be a moron and screw up the best thing that's ever happened to you."

I yanked my foot clear of the door and almost lost my shoe. I shoved my foot back into it and started walking along the sidewalk away from his apartment.

"Hey, Zoe!"

I stopped and turned around to see what Gavin wanted.

"Maybe you should think about taking your own advice."

CHAPTER THIRTY

Obviously I did some good, because later that evening as Lexi and I watched a Hallmark movie, somebody tried to break down our front door, making us both shriek.

"I have a gun!" Lexi called out as she grabbed her phone, ready to call 911.

"You do not."

"Gavin?"

The chain was on, but the rest of it was unlocked, so he'd managed to open the door a couple of inches. "This was a lot less dramatic than I had intended."

Lexi stood in his sight line, her arms crossed. Her face was defiant, but I could see her trembling. She wanted to hope but was scared to.

"Lexi, I love you." I watched as her posture changed at hearing those four words. "I never should have accused you of having feelings for Chase Covington. I was so afraid of losing you that I broke it off, thinking it would hurt less if I ended it before you could leave me. It didn't. I screwed up. Open the door, sweetheart. Let me make this right."

She walked over to the door, gazed into his eyes, and then gently closed it on him.

Two heartbeats later she reached up and undid the chain lock to let him in. He grabbed her in his arms and lifted her against him. If my heart had to be broken, I was so glad my best friend's would be mended. But it made me ache to see how much they loved each other, and I missed Chase all over again.

I went into our room and closed the door to give them some privacy for their reconciliation. I took my phone off my desk and looked at it. I had left it off because I was both afraid Chase would call and afraid he wouldn't.

Holding my breath, I turned my phone on. The pings started almost immediately. Out of habit, I went into my Twitter app first. Nothing from Chase, but I had more than ten thousand notifications from people who had tweeted at me. I started scrolling through them, feeling sick. Some people hated Amelia the way Lexi did and declared themselves #TeamZoe or #TeamZase.

But then there were the people who believed the article. Who thought I was a home-wrecking gold digger. They said . . . not nice things. Including the ever-popular death threat. I knew I should put my phone down, stop reading. But it was like a car wreck I couldn't look away from.

Finally, I forced myself to get off Twitter. I had a bunch of e-mails to go through and thirteen missed calls. One from my mom, one from Stephanie, and the other eleven from Chase. There were voice mails, but I couldn't bring myself to listen to them. Hearing his voice . . . it would be too painful. Just seeing that he'd called made my hands shake.

I needed to focus on something else. I wondered what Stephanie wanted. I was planning on leaving in an hour to go into work. Couldn't she just tell me then? It seemed odd.

Thinking of her reminded me of what had happened with Chase, and I tried to block my thoughts of his accusations and his cold expression, as well as the nauseating feeling they created in the pit of my stomach. I thought of what Stephanie had said. How she knew Chase and

I were in a relationship, something she couldn't possibly have known. I'd been so caught up in my heartache that I hadn't stopped to consider how she got her information.

Then I remembered finding my laptop open after that design meeting when I was pretty sure I had closed it.

Lexi burst in the room and rushed over to hug me. "Gavin told me what you did. Thank you. You are the best friend in the whole world. If there's ever anything I can do to repay you, you let me know."

"There may be something Gavin can do."

I brought my phone and laptop out to Gavin. "Can you tell if these were hacked? Or if somebody stole pictures from them?"

"Yeah," he said, seating himself at the kitchen table. "What's your password?"

"I don't have a password."

He glanced up at me, his eyes full of disbelief. "You don't have a password? On either one?"

"Why would I?"

"Oh, I don't know," he muttered. "Maybe so somebody wouldn't swipe pictures of your movie-star boyfriend and post them online."

He was having an emotional day, so I decided to give him a pass.

"Did you open the pictures on your laptop?" he asked.

"I transferred them to my laptop after I got them, but that was it."

He nodded and went to work. After about twenty minutes, he leaned back in his chair and sighed. "Okay. So you weren't hacked. I can't find any trace of software or viruses or worms or anything else on your phone or laptop that indicates this was done remotely. But when I went into your Event Viewer on your laptop and checked the logs, I can see that these files were accessed by somebody who didn't know enough about computers to cover their tracks. This was really easy to find."

Gavin turned the laptop toward me and showed me the pictures that had been accessed. He told me the date and time.

And my theory had been right. It had been during the design meeting. I didn't know whether to be angry or sick.

I grabbed my phone and purse.

"Where are you going?" Lexi asked.

"The Foundation. I'm going to find out what happened."

"I'm putting a password on your laptop!" Gavin yelled behind me as I closed the door. I stormed down the stairs, not caring if the paparazzi took pictures that showed me angry and upset. Because I was seriously pissed off. In an it-took-me-far-less-time-to-drive-to-the-Foundation-than-it-should-have sort of way.

I entered the building and headed straight for Stephanie's office. She was responsible for this. Either she had done it herself or she'd put somebody up to it.

Before I could start screaming at her, she had the audacity to look up from her computer and smile at me. "Zoe. I'm glad you're here. I wanted to talk to you about Chase Covington. Please take a seat."

I was so surprised she had brought it up directly that when she indicated I should sit in one of her chairs, I did. Stephanie closed the door and settled back behind her desk.

"I'm concerned because it seems you've had a bit of a falling-out with Mr. Covington. I hope you were able to patch things up, and this won't affect him coming to our benefit."

Was she serious? "How did you know we were dating? I didn't tell anyone."

"Noah figured it out."

Noah? How could that have possibly happened? We hadn't even spoken since our failed dating attempt. "How?"

"He saw a picture of you on *The Helen Show*. The one from Disneyland? He couldn't see your face, but you had your keys out, and he recognized the fish key ring I'd given you. You're the only person in the office who's the right age and height, so we made an educated guess. I called my cousin Jerry. He works at ENZ. He said he would help prove it was you."

The paparazzo I'd seen in the crowd. The same guy from the gas station. "Does Jerry have a red, white, and blue denim jacket?"

She pursed her lips, puzzlement shadowing her features. "I don't know. But he found proof that you've been holding out on us, even though I told you over and over again how important this year's fundraiser is. Jerry discovered you'd been going into Chase's neighborhood. A guard told him."

I knew I shouldn't have handed my license over to that security guard. This Jerry had probably bribed him for it. Had Jerry been following me? Was he the one who had set off Chase's perimeter alarm? Had he seen my car?

But Jerry wasn't the one who'd found the Disneyland pictures. "And the photos from my computer? Who did that? Was it you? You sent me to that meeting, making sure I was away from my laptop."

Her eyes narrowed for a moment, like she was deciding whether to tell me something. Finally, she admitted, "Noah forwarded them to me."

A lump formed in my throat. We weren't friends any longer, but I had never imagined Noah would stoop to something so low. "Noah stole pictures from my laptop? Why would he do that? To make sure he was the one who got the full-time job instead of me?"

"I wouldn't consider it stealing," she snapped back, her eyes narrowing. "It was on the Foundation's property, and he used a resource to help our cause. Do you know that over a million seabirds and a hundred thousand sea mammals are killed by pollution every year? It was so selfish of you to not talk to Mr. Covington about our event. We desperately need people like him supporting us."

"Are you serious right now?" I had been raised to be respectful, especially to authority figures, but I couldn't believe what was happening. "I was selfish? Noah posted pictures of me all over the Internet and made my life a living hell, and you knew about it! And I'm selfish? You are unbelievable!"

"I'm committed. There's a difference. And I didn't know Noah was going to post the photos. I only knew that you had a serious connection you were withholding from us."

Anger coiled inside my gut, roaring to be set loose. She should be committed. "And yet you didn't say a single word to me about what he did. You thought it was worth sacrificing my relationship and my privacy for?"

She folded her hands primly on her desk. "I would sacrifice even more if it meant saving the life of one sea creature."

That set the anger free. It coursed through my entire body until I was so full of rage I could barely see straight. My grandma would roll over in her grave if she knew the kind of words I wanted to use. I stood up. "You are a truly terrible person. I know you've made yourself believe you're the hero in this scenario, but you are the villain. You condoned stealing, you used me, you hurt people. You're supposed to do good here." I threw my security badge on her desk. "I won't work for someone as manipulative and horrible as you. And when I get the chance to tell the entire world about what you've both done, I'll do it. We'll see how long you and Noah keep your jobs after that."

For the first time, she looked scared, but I was too angry to even enjoy it. Especially since I didn't actually have a way to tell the whole world about her.

One last barb. I leaned across her desk and put my face close to hers. "And just so you know, fish are *delicious*."

That had her gasping and sputtering angrily. I slammed her office door on my way out. Everybody in the office had clearly heard every word; they just stood there, frozen, staring at me. I saw Noah with his stupid bow tie and his stupid suspenders. "You're pathetic," I spat at him. "You truly deserve every bad thing coming your way."

I briefly thought about slashing his tires or throwing something at his head, but given that he hadn't even had the decency to look guilty, I knew it wouldn't do me any good. Besides, I should behave better than that, even if I didn't want to.

I had to get home. I needed to be in my bed, eating ice cream and watching my favorite shows. I figured muscle memory led me back to my apartment, because I couldn't remember the drive. I had been so hurt and so angry.

I didn't see the paparazzi in my parking lot. It would be the first time in a few days that I'd be able to walk into my building without being inundated with flashes and questions. I took my keys out of the ignition, and the sunlight bounced off that stupid, sparkly fish. The fish that had ruined my life. I rolled down my window, intending to throw the fish key ring into the parking lot. I tried to tear if off, but it wouldn't budge, and my fingers trembled too much to slide it off correctly. I settled for crying in my car, resting my forehead against the steering wheel.

"Zoe?"

My heart pounded so hard I thought I might faint.

Chase was leaning into my window wearing sunglasses that covered half his face. I couldn't see his eyes. "Are you okay?"

"Am I okay? Am I okay? I'm obviously not okay." *I'm in the middle of having a nervous breakdown, thanks so much.* I opened my car door, and he had to move out of the way. I slammed the door shut and brushed past him.

"Zoe, wait. I need to talk to you. Please."

I whirled around, folding my arms. "Fine, talk."

"I would have come sooner, but I've been going to AA meetings. It's why I haven't been over yet." He stopped as if unsure what to say next. He held out a bouquet of pale-pink tulips. "These are for you."

"You think flowers are going to make this better?"

"No." He lowered the bouquet to his side. "I need to apologize. I didn't mean any of those things I said."

"Well, no wonder you have an Academy Award, because if you didn't mean them, you sure made me believe you did."

He looked so crestfallen that even though I was furious with him, it took all my willpower not to comfort him. "Zoe, I know I can trust you. I do."

"That's the problem, Chase. Now I don't know if I can trust you. I gave you my heart, and you broke it." My voice caught. I would not allow myself to fall apart in front of him. "I can't talk to you right now. I need to go."

His hand was on my arm, and I had to move away from his touch. It was too much. "Please tell me what I can do to make this better. I love you. I need you in my life."

"I don't know how you can fix this. For now, I need some space. And some time."

Each step I took away from him made my feet feel like they were encased in concrete, wading through a swamp. My heart wanted me to turn around and run back into his arms and tell him all was forgiven.

But my head wouldn't let me forget what he'd done.

CHAPTER THIRTY-ONE

He listened to me. Chase gave me all the space in the world. He didn't text, tweet, call, or try to see me in person. As time went on, my anger started to dissipate. I thought about our meeting in the parking lot and how differently it might have ended had I not been all churned up from my confrontation with Stephanie.

I finished finals and graduated from college. I felt so sad that Chase wasn't there, because we had planned for him to come. After I was handed my diploma, I looked out to see my family cheering and calling my name. For a moment I thought I saw Chase leaving through the doors at the back of the auditorium but decided I must have imagined it.

I really missed him.

Now that college was done, I started looking for a full-time accounting job. Problem was, everybody seemed to know me. And they asked inappropriate and probably illegal questions about what it was like to date Chase Covington. It didn't matter that I'd gone to an excellent school and earned a degree. They just wanted to gossip like we were girlfriends. Even the men.

Finally, I found a little start-up that made software applications and was in need of an accountant. I wanted to work with an ocean conservation nonprofit, but I needed a job. They offered excellent benefits and a good salary. And not once during the interview did Brenda, the woman interviewing me, say anything about Chase. I absolutely killed it. It was probably the best interview I'd ever had. When it was over, Brenda enthusiastically shook my hand and said, "We will definitely be in touch, Zoe. It was such a pleasure to meet you."

Feeling good about myself for the first time in a long time, I stopped in the restroom to use the facilities and planned to call Lexi when I got to my car to let her know how it had gone. My first inclination was to call Chase, and I felt sad for a moment when I remembered he couldn't be my first phone call anymore.

I had made it to the front of the building when Brenda came running after me, calling my name. "Zoe!"

Confused, I stopped, wondering if I'd forgotten something.

"I had to call the CEO and get his approval, but if you want the job, it's yours."

No way! "Yes. I would love to work here!"

Brenda held out her hand, and I shook it with enthusiasm. "Fantastic. Can you start on Monday at eight?"

"I can."

"Great! We will see you then."

"Absolutely." There was something I needed to know first. "I have a weird question, but did anyone pull strings to get me this job? Call you?" I didn't want this to be because Chase had made a phone call.

"No." She said the word like I was a crazy person. "You earned this on your own merits."

Relieved, I decided to leave before she rescinded the offer because of my weirdness, and I told her I'd be there early Monday morning.

Lexi and Gavin said we should celebrate, but I hated being their third wheel. It hadn't been an issue before Chase, and even though I adored them both, they were a constant reminder of what was missing in my own life.

When they were home, I tried to steer clear and stay in my room. Now that school was over, I didn't have quite as much to occupy my free time. I did my best to remain off-line, and despite her disdain for most social media, Lexi put it aside to act as my Internet police. "Didn't anybody teach these people if they don't have anything nice to say, they should just shut up?" I heard her say more than once.

She also teased me about the #TeamZase hashtag.

"Zase sounds like a bar of soap," I agreed.

"You don't get to pick your couple name. You're stuck with what fans give you."

When she came into the bedroom with her phone, I thought she had another update about social media. Instead she said, "Chase did an interview."

I gulped down the knot that had quickly formed in my throat. He did press only when he had a new movie coming out, and I knew he didn't have anything being released soon.

"It's about you."

If I didn't want to watch it before, I definitely didn't want to watch it now.

"Well, not really about you. It's about how he isn't dating Amelia Swan, and how everything that's been said about them is a lie. How he was in love with someone else but wanted to keep the relationship private. You should watch it."

Our doorbell rang before I could reply. Lexi got up to answer it.

She came back into the room, her eyes wide. "Zoe, it's for you."

Beneath my heartache, a surge of happiness welled up inside me at the thought that it might be Chase. But One-F was standing in the living room instead. "Hey, Zoe."

"Hey. What are you doing here?"

Lexi had made herself scarce to allow us to talk. I knew I should offer him something to drink, but the shock of seeing him made me forget my manners. "Did Chase send you?"

"No. Chase did not send me." He rocked back on his heels, looking distinctly uncomfortable. "In fact, he would probably fire me if he knew I was here. Look, he knows he screwed up. But everybody in his life uses him. Everybody. Even his own mother. Can't any part of you see how he could have jumped to that conclusion? To everyone around him, he's a product, not a person. I think you were the first woman who ever loved him for who he is. He's never loved anyone like he loves you. And he is completely miserable without you."

One-F's words caught in my heart and burrowed down deep. I'd been so caught up in my own pain and sadness that I hadn't given any weight to Chase's perspective. I could see how I would be the obvious suspect when photos only the two of us had were leaked, and he knew he hadn't done it.

"Just so you know, one of my coworkers at the Ocean Life Foundation posted those pictures. He stole them off my laptop in some misguided attempt to beat me for a full-time job by making it look like I was holding out on my boss. But I never intended to ask Chase to go to the fund-raiser, because I didn't want to be another person who used him. I wasn't keeping anything from him. It was never going to be an issue, because I wasn't going to treat him like a product."

One-F nodded. "I know you didn't do it. I think he knows that, too. And I understand you had this painful thing happen between you, but is that really more important than all the good times you guys shared?"

That lump in my throat that appeared whenever I talked about Chase showed up, making it hard to talk. "It doesn't matter. There's no point. He doesn't believe in marriage. There's no future for us. It's better to just end things."

He wore a bleak expression, and the cajoling smile dropped from his face. "That's all I wanted to say. Have a good night." He let himself out, and Lexi came into the room with sad eyes.

"I want to remember the happy times," I said. "But all I can remember is when he hurt me. Why is that?"

"Probably because happiness doesn't leave scars."

She stayed up with me while I cried and talked about Chase. When we finally went to bed, I tossed and turned, unable to sleep. Despite what I'd said earlier, now all I could think about was our good times. The way he made me laugh. The light in his eyes when he saw me. How right it felt to be in his arms. His surprises and outlandish dates. What a good, loving, smart, funny, thoughtful, charming, and patient man he was.

I had almost drifted off when Lexi woke up. She tried to tiptoe around the apartment, but I could not get back to sleep. I was about to get out of bed when I heard my phone ring.

"Hi, Chase," I heard Lexi say. "This is Lexi." Then she began to talk, but I heard only her side of the conversation. She would say a sentence and then pause, listening. "She's sleeping. Yeah, he stopped by tonight. She knows you didn't send him. I know. Can I give you some advice? Zoe is a person who doesn't get mad easily, but when she does, it takes her a long time to calm down. And you really hurt her. She needs to know you won't do that again. She's lost too many people she loved. I know it was a mistake. She knows it, too. I don't know. Maybe show her how serious about her you are. A big gesture. You work in Hollywood. I'm sure you can figure something out. I know she misses you. And she still loves you. Okay. Yeah, I can do that. Okay. Bye."

I came out of our room as she was putting down my phone. "That was Chase?"

"Yeah." She didn't say anything else, but I could see that whatever he'd said had affected her.

"You think I should talk things out with him, don't you?"

She tapped her fingers against the countertop, like she was uncertain what to say next. "I do, Zoe. Even if you think there's no future, you should at least give him the chance to tell you what he thinks and what he wants before you make a permanent decision. I just don't want you to look back on this and really regret it. I know you don't want to be hurt, but that's life, you know? It happens. And I think he's worth that risk."

I realized she was probably right.

"So what will it be tonight?" I had been at my new job for about a week, and even though it wasn't a nonprofit, they were committed to community service and encouraged their employees to volunteer, which I appreciated. Gavin had also found an excellent job after graduation, and he was at a training seminar in Washington. Which meant Lexi and I had been watching a lot of TV.

"How about *Marry Me*? I love that show." Lexi scrolled through our DVR with the remote.

"Nah. They haven't had a good season since they had those Monterran princes on it." Plus, I wasn't really in the mood for a sappy, romantic show. I had been trying to decide what to do about Chase and didn't want to watch people falling in love.

"Let's watch *Jeopardy!*" she suggested. "You get the ice cream, and I'll get it queued up."

I went to the kitchen and opened the freezer. I thought I heard a metallic whirring sound. Like our DVD player. Which we never used. I stuck my head around the freezer door, but Lexi hadn't moved. She smiled at me, and I decided I was hearing things. I grabbed us pints of rocky road, along with spoons.

"Thank you," she said when I gave her the ice cream.

The theme music started, and the board appeared. Lexi glanced at her watch. She looked a little anxious. "Do you have somewhere you have to be?"

"No." She smiled again as she opened her pint and put the lid on the coffee table.

As the host chatted with the contestants, I said, "Alex Trebek is really nice, by the way. I made a total fool of myself when I met him, but he was so polite." It had been a relief to fill her in on all the things she'd missed, but it kept reminding me of those good times.

"I'll take 'The Long Game' for two hundred."

"This National Hall of Fame Junior outfielder, whose career ended in 2010, played in four different decades."

"Who is Ken Griffey Jr.?" I said with a mouth full of chocolate.

Which, of course, was the right answer.

"You know you're super annoying to watch this show with," Lexi teased me, poking me with her toe.

"I can't help it if I know stuff. And that one was easy. They had part of his name in the answer."

The contestant named Karl selected another category and dollar amount. "I bet he lives in his mom's basement," Lexi noted. I had to agree.

"Bluetooth was named after this tenth-century Danish king."

"Who is King Harald 'Bluetooth' Gormson?" I said a half second before Karl answered, "Who is King Harald the First?"

"Mine was more precise," I said. Lexi just rolled her eyes and ate her ice cream.

Karl chose "It's Prime" for one hundred.

The host said, "The only prime even number."

"What is two?" I called out. "Jeez, this is easy. It's like the celebrity version."

Karl was fastest with the buzzer again, gave the correct question, and selected a new category. "Let's go with 'Cut to the Chase' for two hundred."

"This movie star," the host said, and a picture of Chase popped up. I almost choked on my ice cream.

"Who is Chase Covington?" Lexi yelled out. "Ha. I knew that one!"

Another right response for Karl, who seemed to be the only contestant who had figured out how to work his buzzer. "'Cut to the Chase' for four hundred."

"We have special guest Chase Covington reading the clues in this category," the host announced, turning to the monitor. There was a video of Chase, talking. He looked so handsome. My heart sped up, and my lungs felt too small.

"The first name of the actress who plays on-screen aliens Gamora and Neytiri."

The answer to that was *Zoe*. Somehow my heart beat even faster.

"Who is Zoe?" Karl said, winning the money. "'Cut to the Chase' for six hundred."

"This Bryan Adams song released in 1993 was the only single from his greatest hits compilation *So Far So Good*."

"What is 'Please Forgive Me'?" I whispered, my heart rate continuing to increase.

Another right response from Karl. "Same category, eight hundred."

Every time Chase spoke, it was like a tiny dagger piercing my soul. "This 2007 movie that begins 'P.S.' featured Gerard Butler and Hilary Swank."

"What is *P.S. I Love You*?" Karl said smugly. "One thousand."

"Jordin Sparks appeared in the video for this 2013 Jason Derulo song; the first four words following 'I'll say.'"

"What is 'Will you marry me?'"

I put it all together despite the rushing sensation in my head. *Zoe, please forgive me, I love you, will you marry me.*

What was happening?

Then Chase walked out from behind the huge *Jeopardy!* board, looked right into the camera, and said, "Zoe, open your front door."

CHAPTER THIRTY-TWO

"Do it, Zoe!" Lexi bounced up and down in her seat, grinning at me.

As if they had a mind of their own, my feet took me to the front door. I opened it and saw Chase standing on the other side. "Hi."

"Hi." I stood back and allowed him into the apartment. I just stared at him, unable to put together what was going on.

"And that is my cue to exit stage left," Lexi said behind me. She pulled a DVD out of the player and left it in a case on the coffee table, and that was when I realized she'd been in on whatever this was.

Chase said, "Thanks," and she nodded and gave me two thumbs up before she closed the door. Leaving us alone.

My heart pounded so hard I was sure he could hear it. I wrapped my hands around my arms, afraid to say anything. Afraid I had somehow misunderstood what was happening.

He spoke first. "I know I've said it before, but I'm sorry you felt like I don't trust you. I do."

"I didn't do it. I would never betray you." The words slipped out.

"I know. I know you didn't. One-F told me what happened. The thing is, even if you had? I don't care. Because it doesn't matter. You're what matters." He took a step closer to me, and I stayed put.

"That first night when you stayed over, I already knew I was in love with you. And it scared me to feel that way, but it was okay because it was you. I woke up with you in my arms, and it was the best thing that had ever happened to me. I want that. Every day. For the rest of my life. To fall asleep at night holding you and wake up to you every morning and everything that happens in between."

Another step toward me.

"I wish I could promise to never hurt you again. But I'll hurt you. And you'll hurt me. That's what happens when people love each other. What I can promise is to never act like such an idiot again. To trust you completely and never give you a reason to doubt me, either."

One more step and we were almost touching.

"I am committed to you. I'm committed to us. You've made me want things I never thought I wanted. I want you to be my family. I want you to be the mother to a houseful of our kids. I want you to be my first and only love. I want you to be my wife."

He got down on one knee, and even though I'd figured out where this was headed, it still made me gasp.

"You told me once that people get married because they have hope that they'll get their happily ever after. That's what I want with you. Zoe, will you marry me?"

He took out a light-blue ring box, opened it, and nearly blinded me with the massive diamond inside.

"Did you hire someone to write all that for you?" I asked in a whisper.

Chase rewarded me with a smile even brighter than the diamond. "No. That was all me. I wanted to come here and tell you everything you make me feel."

I knelt down in front of him and wrapped my arms around his neck to hold him tight. He crushed me against him so firmly that for a second I couldn't breathe.

I'd thought we didn't have a future, but Chase had just offered me the best possible one. And I knew he meant every word he'd just said. This wasn't some Band-Aid he was using to fix us. He loved me and wanted a life with me.

Just like I loved him and wanted a life with him. I knew our lives wouldn't be perfect, but we would be perfect for each other, and that's what mattered. As long as we trusted and loved each other, the rest of the stuff would work itself out. I would figure out a way to deal with the paparazzi and privacy invasions and harassing Internet trolls or him going on location.

Because I loved him, and he was worth anything I had to go through in order to be with him.

"You still haven't given me an answer," he said against my shoulder.

I leaned my head back and looked deep into the eyes of the man I loved so much. "Have you ever actually watched the show? You don't give answers. It's in the form of a question. And I say, what is yes?"

That made him laugh, and he pulled me into the most loving, amazing kiss I'd ever had in my life.

And as Lexi liked to say, the best kind of happy endings were the ones that also came with a gift.

 **Zoe**
@zomorezoless

Babylonia: groom drank mead nonstop (honey beer); they had lunar calendar & it was called the "honey month" or "honeymoon" #Trivia

 ⟲ 4.3K ♡ 8.6K

We were married three months later. Chase didn't see a point in waiting, and to be honest, neither did I. We hired a wedding planner, Madison LaRue, who charged us an arm and a leg because of the short notice, but she was famous among the Hollywood set for keeping everything private. And we both wanted that. A private day that was just for us and our loved ones.

Except for my immediate family, One-F, and Lexi, our other guests thought they were coming to a summer barbecue at Chase's house. Chase's mom sent her regrets, as she was on her honeymoon with Husband No. 10. But it meant our guests dressed casually, and it fit perfectly with what Chase and I wanted. Something low key and informal. Which made Madison nuts, as I kept vetoing her ideas (which included, among other things, swans, ice sculptures of us, fireworks, a gospel choir, and a fifty-piece orchestra). I did give in on the air-conditioned tents. I didn't want to be sweaty and gross on my wedding day. Honestly, the details didn't matter that much to me. I asked only that I have pink tulips, that she not go completely overboard, and we followed her lead. Even with the dress—I just said okay to the sketch Madison showed me.

Because it wasn't the wedding that mattered. Only the marriage.

Right after we got engaged, a part of me had worried that my friends and family might hold a grudge. But when I forgave Chase, so did everybody else. Even Zia. After she'd hit him once as promised, she was good.

In fact, during the ceremony my mom had to pull her off Chase's leg when she realized she was the flower girl and I was the one marrying him.

Zelda was the other flower girl, and Zander and Zane served as our ring bearers. Lexi was my maid of honor, and Chase asked One-F to be his best man. And that was the entire wedding party.

My mother walked me down the aisle, and just before we started, she hugged me tightly. "I am so proud of you. You look so beautiful."

And I thought I felt beautiful until Chase turned and saw me, and the expression in his eyes was one I'll never forget. He looked at me like I was a goddess, one he worshipped and adored. The ceremony was short and traditional, and the minister told Chase to kiss his bride.

"Why do the bride and groom kiss at the end?" Chase whispered, with everyone watching us.

He wanted to know this now? "Because Romans used to seal all their contracts with a kiss," I whispered back, my eyes flicking toward our guests.

"I love it when you talk nerdy to me," he said, finally doing as he was told. He dipped me back and kissed me soundly.

We were officially husband and wife.

I thought Zoe Covington had a rather nice ring to it.

We danced and ate and laughed with all the people we cared about (which included a huge number of celebrities I can't mention by name because of nondisclosure agreements). And everywhere I went, I felt my husband's gaze on me.

Lexi twirled me around in a circle as we danced to an old Spice Girls song. "Could you ever have imagined when we were twelve years old that someday you'd be Chase Covington's wife?"

No, I couldn't have. I looked up to see him dancing with Zelda, who stood on his shoes as he turned her in a circle. Every time I thought I couldn't possibly love him more, he did something to prove me wrong. The reality of being his wife was so much better than I could have ever dreamed up.

We cut our cake, which was not gray but a beautiful traditional white buttercream with pink edible tulips. I had warned him a bunch of times not to shove it in my face. Smart man that he was, he listened. Then it came time to throw the bouquet, and to my satisfaction, Lexi caught it.

Which worked out well, considering Gavin planned on proposing to her after the reception with the ring I'd helped him pick out.

Then my new husband hinted that it was time to go, and we made the rounds to say goodbye. One of his classic Porsches was parked out front, and we were showered with pink tulip petals as he picked me up and carried me out to the car.

"You're not supposed to carry me yet," I said, unable to contain my laughter.

"We were already in the threshold, so I figured carrying you in this direction works, too."

Chase had a director friend who owned a private island in the Bahamas, and now that I owned a passport, we were going to spend our honeymoon there. But tonight we were checking in to the Viceroy L'Ermitage in Beverly Hills. It was gorgeous, had views of the Hollywood Hills, and best of all, a private entrance for celebrities so no one would even know we were there.

"Let's go upstairs and slip into something a little more married," my husband said. He nuzzled my neck as the bellhops grabbed our luggage.

The suite was amazing, and I had only a second to take in the expensive furniture, the dark grays and white onyx marble, before Chase picked me up again and carried me into the bedroom.

"Are you nervous?" he asked as he set me down, turned me around, and pulled me flush against him, my back to his front.

"A little," I admitted. "But I'm glad I waited."

He kissed my neck where it met my shoulder, making shivers dance along my skin. "I'm glad the waiting is over."

I felt his fingers run along the hundred tiny pearl buttons that fastened my wedding dress. He went to the top button and unhooked it. I heard him let out a sound of frustration. "How much did this cost?"

"Like ten thousand—" I didn't even get to finish my sentence before Chase ripped the buttons apart.

"I can't believe you just did that!" I protested, laughing. "I think that was handmade silk lace. Vera Wang is going to punch you in the face the next time she sees you."

"It's not like you're going to wear it again. I'll buy you a dozen more," he promised as he undid the last few buttons.

"What am I going to do with twelve wedding dresses?"

"Don't know, don't care. But I have been waiting to rip your clothes off for months."

Then he was placing a trail of warm kisses down the top of my exposed spine that made me slump against him and my eyelids flutter shut. "Wait," I said, out of breath. "I have something I want to change into first."

"Really?" That got his attention. "I guess I can wait a few more minutes."

I grabbed the bag from my purse. Just before I went into the bathroom, Chase said, "Just a second. I have something for you."

He pulled a ring box from his tuxedo jacket.

"I already have one of these," I said as I opened it, waggling my left ring finger at him.

But there wasn't a ring inside. It was a set of keys. I held them up. "Is this for the house?"

"For your new car. Now that you're my wife, I get to buy you one."

That was so Chase. "I love you, Mr. Covington."

"I love you, Mrs. Covington."

I kissed him as a thank-you, and his intoxicating lips almost made me forget my plan. Breathing hard, I promised him I'd be right back. I closed the bathroom door behind me. Considering I was able to step out of my unfastened wedding dress, it didn't take long to do as my new husband had suggested and slip into something a little more married.

When I came out, he'd taken off his vest, tie, and jacket and was in the process of undoing his cuff links. He stopped cold when he saw me.

"Like it?" I asked, twirling around in the awful blue *Little House on the Prairie* nightgown I'd worn the first night I'd stayed at his house. I put a hand on my hip, posing. "I was thinking tonight maybe we could just cuddle. Or get a bundling board."

"That is not funny." He crossed the room in a few long strides, picked me up, and tossed me on the bed while I giggled.

"Don't rip this one," I warned him.

"I won't. I plan on taking my time," he said as he climbed onto the bed next to me. "This nightgown seriously drives me crazy."

And then, to my great delight, he proceeded to show me just how crazy it made him.

Two years later

"Are you nervous?" I asked him.

"I'm fine," he said, squeezing my hand. "I'm really glad you're here."

"Where else would I be?" I leaned over to kiss his cheek and then wiped away the lipstick I'd left behind. "What do you think about Zeth?"

"I am not naming our son Zeth," Chase said, but my distraction seemed to be working. His grip felt less tense.

"You don't even know if I'm having a boy."

"I know. And he's not going to be named Zeth."

I had no intention of using that name, either. I just liked to tease Chase with outlandish possible boy names like Zadam or Zefron because of how panicked he looked each time I did. He was partial to Oscar, his maternal grandfather's name, and I thought it was cute. Especially paired with Zev, my grandfather's name. But I let him sweat it out a little. Considering I was the one doing all the puking and pee-ing, he deserved some suffering.

My phone buzzed with a text from the CEO of the nonprofit Chase and I had started together dedicated to ocean conservation. She was wishing him good luck. I was the CFO and had raided Ocean Life

Foundation for the good, dedicated employees for our staff, and things were going really well. We had a fund-raiser planned for next month.

I showed Chase my phone, but he just nodded, distracted. He was nominated for Best Actor for the movie *Spectrum*. It was the one I'd encouraged him to do while we were dating, the one he'd invested his own money in that had almost fallen apart. It had been a long labor of love, and Chase desperately wanted it to succeed.

It had already won Best Director and Best Original Screenplay. Chase's category was up next.

The presenters came out and ran through the list of nominees. Chase's fingers tightened around mine.

"And the award goes to . . . Chase Covington!"

The audience erupted around us in applause. He leaned over to kiss me, his face full of shock and excitement.

"You have to go up there!" I said, beaming at him. He kissed me again and then went up to accept.

He started by thanking the Academy, and the producers, writers, director, cast, and crew—everyone involved with the project. I saw one of the mobile cameramen point his camera at me, wanting my reaction. After we'd announced our wedding and how we met, social media turned in my favor. Suddenly I was the poster child for every girl out there who'd ever had a crush on a celebrity. Which meant I got a lot of unwanted attention, too.

I ignored the camera, focusing my attention solely on my amazing, talented husband.

"And finally, I want to thank my wife. She encouraged me to make this movie." He looked directly at me. "You make me a better man. I love you, Zoe. I wish I could say that winning this award was the best thing that's ever happened to me. It's not. The best thing that has ever happened to me is sitting in the audience, pregnant with the second best." As if he'd realized what he had done, his eyes went wide. "I think

I just let the cat out of the bag. Sorry, babe. Although now we have a pretty good reason to name him Oscar. Thank you!"

Honestly, I was surprised he'd lasted this long. Chase was so excited to become a dad he wanted to tell everybody he came across. The clerk in the grocery store, the flight attendant, our gardener, etc. He was also the most overprotective father-to-be I'd ever seen. After he'd talked to the press backstage and returned to his seat, he turned to me and said, "Let's skip the after-parties."

"No," I protested. I would hate them, but I wanted him to have every moment in the spotlight he deserved. "I don't want you to miss any of the celebrations of how amazing you are."

He took my hand and brought it up to his lips. "I already have the only person I want to celebrate with."

So instead of going to a fancy hotel or someone's decked-out mansion for an elaborate party, we went home. My feet had started to hurt, so my husband insisted on carrying me up the stairs. He laid me in our bed.

"There's something I haven't told you."

Chase stopped pulling off my shoes to look at up me. "What's that?"

"Yesterday while you were at rehearsals, I had some light spotting."

He abandoned his attempts and climbed onto the bed next to me to take me in his arms. "What? Are you okay? Is everything—" He put one hand on my stomach, as if he couldn't bring himself to say it.

"Everything's fine," I reassured him. "We're fine. It's totally normal. I just wanted to get checked out. Just in case. And before you ask, I didn't tell you earlier because I wanted today to be about you."

Chase waved one hand, as if winning the most prestigious acting award in the country was no big deal. "And?"

"And they were able to see the sex of the baby."

"I thought we had to wait another two weeks?" He read more books about pregnancy and babies than I did.

"Sometimes they can tell this early." I gave him a neutral smile, hoping he couldn't guess what I was about to tell him.

"You're not going to make me cut open some blue or pink cake, are you?"

"I'm not." I put my hand on top of his where he rubbed my swollen belly. "You were right. We're having a boy."

"I knew it!"

I couldn't wait to see his face when I told him the next part. "And a girl."

Chase Covington ☑
@realchasecov

Following

Please welcome our little tweethearts--Oscar Zev Covington and Olivia Zadie Covington.

💬   🔁 198K   🤍 567K

NOTE FROM THE AUTHOR

Thanks for coming along on this journey with me. I hope you enjoyed reading Chase and Zoe's story. If you'd like to find out when I've written something new, make sure you sign up for my newsletter at www.sariahwilson.com. I promise not to spam you. It's all I can do to get a newsletter sent out even once a month.

Every time you leave a review on Amazon, an angel gets its wings. Or, more accurately, a writer breathes a sigh of relief that at least one person liked something she wrote! I would be so appreciative if you leave such a review. I bet the angels would be appreciative, too.

ACKNOWLEDGMENTS

To all my readers—thank you. Thank you for buying what I've written and making this my actual job. It's a dream come true.

Thanks to Megan Mulder for stepping in and taking over this project. I am so, so excited to keep working with you and see where this professional relationship takes us both. Thank you to Jennifer Glover for helping me procure this contract. Big thanks to the entire Montlake team for all your hard work on my behalf, for getting this book out there, and for always taking such good care of me (especially Sally, Elise, Kelsey, Kris, Jessica, and Le). Thank you to my developmental editor, Melody Guy (this is our fourth book together!), for pointing out the things I meant to say and the things I said too much of and to my copyeditor, Sally, and proofreader, Jill. Thank you to Michael Rheder for his cover.

Thank you to Zak Knutson for telling me what really happens on movie sets and for sharing details about a day in the life of a movie star. And thanks to all those real-life people out there who have fallen in love on Twitter and shared their stories—you were a big inspiration!

To my kids—I love you and appreciate that you've learned how to let your mom have quiet time to create worlds but also don't let me get too lost in them.

And, as always, my thanks and adoration to Kevin—you're my best friend and my soul mate, and every word of love I ever write is because of you.

ABOUT THE AUTHOR

Bestselling author Sariah Wilson has never jumped out of an airplane or climbed Mount Everest, and she is not a former CIA operative. She has, however, been madly, passionately in love with her soul mate and is a fervent believer in happily ever afters—which is why she writes romances like The Royals of Monterra series. After growing up in Southern California as the oldest of nine (yes, nine) children, she graduated from Brigham Young University with a semiuseless degree in history. She currently lives with the aforementioned soul mate and their four children in Utah, along with three tiger barb fish, a cat named Tiger, and a recently departed hamster who is buried in the backyard (and has nothing at all to do with tigers). For more information, visit her website at www.SariahWilson.com.